Luce Women

Luce Women

Liz Kisacky Severn

40

PRESS

Design: John Toren
Front cover photo credit: Grass Roots Team
Author Photograph: John Early

Forty Press, LLC
427 Van Buren Street
Anoka, MN 55303
www.fortypress.com

ISBN 978-1-938473-22-7

In Memory of Carol Bly
1930 - 2007

Writer, Teacher, Mentor

1

I propped my foot on an old apple crate as I rubbed my aching knee and pressed the cold comfort of an ice cream carton against my bruised head. I didn't exactly have blood on my hands but I had some explaining to do. I shifted my heavy frame. The chair's joints groaned and springs poked through the threadbare cushion. A deer's head mounted on the wall gazed toward the kitchen as if calculating escape.

"Why didn't you partner up to deliver meals?" Chief Huntermeister asked.

"Don't need anyone tagging along. I set my own pace."

"And you came inside even though you were suspicious about the unlocked door?"

"Like I said, I figured Lois got distracted, maybe had her hands full, like I had mine full with his lunch, and she forgot to lock up on her way out." I smiled at Lois who looked like she was chomping at the bit to say something but kept quiet as instructed by the chief.

"Tell me again how you got that bruise?" Huntermeister wiped sweat from his forehead and dropped his hat on a box of player piano rolls.

"This is real funny, you making me repeat myself like I'll forget my first answer, give you some confession or something you want to hear. Like I said, I got shoved from behind and whacked my head." I shifted my weight in the chair and glanced around at the piles of seed catalogs and books with tattered covers. Birch logs were stacked against a dresser shoved in front of the fireplace. Lyle was a recluse and a hoarder and whenever I entered his house, I imagined it screaming to be freed from accumulation.

"And never heard or saw anyone?" Huntermeister said.

"I got here like usual—around noon—with Lyle's lunch. It was already hotter than all get-out. I stood on the porch catching my breath before coming in because, well, you can smell how rank it is in here; makes it hard to breathe." I turned to Lois. "Little FYI; those fake pine air fresheners you stick in the outlets only make the place smell worse."

"So ... the door was unlocked?" Dwight prompted impatiently.

"Now that I think about it," I said, "maybe those agitated crows making a racket in the tree were trying to warn me of foul play."

Dwight checked his watch. "Doubtful."

"Anyways," I continued, "Inside, I banged into that anything-but-gilded birdcage hanging in the entry. Knocked it over, wondered why the noise didn't bring Lyle to the door. I set his lunch down and called for him. No answer. Called again. Then I heard floorboards creak upstairs. I climbed the steps with aching knees."

"What did you find?" Dwight asked.

"I walked into Lyle's bedroom. Something didn't feel right. The room smelled weird, like something burnt and skunky. It was dark, so I lifted the shade. That's when I saw dresser drawers hanging open and papers and stuff piled on the floor. A jar was tipped over and pennies were all over the place. Things were tossed around the room."

"Things?" Dwight said.

"Yeah, jewelry and stuff, safety pins, twist ties, rubber bands, combs. Like someone dug through boxes and tossed it all aside while ransacking the place, though ransack might not be the right word. More like someone looking for something specific."

"It was not like that this morning," Lois piped up.

I ignored her. "At first I figured Lyle had searched for something and gave up, left the mess. But now, clearly, someone else must've done that, broke in looking for who knows what." The deer's head appeared to eye me suspiciously. I took a deep breath.

"At that point, didn't you realize Lyle was dead?"

"Like I said, I thought he was sleeping. The fan was rattling, blowing right at the bed. I touched his shoulder, asked if he was hungry. I couldn't see his face because of the pillows. When I shifted them, I saw he was waxy. His color was off and his lips were blue. He just stared. Then I knew he was dead. Busted my heart to realize it."

Dwight gave me a sympathetic look. Lois didn't.

"Then what did you do?" Dwight asked.

"I got real shaky, couldn't think straight but got my wits about me and remembered that since Lyle was under hospice, I'd been instructed to call them if anything happened to him while I was there. So, I called Lois."

Dwight raised a bushy eyebrow. "That the procedure?" he asked Lois for verification.

"What the heck, Dwight?" I protested.

Lois nodded and then said, "Trudy's telling the truth on that." She was being a royal foe when she should've been defending me on every level. As Lyle's hospice nurse, she crossed my path often when I delivered Meals-on-Wheels. I figured she'd be my alibi and defender, inform Dwight about my good deeds: hauling boxes off Lyle's back porch so he could sit in the sun out there, planting a vegetable garden, bringing ice cream. I was his friend with a real soft spot for the old guy.

"Of course I'm telling the truth. Geeze!" I glared at Lois. "Your phone rings a bazillion times before your voice mail kicks in. So annoying and it took you forever to call back."

"Your message did not say he had passed away."

"I said it was urgent."

Dwight intervened. "What else occurred while you waited?"

"I nosed through the pile of stuff on the floor."

Dwight frowned. "Why didn't you call me about Lyle?"

"I was waiting for Lois to call back. Aren't you listening to my story?"

"Sure am?"

"Saw Randall Short's card in a stack of stuff. Why not ask him why he's been snooping around the place? Everyone knows he's chomping at the bit to get Lyle's land, carve it up for condos and—"

"Let's just hear what you know," Dwight said. "No need to speculate."

"Truth isn't speculation," I shot back. "Oh hey, I saw a letter from the city offices. Jerry Wanderi was contesting the line between his Mini-Mart and Lyle's fence. He's been crying in his beer for years about Lyle's house, calling it a property-value-lowering eyesore that's preventing progress along Highway 10. You ask me, tearing down trees to put up strip malls isn't progress. That's how Lyle saw it too. He knew Emma Lake and his land were the crown jewels."

"What else did you see?"

"Old photos." I pulled one from my pocket. "Like this one. Looks like Lyle standing by the old granary on the north side of the—"

"You shouldn't just take things," Lois said.

"Whatever," I used my teenage daughter's favorite come back.

"So between the time you realized Lyle was dead and the time you contacted Lois, you went through all those papers?" Dwight said. "Which would have given you chance to call me."

"I was waiting for Lois to call back so I stayed close. Him and me were friends, you know."

"Duly noted."

"Anyway, I lifted a bowl from the bedside table. It had melted ice cream and something else, like powdery sand that stuck to my fingers."

"Is there anything you *didn't* touch?" Huntermeister scowled.

"Geeze, Dwight. I didn't know what to think when I saw that, just curious why it was there." Sadness then hit me like a hammer as I sat seeing Lyle's dead face. "I lifted his hand and checked for a pulse. The room was quiet, not even traffic noise, so it was kind of unsettling. I'm agnostic, you know, but the idea of a spirit floating in the room put me on edge."

"Then what did you do?" Dwight said.

"I set the empty OxyContin bottle on his nightstand by another container. I lifted a spoon coated with some kind of white granules that smelled bitter. Then I saw a bunch of medicine bottles on the floor and read the labels: Ativan, Morphine, Haldol; a real smorgasbord. That's when I thought, oh no. What did he do? I saw the message, a piece of torn paper. It said, '*I have to go* ...' I realized it was my handwriting."

"What do you mean?" Dwight asked.

"I'd leave him notes. And like everything else, he didn't throw them away. He must've torn that scrap from a longer note."

"What would the rest of the note have said?"

"Oh, something like '*I have to go to White Drug. Need anything?*' Anyways, after I saw that note, I thought oh no, he killed himself! My hands were really shaking and I kept waiting for Lois to call back." I held my hands up and showed Dwight what I meant, forcing a shake back into them. "I was sitting there and noticed a dead mouse of all things under his dresser. I was scooping it into a grocery bag when my phone rang. Scared the bejesus out of me. But before I could even answer Lois's call, I got shoved from behind into the dresser drawer. Then someone ran out of the bedroom and I heard the back door slam."

"So why didn't you call me then?" Huntermeister asked. "If you were assaulted."

"*When* I was assaulted. Not *if*. I didn't call because when I got shoved, my phone went flying. I had to dig around for it and call Lois back."

"Take you long?"

I shrugged. "When Lois finally arrived, she called you, which is how I understood it was supposed to work."

"How'd that *Do Not Resuscitate* order on the door make you feel?" Dwight asked, with a hint of accusation.

"How'd it make you feel?"

"Trudy—"

"Look man, I'm forty-one, in good health except for excess weight and bad knees, so it's not up to me to deny someone who's suffering the right to give up the ghost, so to speak."

"He didn't want to—as you say—give up the ghost," Lois said. "He was terminal!"

"And in constant pain," I said.

"The meds controlled the pain," she countered.

"When I'd see him double over with pain and—"

"Not denying that pancreatic cancer—"

"Was a death sentence he was supposed to endure. Wasting away and suffering."

Lois straightened at that. "He kept his dignity."

"And his ability to plan," Dwight interjected. He held up a document. "Did you pin this to Lyle's shirt?"

"What is it?" I asked.

"His will." He studied me for deceit.

"Heck no. Why would I?" I was sweating and propped a portable mini fan between two marble-filled cigar boxes to let it blow air. "Could we go outside? I'm suffocating."

Lois tried to open a window but it was stuck until Huntermeister hit the frame to free it. Lois propped the front door open. A furnace blast of hot air pushed inside.

"Did you know Lyle named you as beneficiary?"

"Of?"

Huntermeister rocked back and forth all nonchalant, like

he was watching for telltale signs of lies. "You really have no idea?"

"Completely clueless as to what you're talking about."

He leaned forward and something about that movement, or maybe it was the squeak of the chair, put a big lump in my throat for Lyle. I remembered him sitting in that rocker slurping melted ice cream, not interested in eating the lunches I kept delivering to him. I told him at one point we could stop the lunches; but he said he'd just as soon try to eat as not, but could I bring chocolate ice cream the next time.

"Trudy?"

"Yeah?" I said, shaking off a memory and snapping back to the present.

"You didn't convince Lyle to change his will?"

"No. Why would I? He said the state was getting it all for a refuge. A great idea. A thousand lakes surrounding this town and spring-fed Emma Lake is the only virgin left."

"He didn't tell you about his house?"

"The state was getting it lock, stock, and barrel. That's all he told me."

"But you had no idea that he changed the will?"

"How many ways are there to ask the same question?" I usually held Dwight Huntermeister in high regard since he had to put up with so much jackassery in his line of work, but his grilling me was making me question his cop chops. "Get your hound to track the woods. You're wasting time focusing on me."

He scanned the document then looked straight at me. "Appears he had it changed a month ago."

"You care more about the will than tracking the person you want?"

"The will is circumstantial evidence," he said.

"What're you talking about?" I looked at the paper in his hand. "Can I see it?"

"In due time," he said. "He's included you in the will."

"Get out!"

"Is there a reason this photo of you and your volunteers was clipped to it?"

"How the heck should I know?" I protested. He bit his lip as if considering something about me that I imagined I wouldn't like. I figured I had better try to present some logical response to his question. "He asked me about Homes for Dwelling. He must've cut that from the paper. Can I at least see that?" He obliged and I studied the picture of me and seven volunteers in front of our most recently renovated house. We were giving keys to the new low-income owners. That was always a great publicity move, but mostly just a great moment to showcase our achievement. Afterward, we women celebrated at the Cactus Corral before meeting again, ASAP, to plan our next renovation project.

"So there was no suggestion on your part? No coercion?"

"Would you just say what's on your mind?"

"He left the house to Homes for Dwelling."

"Seriously? Get out!"

"Why do you suppose he did that?" he prodded.

"How should I know? Maybe he was afraid the state would raze his house rather than maintain it, so he figured giving it to me would save it."

"Technically, the house was left to Homes for Dwelling," Huntermeister said, "but you personally get more."

"More?"

"Everything else." He waved his hand through the air like he was stirred up over the idea. "To use your term: lock, stock, and barrel."

"Everything inside this house?" The stacks of junk blurred before my eyes into one huge lump of work to wade through.

"Yes, and two hundred and forty acres of grass, cotton-wood, oak, poplar, pine, birch, and Emma Lake."

"Are you messing with me?"

"I assure you I am not. He left you every single acre."

"Doesn't seem possible," I muttered. The magnitude of that news spun my head. "What about the state? They must be ticked over this."

Lois looked at me; her eyeglasses crooked and worry lines deep in her face. She appeared stricken by some thought. Maybe she was worried that she'd be implicated along with me for whatever Dwight had on his mind, guilty by association or something like that. She ran her hand through her thick, copper-colored hair but didn't say a word.

"Still receiving grants from the state for your projects?" Huntermeister asked.

"Hell's bells, Dwight. Why don't you just cuff me and throw away the key?"

"Now why would I do that?" he said.

"I don't like the implications of that question. I got denied a grant this year. Only funds come from local donations, my own pocket, and skimming from the hardware store, which is dying in the face of Tool Mart. If you're insinuating I was worried about money and would harm Lyle or swindle him— or *worse*—you're wrong with a capital W." I wrote a *W* in the air and stared him down. Truth was, me and Don were in pretty bad financial straits since Tool Mart added another link to its big box chain two years ago, opening a home improvement store on Highway 10. It cut deep into our bottom line. We borrowed against our house. If word got out about that, maybe the law would… well, I didn't want to think about it.

"Dear, dear Lyle." Lois stood by the player piano stacked with *National Geographic* magazines. "May he rest in the peace he deserves." She dabbed her eyes.

"That's what he wanted," I said. "Some peace, once and for all. First they widened Highway 10 to four lanes, then they added the frontage road. Practically took his entire front yard, ruined his front porch sitting."

Lois stood with hands on hips like a brick wall I needed to bust through to prove my innocence. "He could *not* have gotten all the meds without help. I did not leave the comfort kit out for him. It wasn't time for him to have that. Yet, someone found it and forced him to overdose. He was not ready to die."

"Then why'd he post *Do Not Resuscitate* orders?" I asked. "He said, 'No heroic stuff.'"

"Is that reason to kill him before it was time?"

"Seems the cancer was doing that," I said.

"And you knew it." She got a little red in the face but kept her professional composure, her voice level. "He could not have done this on his own."

"He was a pretty willful old guy," I said. "A survivalist, too."

"What in Heaven's name does that mean?" Lois asked, impatiently.

"He practically lived off this land. Once had chickens and goats, two cows. Slaughtered his own pigs. Raised corn, beans, squash, potatoes, carrots. Canned it all to see him through winters. Pickled and canned pig's feet, sauerkraut, too. Beets, those were his favorite. Self-sufficient and avoiding town."

"He told you all that?" Lois looked like she wanted to call me a liar.

Then I said, "Sad really, a survivalist no longer wanting to survive."

Lois got back on her high horse. "I just want to be on record as saying I *always* manage my patients' meds properly. I go the extra mile for them. *Always*." Her voice broke. She walked to the door and leaned against the frame, staring right at me, chewing on her pink lipstick. "He clearly had assistance to take his life. Or someone murdered him wanting it to look like suicide," she said and shivered.

"Exactly what I'm saying. Someone was here and I got assaulted." The ice cream carton I had used on my bruised forehead sat soggy on a box. The room was caving in on me. I picked up the carton and walked to the kitchen where I tossed the mess into an overflowing garbage can and then leaned against the refrigerator to clear my aching head. I rearranged a stack of Butternut Coffee tins to calm my nerves. For crap's sake. One minute I was doing a good deed, next minute I was getting interrogated. I stepped onto the back porch and took some of what my friend, Iris Tucker, called calming breaths. A couple of crows were pecking at something at the edge of the woods. One flew up and made a racket; the cawing seemed to mock me. I knew one thing for sure, it sounded a lot better than what I was hearing from Dwight and Lois. I called Don to tell him I was running late for Courtney's swim meet and had something important to tell him. My forehead was throbbing along with my bad knees. I took deep breaths and went back inside.

Dwight looked up at me, "Trudy when you—"

"I need to leave," I said.

"Assisted suicide is a crime," Lois said.

"Yeah. So?"

Dwight was turning a gigantic ring 'round and 'round on his finger, looking really solemn. I got a little freaked out by the way he was so deep in thought. "Trudy how is it you have a key to the house?"

"Lois gave it to me."

"Against my better judgment, I now realize." She ignored my glare. "Actually," she said, "Lyle insisted. No doubt because Trudy coerced him into thinking it a good idea."

"Whoever ran into the woods set me up," I said. "They knew I delivered lunch on Wednesdays."

"Hmmmm." Lois seemed to consider that possibility. She sat back down, tugged at the hem of her skirt and then played with the seashell buckle on her tightly cinched belt. Her foot tapped on the floor like she was playing organ at church. I imagined her feet working away at the pedals, her hands as adept on the keys as they were injecting morphine into patients' veins.

"Trudy, where were you before coming here?" Hunter-meister asked.

"Delivering meals."

"Where?"

"Oh for crying out loud," I said. "There's two stops before Lyle's. I was at—"

"Is there a problem?" he asked.

"They weren't home," I said.

"Who's that?"

"Alva Techemeir and Opal Harvala."

"Where do you suppose they'd be if they knew you were bringing lunch?"

I shrugged. "Don't know. They didn't answer and their doors were locked. Alva blares her TV and I didn't hear it so I figured she was out. I didn't leave the food."

"So it's in your car?"

I blushed. "No."

"Where?"

"I ate it."

Huntermeister frowned.

"*What?* I was hungry and why waste roast turkey?"

"You ate two meals?" Huntermeister said.

"Well look at me. Don't I look like I could eat two meals?" I gestured toward my body, pushed at the fat around my waist. I don't pretend I'm not a big woman. Dr. Schemp told me if I'd lose at least thirty pounds, it'd be better for my knees… and my waist. Believe me, I got plenty of failed diets under my belt. "Besides," I defended myself. "Those are mighty small portions Bertha Hewitt allows."

"What time did you pick up the meals?" Dwight asked.

"Oh, well, ummm," I said. "I got there earlier than usual."

"How early?" he asked.

"Nine."

"And you came here at?"

"Noonish."

"Why'd you pick up early?" he asked.

"Efficiency. I had other things to do in Gorman Township. Didn't want to waste gas or time driving all the way back to town. I called Bertha. She said I could get the food early if I put deliveries together myself. Said I'd need to reheat the food because she didn't want any of her clients eating it cold. I put my seven meals together and drove out to the old Reuben Matz farmstead. The river keeps flooding the house, foundation's shot. His son's going to raze it now that Reuben's in the nursing home. A real shame but it's impossible to move a stone house. Anyway, Marlin's donating the wood floors. That's what I was doing, removing floorboards. Before I left, I warmed the lunches in Reuben's old trailer oven."

"About what time?"

I shrugged. "Don't know exactly."

"So Marlin can back your story?" Huntermeister asked.

"That he said I could remove the flooring?"

"That you were working there this morning."

"He wasn't there."

"Who was helping you?"

"No one."

"You usually do that work alone?"

"No."

"Then why today?"

"I felt like it." Truth was, I didn't want anyone with me when I walked through the house, making note of what else I could talk Marlin into donating. Had my eye on some porcelain doorknobs and leaded glass windows. The biggest truth was I'd hoped to salvage tongue-in-grove pine for my own porch ceiling that got wrecked when a busted gutter leaked. Don wouldn't agree to order new materials through the store, said it would be a bill he couldn't afford. Made me anxious that I wasn't able to maintain my own house.

Lois answered her phone and told the caller the medical examiner had not yet come. She hung up and we had a little stare down until she blinked. "Assisted suicide is a serious crime." She tugged at the sleeve of her blouse.

"No kidding, Lois. You already told me that." I looked at Huntermeister. "Can I go? I have things to do. I got four people waiting for lunch and Courtney's swim meet to attend."

Huntermeister looked at his watch. "Nothing's holding you," he said. "Chances are the others found something else to eat by now."

"No thanks to you," I said.

"By the way, know anything about this?" He pointed to a gravy boat. It was white with gold edging. Lois seemed startled, made a weird noise, a quick intake of breath like maybe she had stumbled upon a long-lost family heirloom.

"No," I said, keeping my eye on Lois who looked weirdly unbalanced rubbing her thumb along her seashell belt buckle. I reached for the boat.

Dwight grabbed my hand. "Stop touching the evidence. You'd think you'd get that by now."

"How else would I have figured out why Lyle was dead if I didn't examine things?"

"Not up to you to examine anything. Common sense would've told you that."

"One would think so," I said. They were sitting on my last nerve. Man it would've felt good to slam a sledgehammer into an old plaster wall right then. "So what's in it?"

"Marijuana."

"Seriously?"

"Know anything about it?" Dwight asked.

I turned to Lois. "Yours maybe? To keep you mellow on the job?" I clucked my tongue. I'd been sitting under the gun way too long and needed the focus off me.

Lois rolled her eyes. "Oh honestly," she said.

That really irritated me. "Where were *you*, I wonder, when all this was going on? Maybe you're one of those angels of mercy," I accused.

"How dare you!" Her hand flew to her heart. "Unlike you, I have a solid alibi and a sterling reputation above such suspicions."

"Yeah, well, I have a headache." Of course she had a sterling reputation. Lois Urho was practically royalty what with the town named after her great-great grandfather Josiah Luce, first President of the Northern Pacific. I got up, walked across that room, and slammed the door behind me, glad to be out of the hot seat and into the hot air.

"Trudy, wait," Huntermeister shouted.

I held out my wrists. "Go ahead. Cuff me."

"Stop being dramatic," he said. "You know I have to ask you questions."

"And you know I'd never murder anyone. All these years you've known me, Dwight, think of all the good we've done side-by-side: fundraisers, river clean up, *Picnics Against Poverty.* I'm not a murderer!"

"Assisted suicide, well that's more likely—"

"How do you know Lois didn't do it?"

"It'd be hard to say no to someone you care about asking to help end his pain. I get that you were fond of Lyle."

"Well get this, Dwight. You might think I'm capable, but you know I'm not stupid, and I'm not talking to you anymore about Lyle."

Dwight leaned in close. "Get a lawyer, Trudy. You're implicated at the scene of a crime *and* you'll have a fight coming as potential beneficiary of all this." He motioned around and then held my shoulder. "As your friend, I'm—"

"Friend?" I laughed. "That ship sailed." I felt shaky and wondered if I'd already said more than I should have. "Friends don't turn on each other," I said.

"I'm not turning on you, Trudy. I'm telling you. Get a lawyer."

2

I got in my car and gagged. The warming carrier had over-heated in the sun on my back seat and the undelivered lunches smelled gross. Screw it, I thought. Just screw it. My hands were shaking. *Implicated at the scene of a crime.* I pounded the steering wheel thinking of how I'd cooked my goose and imagining how upset Don would be.

I was about to drive away when I saw Huntermeister cut across the muddy yard, around the chicken wire fence to Wanderi's Mini-Mart parking lot. He stopped, turned, and seemed to scrutinize Lyle's house. Maybe thinking it wouldn't be hard for someone with murder on their mind to hide. Overgrown shrubbery and thick pines with low-hanging branches grew close to the sad, shabby house.

Huntermeister went inside the store. I needed something for my throbbing head. I cut across Lyle's yard to the Mini-Mart. Through the window, I saw Huntermesiter head to the rear of the store. I ducked inside. I may have been large, but I was good at hiding. I kept low and off to the side, scanned shelves by the pop coolers, inching up enough to see Dwight pumping out coffee. He tilted the creamer container, fiddled with the top, tipped it again, and then walked to the front counter. "Mind filling this?" he said.

"Not at all, officer," Nunda Ward said.

I inched up as Nunda reached into a cooler behind the counter. Her waist-length hair was as blonde as she was skinny. A runaway with an abusive father and a dead mother, she landed with her grandmother who owned and operated the town's only movie theater. Nunda had nervous tics, like licking her lips and biting the ends of her hair. She had shifty eyes that never seemed to land on customers. I pitied her. I mean what chance did a girl like that have in life? Still, I always watched her count out my change.

"Nunda," Huntermeister said. "You have a pretty good vantage point—"

"A what?"

"A good view of Lyle Staybler's house."

Nunda leaned on the counter and turned toward Lyle's. "You mean that gross haunted house that'll get bulldozed?"

"I mean Mr. Staybler's house."

"Oh, yeah, guess so."

"You see much comings and goings?"

I lifted a box of Aleve then inched closer to the end of the aisle near a cosmetics display; figured I could use some Cover Girl on my bruise.

"It's not like I sit on my butt, you know. Gets freakin' busy around here."

"I'll bet. Just thought maybe if you ever looked over there you might've seen something strange."

She scratched her skinny arm. "It's super creepy and totally bitchin' about the ghosts."

"You've seen ghosts over there?" Dwight asked, surprised.

"What if I have? Not against the law to see ghosts," Nunda said. "There's lots of cars around there this morning. Probably having one of those séances."

"Who says?"

"Who doesn't? The old guy kills animals and buries 'em in his woods. People's dogs disappear. Nobody swims in the lake 'cause you sink to the bottom and never come up."

"Who says it'll be bulldozed?"

"Huh?"

"You said the house would be bulldozed. Where'd you hear that?"

"The boss."

"Jerry?"

"*Mister* Wanderi to me," she said.

"When did he say it?"

"When doesn't he?" she replied. "He's always cussing at the house. Gets all emo. Throws stuff at it."

"Stuff?"

"Rocks and stuff, says to shut the crows up but sometimes I don't hear no crows."

"If he mentions it again, you can tell him I said not to bet on that bulldozing."

The door opened. "Tell him yourself."

"Looks like another downpour coming." Jerry limped toward the counter. "Feel it in my bones." A farming accident left him with a bum leg. Huge medical bills wiped out his bank account, forced him to auction off his family farm. A small settlement he got from a lawsuit against the manufacturer of the faulty combine bought him his Mini-Mart. He had a pretty good monopoly along this strip until big box stores moved in. On that we shared common ground. I pretty well figured he'd been bitter toward Lyle for managing to hold onto his family's land and fortune, probably the real reason for his lack of neighborliness.

"See anything suspicious at Lyle's this morning?" Dwight asked.

"Don't pay no attention to the place," Jerry said testily. "I'd put up a ten-foot fence if it'd keep that eyesore out of my sight. Roof shingles blew over here after yesterday's storm. Place should be condemned."

My phone dinged a text message from my daughter: *Call me back!*

I texted: *In a minute.* I stood up to see Dwight smirking at me.

"You ought to buy some ice for that bump," he said, pointing at my head. He started to walk away, then turned. "And,

Trudy, you ought to hide where the security mirrors can't find you." I looked up to see our distorted reflections in the fish-eye mirror.

I held up the Aleve and Cover Girl. "Ten four Good Buddy."

"Hey Dwight." Jerry shuffled over to us. "Something might interest you. Trudy was hauling stuff out of there a few days ago."

"Thought you didn't pay attention to the place," I said.

"Trudy, that true?" Dwight kept the focus on me.

"To make way for the hospital bed," I quickly defended.

"Didn't see such a bed there," Dwight countered.

"Supposed to be delivered tomorrow. Ask Lois. I took out a bunch of newspapers, a beat-up chair, a gazillion Red Owl grocery bags."

"Looked like more than that to me," Jerry said.

"Yeah, well looks can be deceiving."

"No. Pretty sure it was more."

My skin was crawling and I needed to get out of there. "Your word against mine. Maybe you just like accusing me of what you've been doing for years."

"Don't follow," Jerry said.

"Lyle suspected you were stealing wood from his land." I nodded toward the stacked firewood for sale outside the Mini-Mart.

"He never pressed charges," Jerry said.

"Because he pitied you," I said. "You gave him a hard time; he offered you pity. That's how good he was."

"Was?"

"Lyle passed away today," Dwight said. "Been sick with cancer."

"Sorry to hear it," Jerry said.

Dwight touched the brim of his cap. "Might need to talk to you later, hear more about that wood."

"Anytime, Chief," Jerry said unconvincingly.

Just then Wanda Laconda came into the store and stood close to Dwight who stepped around her and then hurried out the door. I was paying for my purchases when she looked at me and shrugged like I'd get what she was thinking. Wanda was a skinny, nervous woman in her fifties working in the grain elevator office and rumored to have a meth habit.

A month earlier, I'd spotted her at the town's recycling center, bent over inside the magazine bin, apparently searching for something good to read. Now she stood in the Mini-Mart doorway blocking my exit and watching Dwight walk toward Lyle's house. "Excuse me," I had to say twice before I got her attention off Dwight's back and her body out of my way.

In my car, I swallowed two Aleve with stale travel mug coffee. I looked in the rear view mirror at my bruise, opened the package, and applied the liquid make-up. The air conditioning was running at maximum and the car finally stopped stinking like roast turkey sitting too long in the heat. I was going to put the car in reverse when I saw one of Dwight's men come out of the woods with a dog and then up the porch stairs and through the front door, the bright orange DO NOT RESUSCITATE orders still posted there.

Then a white van pulled up. It looked official, a no-frills government-issued vehicle. A tall, broad-shouldered man dressed in a serious-looking black suit and a lanky woman wearing a somber black pantsuit got out. They looked like two crows. They glanced left and then right, before walking up the steps and into the house. I had a mind to go up and rap on the door, pretend that I'd forgotten something, and find out what was going on. Then some wiser side of me decided I did not want to talk to those people and should drive off. My cell phone dinged a message: *Mom. I need the check for the swim meet!*

3

I had to call Don and tell him I was running late, write a check for Courtney, and yes I had a good reason. I'd explain later.

After stopping home to grab my *Luce Swim Team* cap and re-apply make up over my deepening bruise, I drove to the outdoor community pool. I walked through the shabby concrete entrance building that smelled like mildew and chlorine and out to the pool surrounded by chain link fence. I looked around for Courtney, wanting to catch her eye, let her see I made it. She was huddled with teammates under an umbrella. The sun beat down as I scanned the crowd sitting on lawn chairs and blankets.

Above the shouts of the cheering crowd, I heard someone yell, "Hey, Trudy." Sandy Mattfield, one of my volunteers, was waving through the chain-link. I walked over to her.

"Aren't you coming in?" I asked.

"I can't. Just got a call to show one of my listings." She reached into her canvas bag and pulled out sunscreen. "Would you give this to Allison?"

"You bet."

"She's so busy with her friends, I can't get her attention." She tossed the tube over the high fence.

When I looked up to catch it, my cap fell off. I quickly put it back on. "Got it," I said, waving the tube.

"Make sure she puts it on, would you? She'll fry to a crisp if she doesn't." She looked hard at me. "What happened to your face?"

"Born with it." I laughed while she stared. I pulled my cap down to deepen the shadow over the bruise.

"Put some on yourself, too. The back of your neck is red."

"Yes, Mom. Whatever."

"You sound like Allison. And please assuage my guilt over having to leave by cheering extra loud for her."

"You bet."

"Oh, say. There's a lot of action at the Staybler place. News over the police scanner indicates a 10-56 or 187."

"A what?"

"Possible suicide or murder," she said. "Don't you visit him?"

"Yep. Well better get this to Allison." I heard my voice break as I stuck the sunscreen in my shirt pocket. I felt suddenly shaken by such news coming at me through a fence. I had to force back an image of myself behind prison bars, not let my nerves undermine me and my story.

"Let me know if you hear anything about it," Sandy said. "Witch hazel is good for bruises." She touched her forehead. "You could use some on that."

"Will do." I squeezed sunscreen into my palm, rubbed it into my skin. Don was standing behind lane four, his *Luce Swim Team* tee shirt wet and his running shorts even wetter. He looked all the more appealing, the yellow of his shirt bringing out the tan good looks of his face. The swimmers flipped for the final turn and headed to the finish. Don leaned over the edge of the pool, waiting with stopwatch in hand. The swimmer came in hard, taking first place and dousing Don. I was about to walk over to him, tell him I'd take over timing if he wanted to shoot photos—he was the so-called official team photographer—when Darcy Loking placed her hand on his shoulder and offered him a towel. After he wiped his face, she whispered in his ear, stepped back, and they both laughed until she walked away. I put my sunglasses on and stared. Darcy was owner of the new Sassy Spa and

Exercise Studio and on the hunt for some male to pick up the slack her ex-husband left behind. She put together the swim team's newsletter and often called Don to request photos. Her daughter Justine had a reputation for being fast, and not just in the pool.

"Mom!" I jumped at Courtney's voice behind me. I turned to see *Pluth Rocks* written on her beautiful cheeks. I really wished the girls wouldn't write on each other with markers, but other parents didn't seem to mind. Don defended the ritual as spirited. "Didn't you see me waving my head off at you?" She tapped a marker against her palm.

"Sun must've been in my eyes."

"Mom, you're totally wearing sunglasses. And a cap."

"Give me that pen," I said.

"What for?"

"Courtney, give it to me."

She relinquished the pen. "Other moms don't care that—"

I grabbed her waist, pulled her close, and wrote *FIRE UP* inside her arm.

She laughed. "That tickles."

Courtney had her father's easy smile. Sometimes, I'd catch rare glimpses of me in my daughter, like how she squinted before losing her temper or bit her lip when deep in thought. Courtney is dark like Don and has his long, slender nose and high cheekbones. I'm short and busty. She's tall and thin. Iris Tucker, friend and Homes for Dwelling volunteer, noted the similarities Courtney had with Don the first time she met my family, commenting that Courtney's brown eyes were kind, like Don's. Never did my faded red hair, drab green eyes, and fair freckled skin get me such compliments. It was not easy being the red-headed step child in the family; though when I told Iris that, she said I had a pretty face. I told her she needed glasses; a high forehead and double chin were not ideal.

I suddenly felt like hugging Courtney, which took her by surprise. "Love you."

"Mom!" She looked around, probably concerned that her coolness factor was compromised.

"Pizza tonight," I said. "Remember to invite your friends."

"Totally."

"Now go get 'em girl."

She hurried back to the group.

Don was sitting with his usual perfect posture in a folding chair behind lane four watching the swimmers slog back and forth through the water. One thing I admired about Don, he was always in the moment, not preoccupied with other thoughts or wishing he was elsewhere. He genuinely appreciated people and they gravitated toward him with affection.

Born and raised in Luce, Don brought me to town fourteen years earlier. After completing carpentry certification at Minnesota State Community and Technical College, I worked for a restoration company in St. Paul. Driving on the interstate one afternoon, I spotted Don on the shoulder with a flat tire. I stopped to help. He offered to buy me a cup of coffee.

It was interesting hearing about the family hardware store and Queen Anne house he inherited after his parents were killed when their cruise ship cabin was flooded by a 60-foot wave. His older brother wanted nothing to do with Luce and took off for good after the funeral to roam South America. Don told me how people in town rallied around him in those difficult days while he tried to figure out his life and moved through grief, not knowing how he'd ever endure. As he talked, he seemed vulnerable yet strong, a survivor.

He got to flirting, said he noticed my shirt was unbuttoned and maybe he could open up the next one. When I realized Don was five years younger than me, I felt like I should send him on his way home. But then he suggestively asked me if I'd like to see his three-story Queen Anne with its cutaway bay windows and wraparound porch. I thought, what the heck, why not get in bed with this man? Four months later, I was pregnant and married. I gave birth to Courtney but never shed my excess pregnancy weight, piling on even more pounds because—as I very well knew—I did not take good care of myself.

After the race ended and Don handed his stopwatch over to another parent to take his place timing, I went over to him. "I'm here."

"What took you so long?"

"Oh, man do I have something important to—"

"Hey there," Darcy called out, waved, and walked toward us.

"What do you have to tell me?"

"It's a long story," I said before Darcy was in earshot.

"Was wondering if you'd show up." She stood too close for comfort.

I stepped back and pulled the cap down to shadow my face. "Don't you just hate when a day gets away from you?" I then remembered the sunscreen I was to deliver to Allison. I pulled the tube from my pocket, told Don I'd be right back, and headed in the other direction.

"Trudy," Darcy yelled, "You dropped this. I think it's ruined." She held out the black and white photo of Lyle, now smeared beyond recognition. A flash of our first meeting hit me, Lyle opening the door, me trying not to gag from the stench. I heard his voice saying, *Come in. Come in.*

Then I heard a voice yell, "Go Pluth."

I looked up to see Courtney by the block and then in the water, posed for the backstroke, waiting for the start. She took the lead and kept it the entire time, winning her event, contributing to the overall success of our team taking first place. I was relieved when the meet finally ended and I could avoid the idle chitchat people loved to partake in.

Later at Pizzeria Plus, Don and me ordered pizzas to go and then sat outside waiting and drinking beer. I removed my cap and showed Don the bruise.

"What the heck, Trudy. You get in a fight?"

"Lyle's dead."

"How's that connected to the bruise on your head?"

"I found him dead. Someone was in the house when I got there. They pushed me from behind and ran out."

"That doesn't make sense."

"I was the one who found him. I'm sort of a suspect in his death."

"From cancer?"

"Assisted suicide."

"That's crazy."

"I might be in trouble."

"What kind of trouble?"

"Because," I said, trying to keep my voice even. "I was the one that found him dead and Dwight questioned me about—"

"Questioned you? He should be thanking you for caring as much as you do. Going over there with your concern and—"

"Assisted suicide is a felony," I interrupted him.

"You helped him kill himself?"

"No, I did not, but Dwight said I better get a lawyer."

"Trudy. A lawyer? This is ridiculous. You wouldn't harm a flea."

"A bit extreme, but okay," I said, thinking of the mice I had no trouble poisoning.

"We'll get you a lawyer, pronto."

Soon back home, I was glad when the girls arrived with their chatter and energy. When Darcy's daughter asked about my bruise and the other girls turned to look at me, I laughed and said, "You should see the other guy, Justine."

"Seriously, Mom," Courtney said. "That's mega."

"Just hit my head doing repair work," I said. They lost interest after that.

Their activity kept me moving through the night. A few times I caught Don staring at me and I wondered if he thought I was capable of what Dwight suspected. I wondered if the bruise seemed like a lie to him, so I played my injury up, kept icing it and said several times, "Never saw whoever it was coming from behind."

Later that night, after Courtney and her friends went to see a movie at The Comet Theater, I was not happy to get a call from Huntermeister asking me to please return to Lyle's house first thing in the morning. BCI agents wanted to talk with me.

I forced my hands not to shake as I carried dishes into the kitchen where Don was trying to get the garbage disposal to work. I knew it was no use; the switch was faulty and on my list of things to do. The tray slipped from my hand and clanked onto the counter. "Whoa," Don said. "You scared me."

"Sorry." I felt like leaving the dishes and scraping peeling paint from the windowsill above the kitchen sink. But why bother? Once you began one repair, there was the next just waiting for you. I felt lousy for me and for my neglected house.

"Those girls can put away some pizza," Don said. "Only two pieces left." He set them in a container and opened the refrigerator. When he closed it and turned back to me, I was sitting at the counter with my head in my hands, the dishwasher wide open. "What's wrong?"

"I have to talk to BCI agents tomorrow."

"Take a lawyer with you."

"I don't have one, Don. And we don't have money for—"

"We'll find the money; we'll get a lawyer. This is insane." He took my hand and hugged me. I held onto such comfort for as long as he offered it.

4

Next morning, I walked up the steps to Lyle's house thinking about my story, telling myself not to get my extra-large undies in a bundle over some big wigs interrogating me. I'd simply tell them the same thing I told Dwight.

Inside the house, the man in the black suit I saw yesterday, pointed to Lyle's rocking chair. "Have a seat," he said.

"I prefer that chair over there." I sat down where I'd been interrogated by Huntermeister the day before. At least Lois wasn't around to give me the side eye.

"We understand you claim to have found Mr. Staybler."

"I claim it because I did."

"And that you had free access to the house."

"Free? Not so much. I helped here and there with things, delivered his lunches."

"Nevertheless you were able to come and go as you pleased?"

I nodded feeling really unsure where this man was leading me. He had one of those square jaws and sharp features, like he could take a fist in the face and not feel it. His dark hair was short and trimmed neat above the ears. His partner hovered nearby, not so much a part of the questioning but kind of listening, observing, maybe making mental notes.

"He was a good man," I said.

"Yes and with a very lucrative estate."

"I wouldn't know about that," I said.

He removed his suit coat, slung it over a box, and rolled up his shirtsleeves. Yesterday's heat had returned. "But you

do know about it," he said. "You indicated to Chief Huntermeister that you knew people wanted his land, so you
must've known it was valuable. Why would you say any
differently?"

"What I meant was his money was none of my business."

"And his house? Was his house your business?"

"Just did my good deeds when he needed me. That's all the
business I had here."

"Did you and he ever discuss you helping him take his
life?"

"No!"

"Nothing about a plan for you to do that in case the pain
got really bad for him?"

"I said no and no I did not do it."

"Did you write him this note?"

I took the note and read, *Going to put out mouse poison.
Don't mess with it.* "Looks like my handwriting."

"Where'd you put the mouse poison?"

"Kitchen and cellar."

"Did you lead him to believe his death would be easy?"

"Ridiculous," I said dismissively. I was shaking in my
boots.

"You might need to come in for questioning," he said.

"What for? I gave Dwight answers to his questions already."

"A more formal sort of questioning," he said.

"Am I under arrest?"

"Not yet," he said.

"What's that supposed to be? A threat?"

"Sounds like it," he said.

"If you knew me, you'd know I'd never—"

"Mind if we check your phone?"

"What for?" I patted my pocket feeling for my phone.

"Just like to check your call log," he said. He studied my
phone then passed it to his female partner.

"Should we dust it?" His partner made it sound like a joke, kind of smirked.

"No need." He turned back to me, stared like he could crack me.

"Would you take a lie detector test?" she then asked, her tone more serious. Unable to speak because of nerves, I nodded. "How about a drug test?" she asked.

I looked at Dwight, wanted him to be my friend, say that wasn't necessary but he just looked at the woman like he'd lost charge of his own show while I was in the hot seat. "For what?" I asked.

"Marijuana," the woman said.

I carried their container to the bathroom and peed into it, handing it back to some man wearing a mask and rubber gloves.

"I'm not that toxic," I joked nervously.

If he smiled, I couldn't tell. He wrote on the lid before securing it with white tape.

"One more thing," the man in black said. "Is it true you told the hospice nurse that the day they posted the Do Not Resuscitate orders was the day you thought Mr. Staybler was better off dead than alive?"

"She misquoted me," I said, and then leaned in conspiratorially. "Between you and me, Lois sometimes gets her wires crossed." I'd come to know her as a platitude-reciting woman of good works who carried a cross for Jesus. "She smiles too much."

"That's a problem?"

"Never trust someone who smiles too much."

"You smile much?" the man said.

I shrugged and thought of Lois. I figured with suspicions against me driving her mad, she'd probably lead a crusade to nail my butt to a wall, take anything I said out of context. Her reputation as the best hospice nurse in town was "sterling" to use her word, but I knew she could lean toward

artsy ways of thinking, like her telling Lyle to imagine himself as a Monarch butterfly feeding on milkweed to help him
enjoy that liquid nutritional drink Ensure. She'd have him
chew mint to soothe his stomach and parsley to cleanse his
breath. Real into plants like that. "Maybe she's jealous."

"Oh?"

"Sure, why else would she make something up like that?"

"So you didn't say he'd be better off dead than alive?"

"That's not what I said. She's putting words in my mouth."

"Why would she?"

"Ask her. Maybe she's got some secret she's trying to hide,
so she's all about me being guilty of something."

"So what did you say?"

"I can't remember. But not that."

"What then?"

"Don't remember."

"If it comes to you, let me know."

"What's it matter? Just her word against mine."

"What is?"

"When I said Lyle was better off…"

Damn!

"…Like I said, don't remember."

"So tell me again how you got that bruise."

I wanted to say for crap's sake, ask Dwight since I already
told him all about it, but I cooperated because the man was
staring bullets at me. For the next hour, I told my story again.

5

Two days later, me and Don were arguing over a new brand of paint. Don wanted to run a special. My way of thinking was to sell at full price for a month before marking it down. Don's business degree didn't mean he was necessarily shrewd about making a buck. New inventory didn't need marking down; it needed promotion. And we needed profits. Years ago I suggested we build up our business; learn about the latest technology, gizmos and trends; diversify. As soon as we got whiff of incoming big box chain stores along Highway 10, we should've gone into strategic-planning mode. I told Don, years before Tool Mart's arrival, that I was willing to put the brakes on Homes for Dwelling to help build the business. He didn't want me to, so I let it be and focused on saving old houses, even to the point of my own home suffering from neglect due to lack of funds. I popped two Aleve; my bruised head was really aching.

Developer Randall Short entered the store. "How's business?"

"Could be better," Don said.

"More money in doing nails than in selling 'em," Randall said. "Heard the new spa's profiting like gangbusters."

"Guess that's true," Don said.

"Heard Lyle Staybler died," he added, as if an afterthought.

"That's right," Don said. Randall looked at me but I kept my mouth shut and my bruised forehead hidden with a *Pluth Hardware Store* promotional cap. The bruise had turned an ugly shade of purple and seemed larger than before.

"So the state wins," Randall said.

"Don't catch your meaning," Don said.

"Turning it into a wildlife refuge. What a waste." He shook his head.

"How would you know about that?" I spoke up. Don squeezed my hand, a warning to keep quiet over the facts about Lyle's death and estate.

Randall laughed. "I got sources." I figured Martha, his wife, who is also my friend and volunteer, must've blabbed. He'd been pumping her for information about Lyle's place ever since I befriended Lyle five months earlier. I also knew he'd been stopping by Lyle's harassing him, trying to coerce him into selling his land. "Knew he was sick but didn't think he was that close to dead. Course it seems a bit off. His death."

Don and me didn't say anything.

"Shame about all that land going to waste," Randall said.

I took the bait. "What's it any of your business?" I stupidly pushed my cap back so I could glare at him.

He pointed to my bruise. "Whoa Nellie. You run into a wall or an enemy?"

"Sometimes they're the same," I said.

"Don't follow your meaning," Randall said.

"Something we can get you?" Don asked. He squeezed my hand to calm me.

Randall smiled, presented his most charming handsome self, leaned back a little, then forward as if to pull us into his confidence. I thought of young, naïve Martha snared by his smooth veneer all those years ago. "Thing is. They've got police tape around Lyle's house. Wondering why. No crime in dying of cancer that I know of, unless, of course, rumors about murder are true."

"Maybe it's to keep people like you from trespassing," I said.

"People like me? Upstanding, law-abiding citizen who just wants to take this town into the current century? I'm up to my ass in alligators, all the good deeds I got going now."

"Just got in a new line of paint," Don said. "Interested?"

"Only thing I'm interested in is why there'd be police tape around Lyle's house."

"Ask Dwight," I said.

"Oh I did. Hit a dead end for trying."

I kept my face averted and Randall left the store. Outside, he talked to the mail carrier, patted her back, and laughed. Charming, slick weasel. I knew his true colors, how he talked to Martha like she was a dim-witted dog and played mind games on her. Lyle saw Randall's true colors, too, told me how Randall came knocking, trying to convince Lyle to sell. Kept referring to Lyle's lake and land as pristine, a true tourist attraction waiting for accommodations, like his plan for condos and a lodge. So convenient right off Highway 10, yet reaching far enough back to make it an oasis, a real sweet spot of recreational beauty. I should've told the BCI guys what I knew about that, given them a different trail to sniff.

The next day I called Martha to coax anything out of her she might have heard. She was excited over some new craft she'd seen on a show. I pressed the phone to my ear as Martha asked me about making dried-hydrangea wreaths with her. I didn't have much patience for crafty things; but Martha liked company when she made that stuff, so sometimes I endured it. I told her I'd remember to snip the blooms from my bushes. Then I cut to the chase.

"Randall came to our store yesterday. Such a nice surprise." I tried to hide my sarcasm and sound sincere.

"Was he acting strange?"

"No stranger than usual," I said.

"I'm worried about him."

"He was asking about Lyle," I said. "Wonder how Randall got wind about Lyle's land going to the state."

"I knew it."

"Knew what?"

"I think he convinced Lyle to sell to him before he died," Martha confided in a hush.

"Trust me. He didn't."

"You could be wrong," she said. "I heard Lyle was murdered."

"He wasn't murdered!"

"How can you be so certain?"

"I'm the one who found him when ..." Oh hell I was supposed to keep my mouth shut.

"You were? So the rumor is true?"

"He wasn't murdered. Remember, he had terminal cancer."

"Well that's what I told Randall, but he's all—"

"So what makes you think he convinced Lyle to sell to him?"

"He was on the phone about surveying Lyle's land."

"Talking to who?"

"I don't know."

"Think, Martha."

"I don't know, but I believe if Lyle sold to Randall, I have every right to know."

"For crap's sake, Martha. He did not sell to Randall!"

"Language, Trudy."

"Well he didn't."

"Don't snap at me. Randall's always snapping. I'm tired of it."

"Sorry," I said, wanting to keep her from pouting. I'd told her often enough that pouting never won a battle.

I met Martha years ago when she knocked on the door of a Homes For Dwelling house. I sized her up and expected a mousy little squeak of a voice, but she surprised me when she said all confident like with a deep voice that she wanted to volunteer. I didn't think she'd be able to do much, given her ladylike stance, but holy smokes if she didn't know how to hammer nails with the best of us. Her kind view of things often helped me see the good stuff I might've missed. I guess, like Don said, Martha brought out the best in me, but still I had to be careful. So like I said, she's my friend who couldn't keep a secret, but that also worked in my favor. Randall pumped her about Homes For Dwelling properties. I pumped her for information on Randall's properties in case EPA or DNR might be dogging him.

"Maybe if Randall got what he wanted, he'd be easier to live with," she said.

"Wouldn't we all."

She sighed. "He doesn't tell me things anymore."

"Trust me. He didn't get Lyle's land."

"I found a letter on his desk. There's asbestos in Pugmeyer's building. Demolition's on hold and it'll cost a fortune. The EPA is worthless. Government intruding where it has no business." She was parroting Randall. She continued, "And to top it off, they found arsenic in the groundwater at the old fairgrounds. Who's going to want to develop there?"

"No kidding?" I said, pretending not to have already heard that, "Arsenic at his site?"

"Gosh darn it. He needs something to go right," she said.

I felt for Martha, but I smiled because whenever Randall's company had a set back, it meant less money for him to buy up land and buildings. My skin crawled when I thought about what he did to the 1902 St. Paul Hospital, a three-story, red-brick beauty with bell tower. After a non-descript new hospital went up mid-century, the old St. Paul Hospital's downward spiral began. It was used as a nursing home, then professional offices, then community ed. classes, and finally doomed after Randall Short's purchase. Boom, just like that the beautiful building was rubble. I went ahead and helped myself to bricks so St. Paul could live on in my backyard patio.

"Did you hear me?" Martha asked.

"What?"

"Property taxes go up before he can even begin a project.

But Lyle's land would be different. Investors are ready for it. What a tourist attraction."

"No way, Martha. You said yourself it'd be a shame if Lyle's land got developed."

"I just want him to catch a break. With this economy and all … well … we don't need a state refuge. We need progress. It shouldn't be this hard."

I wanted to say her life would be easier if she'd leave Randall for good. But why stir it all up? Twice it did get bad enough that she left him. The first time, he came home drunk and took it out on Michael, making him sleep on the floor because he wet the bed. The second time was after he took his anger out on Ruthie, telling her she was stupider than her mother and screaming at her until she ran out the door and hid in nearby woods. Both times Martha took the three kids and stayed at her mother's place near the old mill where the Otter Tail River runs along 78. Randall vowed to quit drinking and her mother was all for saving the marriage, saying Jesus would protect them. Sent Martha home with her tail between her legs.

Martha said if you push your tongue against the back of your teeth, you could force yourself to smile for a long time, a beauty pageant competitor's trick. She read the lamest junk in those women's magazines, but I guess that helped her cope to avoid the hard work of changing. Once I tried to get her to read an article I ripped from a psychology journal in the clinic waiting room. It was about the harmful effects on health when people avoid fixing relationship problems. After I gave it to her, she tossed it in the trash, told me I should look in my own backyard, and quoted a Bible passage: *learn to know God's will for you, which is good and pleasing and perfect.* Whatever. I just let it go. Anyway, it's easier to see the weakness in others and what they should change than it is to focus on oneself; I've since come to understand.

"Oh, and," Martha said, "Dwight came on official business to our house."

"Yeah?" I was really interested in that but kept my eagerness in check.

"They were talking in the kitchen. I was at the dining room table scrapbooking. I'm almost done with Michael's book. It's so hard to choose what to include when you have ten years of a child's stuff to—"

"So what about Dwight?"

"He asked why Randall hadn't been playing basketball with the guys. Wanted to know if Randall was still attending AA, keeping in touch with his sponsor. Randall said, 'What're you, my mother now?' Dwight said in a joking way it'd be a hard role for anyone to take on. Then his tone changed. He wanted to know why Randall was out on Lyle's land the other day. Randall said it was a free country—which it is—and he could go wherever he wanted to. Especially if Lyle sold to Randall."

"Martha. I am telling you. He did not sell the house to Randall."

"Maybe the land, then."

"No."

"You don't always know everything, Trudy!"

Bless her heart; she sure was right about that.

6

As the days passed, my bruise itched and turned an ugly shade of yellow-green beneath the Cover Girl make-up. On a service call for the hardware store, I stood on a ladder installing an energy efficient window. Returning to do maintenance work on one of my former Homes for Dwelling houses felt kind of like playing nurse to my child's injury. My knees ached but otherwise I felt good about minding my own business—and the store's. Adept at repair work, I did the service calls and Don tended to the retail side of things.

The house where I worked that morning had sat empty for years after the owner's death. Her family bickered with each other, which kept the property off the market as it deteriorated. Chief Huntermeister—back when he was my friend—said he'd hold them liable if teenagers trespassing and partying inside got hurt. If the family couldn't afford to make it marketable or raze it, they could donate it to Homes for Dwelling. My volunteers thought I was insane to take it on; it being across the street from the Municipal Cemetery, close to the railroad tracks, and downwind from the dog food factory. But I had a vision for that 1910 Folk Victorian home. To help with funding, I got a grant from the county because the house had historical significance. It was the only one left in Luce with its spindle work detailing the porch, cornice-line brackets, and a symmetrical façade. We did a praiseworthy job. A devout fertile Catholic couple moved in with their five kids.

I thought back to the day we turned the keys over to them, all of us gathered on the porch for the newspaper photos and then for a potluck celebration at my house. The couple brought the best rhubarb pies I'd ever tasted as offering to the spread laid out on my dining room table. I gave them a tour of mine and Don's house and they oohed and ahhed over every inch. Afterward we had a croquet tournament in the backyard and laughed when someone hit the ball so hard it flew into the alley. Don took tons of photos and I added some to the Homes for Dwelling families album. We did a lot of laughing and celebrating before Lyle's death unleashed the suspicious turn of events.

I had to stop thinking about the good old days because after news of Lyle's death, my volunteers started giving me the stiff arm, not showing up at a meeting to discuss possible property acquisitions, and leaving flimsy excuses in my voice mail as to why they had to drop from the group.

That all started happening after an article about Lyle's death appeared in the weekly *Luce Bulletin*: *Foul Play Suspected in Wealthy Recluse's Death*. And yours truly was featured in paragraph two: *Trudy Pluth, the last to see Mr. Staybler alive, was questioned*… The reporter got it wrong, naming me as the last person to see Lyle alive, but he did get it right that I'd been questioned by BCI agents and that no charges were filed. Some bigwig hospice administrator noted the gravity of a patient in their care dying under suspicious circumstances and promised there'd be a full investigation. Didn't see any mention of Lois in that article. Dwight declined an interview and refused to provide more details about the death.

By the end of the week, other volunteers left messages saying they were dropping out. One claimed she could no longer work with me under such a cloud of suspicion. It was hard to remember working as a team with those women who were supposed to be my friends. *Don't let the door hit you on the way out*, I thought to myself.

Iris Tucker remained loyal, called me right away, worried

and angry at the idea of someone suspecting me. Said I should contact the others, tell them I was not responsible for Lyle's death. Tell them like I told her the story about finding him. It was tempting, but I said there was no way I'd grovel to get anyone back who suspected me of murder. Martha also called to say she was praying for me against suspicious minds. Said I should cheer up and put my trust in the Lord. He knew I was innocent and so did she. I was grateful for those two. Or should I say three: Iris, Martha, and her Jesus?

I'd finally told them about Lyle's house left to Homes for Dwelling, but I made sure to keep my mouth shut about his land coming my way since Huntermeister insisted on it. Not telling Iris and Martha about the land was harder than removing dried adhesive from wood flooring.

I finished the window work and was folding up the ladder when Dwight came whistling around the corner. "You tracking me?"

"Don said you'd be here."

"Didn't know that was newsworthy." I leaned the ladder against the van: *Pluth Hardware, Paint and Glass: Give Us A Break.* Don thought that was so clever. Yutz Signs lettered it in black and I learned to live with it. The old van was on its last leg anyway, so what the hey. I wiped my face with a bandana and joined Dwight under the shade of a young tree planted too close to the house. Not good for the foundation to have roots so close. I considered leaving a note suggesting they transplant it, but ended up letting it go because the talk with Dwight distracted me.

He looked around. "You working alone?"

"Why wouldn't I be? No volunteers help with store business. Besides they made a beeline away from me since news of Lyle's death."

"Sorry to hear it, Trudy." He sounded sincere. "You still keeping a lid on news of your inheriting the land?" Dwight wore a baseball cap, t-shirt, and jeans. Even out of uniform, he had an air of authority, tan and lean with muscles that bulged beneath his short sleeves. He practiced martial arts, so his hands and feet were dangerous like his gun. One of those viral bald-headed older men who seemed to have more testosterone than men half his age, Dwight attracted younger women. His love life was often in the gossip mill. Hadn't heard anything of any love interest on his part lately. Must've hit a dry spell. I wished he'd take another lover, give people something other than me to discuss.

"Yes, yes. I haven't said a word."

"Good. Don't need that out just yet."

"Got a question for you."

"Shoot," he said.

"Wouldn't Mark Riepe be someone to question? He's claimed rights to Lyle's place for years. Why don't you turn the heat up on him?"

"Ah I see. You want me to quit bugging you."

"Seems about right."

"Lyle ever say if he feared Mark might harm him?"

"Don't know if it was that so much."

"What then?" Dwight leaned against the back porch railing.

"He was a nuisance."

"Do you know if Mark ever threatened him?"

"Why not ask Mark?"

"He won't talk to me."

"That must hurt your feelings," I said. "Can I *not* talk to you?"

"I was at the Mini-Mart and he was just leaving. Nunda said she wondered if he'd keep watching the house now that the old guy was dead. Said she saw him sneak around the back of Lyle's house the other day, suggested I 'investigate.'" Dwight put air quotes around the word. "Thought maybe Mark helped kill dogs in the woods."

"I'd like to know who started that rumor."

"Maybe Lyle did," Dwight said.

"What?"

"To scare kids from coming on his land."

"Yeah, well be careful what you believe with Nunda. She's troubled. Might be playing with your head."

"Could be." He rubbed the back of his neck. "Seems Mark would get coffee, sit in his truck, and stare at the house. Nunda said one day he rushed into the store and screamed at her, said she poisoned the coffee, and he wanted a refund."

"Pathetic," I said.

"Nathan Buck caught the youngest son letting his dogs chase deer." Dwight rubbed his neck harder, like just the thought of Arnold Riepe put a bigger pain there. "Sixteen years old and nothing but trouble for years."

"Mark's a real mean SOB. Wonder if that kid'll leave town when he's eighteen like the two older ones did," I said.

"Can't help but feel for the boy, left by his mother with his father and grandmother, most likely the one that put ideas into Mark's head about rights to an inheritance from Lyle."

"I wouldn't know, but can tell you what Lyle shared about Mark." I stretched my leg and rubbed my aching knee.

"Let's hear it," Dwight said.

◆　◆　◆

Lyle was at the sink rinsing an aluminum lunch container when his cellar door opened and Mark appeared. Said Mark seemed to be hiding something inside his coat.

"Lyle," Mark said, "Left your cellar window open."

"Takes gall to break into a man's house."

"Saw that sign on your front door. You sick?" Mark said. "Need any help?"

"Get out!"

"Don't need to be rude, Cousin."

"Not your cousin," Lyle told him.

"Don't you invite guests to sit down?"

"You're not a guest."

"That's right. I'm relation. My grandmother and your grandfather were—"

"I got no connection to the likes of you."

"Sure you do. People living a hundred years ago just as important as family living right now."

"You got no legitimacy connected to me."

"One way or another family sticks together like glue." He leaned close. "Keeps what belongs to the family in the family."

"State gets what's mine."

Lyle said Mark looked angry but then laughed. "Easy to change that. All you got to do is draw up what they call an intestate will. I done one for Mother."

"I bet you did."

"She asked about you before she died, Cousin. Shame you never visited her. Not once. What kind of nephew doesn't visit his dying aunt?"

"Not my aunt."

"Just 'cause she got denied her birthright don't mean she's not."

"Take whatever you got hidden; makes no difference to me. Just get out!"

"Only need two witnesses to sign a new will. Get my boy, Arnold, to come here and sign; me and him. That's two. Good as anything in a court of law."

"Get out!"

"Well, you go ahead. Think about it. I got time. No sweat."

"Trouble since the day you were born."

"Listen, I'll come back around and see you soon, make sure you're doing alright."

"And steal something else?"

"Steal from family?"

"Get out!"

Lyle said Mark laughed real close to his face and then left.

◆   ◆   ◆

Dwight rubbed his chin. "Mark's never been prone to violence that I know of, but I'm wondering if he might've threatened Lyle?"

"Lyle didn't say. Seems if he did, Lyle would've told me. You know, just thinking about Mark walking out of the house with whatever he slipped under his coat, maybe Lyle's stuff is at risk. Vandals and thieves go right for an empty house. Someone ought to watch it and we ought to remove valuables. I could start clearing the place out. If people know someone's in there, more likely they'll stay away. Prevent breaking and entering."

"Get yourself a lawyer, Trudy," Dwight said. "You'll need help with what you're facing. You can't assume ownership and take it over just like that. Get a lawyer to explain it. Far as I know, word's still not out about the land. When news hits, it'll spread like wildfire. You don't want to get burned by fights heading your way. You'll be smart to avoid Mark."

"I'll keep that in mind." Then something occurred to me. "Maybe Mark and Randall are a team!"

"A team?"

"Lyle said he told Mark he planned to will his land to the state. What if Martha wasn't the one who told Randall about that? What if Mark told him? Maybe those two were in cahoots for some reason, shifty birds of a feather flocking together, stopping by Lyle's house, doubling up on him. Maybe Randall was planning some kind of dirty work against the house.

"It's a thought," he said unconvinced.

"A good one," I said.

We walked around to the front of the house where a white car was parked behind Dwight's cruiser. "This has got to stop," Dwight said.

A woman stepped out from the shade of a dying elm. It was Wanda Laconda. She waved. "Hey there. Brought you lunch."

Dwight turned fast on his heels and hurried to the side of the house. Wanda just stood watching. He made a call, but I couldn't hear because a train was going by and he was turned away from me. He soon hung up. He looked toward the front yard and took a deep breath like he was gearing himself up for something unpleasant.

"Find any leads in Lyle's woods yet?" I asked stalling for time, hoping he'd explain Wanda's appearance as the train slowly moved away.

My question seemed to pull his mind free from something. "Found garbage and a huge junk pile; illegal dumping. Need to get EPA out there."

"Tire tracks?" I asked.

He shook his head.

"Jerry steals wood, so you'd find his," I said. "Maybe look for some others!"

"Trudy," he paused, "Do I look like I don't know how to investigate a case?"

I shrugged. "Just saying Jerry steals wood. Never know what else is going on."

"Far as I know Lyle never filed a complaint so I don't have reason to suspect Jerry of much other than greed." He was walking and I was following.

"Oh, sure," I said, getting mad. "But you, the BCI, and half the town can suspect me of killing a man."

"Just doing my job. You know that."

"I'm just a job to you?"

"It's a lot like working on a house, Trudy."

"Whatever that means."

"Got to focus on what needs attention to do the job right."

"Maybe so, but all your questions amount to a lot of focus on me."

"No charges filed against anyone."

"Yet," I added. I stopped walking as he continued toward his car. He ignored Wanda holding up a fast food bag dotted with grease as if that would clinch his desire and affection. He got into his cruiser and drove away. Wanda soon followed, her radio blaring country music down the road.

7

As my bruise continued to fade, Don filled with worry over things he'd been hearing about me around town.

I held ice to my still-tender forehead. "Like what have you heard?" I asked, ready to take it on the chin.

"You being the last one to see Lyle alive."

"Not true."

"That you'd put saving a house over saving a person any day."

"Seriously? Someone said that?" I tossed the ice cube in the sink.

"Call Julianna," he said. "She was kind after my parents died, guided me through all the estate paperwork when I inherited the store and house." He gazed out the kitchen window then turned back to me. The way he looked, kind of lost in some point in time, made me feel edgy. "I was just a kid, really, and had to give up my dreams to—"

"Don't I need a lawyer who defends criminals?" I shouldn't have interrupted, but I could not just stand there listening to Don's remorse about giving up his dreams when I was feeling the nightmare of judgment on me.

"Don't call yourself that." He looked up a number and wrote it down. I ripped the sheet from the pad and stuck it in my shirt pocket.

"You suggesting I call Julianna doesn't have anything to do with your crush on her?"

He laughed. "She was—"

"I know. I know," I said, "Otter Tail County Dairy Princess—"

"Love at first sight."

"—tossed you some candy."

"Aimed right for me." He held up his hand as if that candy flew straight out of the past and into our kitchen.

"And threw you a kiss from the float."

"Every four-year-old's fantasy," he said dreamily.

"Hmm."

"Guess I always preferred older women." He punched my arm.

I don't like to be reminded that I'm five years older than Don. People sometimes assume he's way younger, with his boyish good looks and easy charm, and that maybe I'm his overweight older sister.

I was on the leaner side of chubby, curvaceous, when we met but grew wider with each year of maternal and domestic bliss. In truth, it was in my nature to focus on projects rather than take care of myself. No matter how often I had vowed to lose weight or to be less driven at work, I could not do it until it was forced on me.

I soon dialed Julianna's number and got a recorded message to call another number. I was surprised when she, not her secretary, answered. "I closed the office for remodeling," she said. "Don gave us a great discount on paint."

"Oh that Don, so darn thoughtful," I said sarcastically. A successful attorney, heir to the Mandle family's timber fortune, and a big shot in the Luce Rotary Club and Chamber of Commerce, she did not need a discount. Was the orthodontist going to give us a discount on Courtney's braces? Was the auto mechanic going to give us a discount on repairs to the store van that threatened to fall apart each time I drove it? No, with a capital N. But Don loved to give a discount. I told myself to calm down; her long-ago kindnesses still mattered to him. After Julianna relocated her practice to a one-and-a-half story Bungalow—one that I'd been chomping at the bit to get—she discovered the foundation was shot. She hired me to do the repair work. Once that was done, she instructed the interior designer to buy all paint and supplies from our store. She stayed loyal while other customers ditched Pluth Hardware for Tool Mart on Ten.

"We'll have to meet at my father's place," she said. "I have free time later this morning. I set up my office in the kitchen. Come to the back door."

The twenty-minute drive gave me time to think about building my case and to enjoy the road parallel to Luce Lake. Resorts and Stewart's Pizza were doing a bustling business on that summer day with cars in the lots and people milling around cabins and the lake. I soon turned onto the road dead-ended at Tom Mandle's makeshift billboard: *Support Local Farmers. Drink Real Milk.* Eccentric old guy had his priorities in order. Martha's house—the first in a long line of new houses going up along Luce Lake Road—abutted his land. The Luce Lake Association had tried to get Tom to tear down his dairy sign, proclaiming it an eyesore. He then placed a rusted out pick-up truck beside it. No one told Tom what to do on his own land, which extended from the point on Luce Lake all the way across the acres from the dead end road to the lake's north shore, including a four-acre island. He was a shrewd man who continued the family practice of investing their logging fortune in foreclosed land in and around Luce. Takes money to make money and it takes money to take advantage.

I turned into Tom's long driveway to see the classic two-story farmhouse, first structure built on the lake in the mid 1800s. It got me charged up thinking about restoring Lyle's house to its original state.

I knocked on the back door and heard, "Come in."

"Thanks for meeting with me," I said. It was cool inside, an overhead fan whirring, and an open window letting in a lake breeze. The extreme heat that hit the day Lyle died had moved on. The kitchen décor seemed to belong to a farm-woman cooking huge meals for crews and tending the hen-houses, gathering eggs for town delivery. The wall calendar should have read 1950 to coincide with the Skelgas stove and Northstar refrigerator. The green mottled linoleum was older than the hills but in good shape. Well, why didn't I just tie on a gingham apron and wash some dishes?

Seeing Julianna in her tailored outfit and silver jewelry placed me back in the present. I couldn't tell if the rumor that she had a facelift was true. She just looked like a well-kept fiftyish woman with sleek dark hair to her skinny shoulders. I wore a pair of khakis and a white linen shirt but still felt shabby in comparison, more in line with the kitchen curtains than with Julianna. She shook my hand as some professional formality, I guess. Her palm was smooth in my calloused one. The *Luce Bulletin* was on the counter. "I was just re-reading Lyle's obituary to my father."

Tom sat at the table with another section of the paper. We nodded to each other.

"Would you like coffee?" she asked.

"Coffee'd be great," I said.

"Help yourself. Cups are in the pantry," she said. I grabbed a mug with a *Luce Implement* logo. "I make it strong, so if you want milk, it's in the 'fridge."

"Black." Tom held out his mug, eyes on the paper. I assumed he wanted me to fill it, so I did. He circled a classified ad with a Sharpie. His hands were large, aged with liver spots and puffy blue veins. His right wrist was wrapped with an Ace bandage.

"He was eighty-six, Dad," Julianna said. "Born same year as you."

"No one cares," Tom mumbled.

"Dad?" Julianna sounded concerned. "Do you think no one will care about you?"

"No. No," he said.

"It says Lyle was preceded in death by a sister, Tilda Matz, and a nephew. Did you know them?"

"Obed Matz and his boy drowned in '58 in Devil's Lake. Widow lost the farm, moved in with Lyle. Died soon after." Tom pushed his seat back and scowled at his daughter. "The past." He looked suddenly stricken, leaned over, braced his forearms against the tabletop, and coughed up phlegm. He spit in the sink. "Past never dies."

"Dad. I asked you not to do that. It's unsanitary."

"Bossy like your mother." He sat back down.

"Yes, Dad." Julianna sipped coffee. "I take that as a compliment."

"Back in 1890, guy from Fargo caught 258 fish in one day!" he said. I realized he was reading trivia in the *On This Day* column in the paper. He coughed loud and hard, brought up phlegm sounding worse than ever, and went out the back door.

In a low voice, as if he might hear her through the walls, Julianna said, "It's gotten so much worse."

"Sounds like it."

"Lung cancer," she said as if I didn't understand the seriousness of the hacking and coughing, the shortness of breath.

"Wretched cancer," I said.

"I hate to see him suffer. After Dr. Schemp's diagnosis, I wanted to hire a full-time caretaker but Dad wouldn't agree. Goes off sometimes and I have to track him down." She shook her head. "And he calls me stubborn like my mother. Now there was a saint." Julianna laughed which sounded as high class as she was. "He refused to make any changes after she died. Her clothes are still hanging in their closet."

"That explains the kitchen."

"Oh I know, it's from another century." She laughed but it had a sad note to it. "My parents were frugal. No need to change what didn't need it." She sat with her bare feet propped on a stepstool. Her linen skirt fanned across her legs and a matching jacket hung from the back of a chair. A thin black band pulled her hair back from her face. Long silver earrings shaped like feathers caught the light when she moved. Tall and slender, she had muscles and curves in the right places like she was custom fit to sit real pretty anywhere at all. Whenever I spotted her tooling down Main Street in her red foreign sports car, something whispered to me: *out of your league.* I could imagine her as a skinny kid climbing trees and chasing after whatever suited her fancy right into adulthood, an independent woman who knew her own mind and wouldn't risk losing it over anyone. Martha told me Julianna was engaged twice but left the guys at the altar, so to speak. Got all the way down to the hour before the wedding and she never showed, both times. Sent a messenger to tell guests to go enjoy the reception, of all things. I bet Don still had a crush on her. Nothing wrong with that, though; I had one on Bob Vila. I used to watch his show on PBS with my grandfather. Then they fired Bob. My grandfather gave me all his tapes of *This Old House* episodes. Bob got his own show on an inaccessible-to-me channel, so I'd watch those old tapes whenever I needed cheering or instruction and it was like I was sitting right next to my grandfather all over again.

"When did your mother die?" I had vague memory that it wasn't so long ago.

"Eight years. What a day, so many people at her funeral. Even Lyle left his house to pay his respects."

"Lyle?"

"Oh yes, he and my mother were once—"

Tom returned and said, "Better now." He sat and scanned the newspaper. When he wasn't bent over with a cough, he still appeared mostly sturdy, a man who could get a job done and knew his own mind. "Some parcels of interest. Randall Short's got acres for sale in Corliss out by the old ball field, mostly bottomland." He circled the ad. "Not worth his price."

"Nothing usually is," Julianna said.

"I'm going out to Lyle's place," Tom said.

"Why?"

"Can't a man just have some peace? Not have to account for his every action. Just want to see the place."

"They were friends in another lifetime," Julianna said. "Re-established a connection last year after running into each other at the clinic."

"He was stubborn like your mother," Tom said. "Took him long enough to accept my offer."

"Offer?" I said, wondering why he was saying that.

"Tried for eight years cause my dying Ida had asked me to make amends and he spurned me. Waits until he's dying to accept, ask for favors for me to—"

"Good to have a friend," I interrupted. "I still have a few left."

Tom lifted a hat from the table. "I'm going out there," he said.

"What do you mean favors?" Julianna asked.

"Doesn't matter," Tom said. "No one cares."

"You're not making sense." Julianna shook her head as if exasperated. "I have an appointment with Trudy. Then we'll go." She watched him fiddle with the bandage around his wrist. "Leave that on," she scolded.

"Ahhh." He waved his hand through the air, coughed up phlegm, and got up to spit.

Julianna turned to me. "I have to go with him. I think he's been falling lately. He got a nasty bruise on his wrist last week and it keeps swelling. Says he can't recall doing it. I think he fell and doesn't want to tell me. Afraid I'll get a full-time care-taker in here." She stopped talking when her father returned to the table. "Finish reading the paper while you wait." She slid the *Luce Bulletin* to him.

"What's the point? Bunch of hooey. New schools, new sewers, new roads, new sidewalks, new library, new historical museum. Town's gone crazy voting to improve what doesn't need it. School bonds passing, taxes going up." His face grew redder as he talked. "Fancy lampposts and what those city council members call *green spaces* for folks to sit and rest from buying what they don't need. Used to be Schultz's Store on Wheels came through town. Chickens in crates, tires on top of the truck. Hardware, overalls, flour, sugar, candy, salt. Good deals on what people needed. Not like the hooey now. Or bring the Sears catalog back, things a person really needed, could even order an entire house. That's what Lyle's father did, ordered a house and brought it in on the train."

"So it *is* a Sears house!" I'd wondered but had not yet investigated. Of course, a Foursquare with a central dormer. But who could really see the house for all those trees and bushes and all the stuff stacked inside?

Tom continued. "Merchants used to put notices in the paper arguing against catalog houses, better to buy in town. 'Course Old Man Staybler was more stubborn than the son he left it all to."

"And a century later, the merchants are still putting notices in the paper urging people to shop at home," Julianna said.

"What goes around comes around," I said. Julianna looked at me like my comment was worth two cents. "Sears catalog stole business from brick and mortar local stores, now bigger online corporations steal from brick and mortar Sears stores. Bottom line is the only line that matters to bigger business and the cheapest price is all that matters to consumers with their so-called loyalty cards that get them special discounts and deals." I shook my head. "Loyal to what? To who? The dollar. Not the storeowner."

"I'll get the mail," Tom interrupted.

"No further than that, Dad."

"Bossy." He pointed to my faded bruise. "Your head?"

"Looks worse than it is," I said.

He got close. "Never can be sure."

"No really, it's fine," I said wanting him to just let it go.

"Did you get it looked at?"

"By a doctor, you mean?"

"Yes."

"No."

"Could be—" He had a coughing jag, which got his attention off me. He left the room.

Julianna opened her laptop. "I assume you're here about Lyle's will."

"His will?"

"I drew it up for him," she said. "Isn't that why you're here?"

I shook my head.

She typed something. Soon the printer was running. "I assumed that's why you called me."

"I need you to be my lawyer. Prove I didn't help Lyle kill himself or worse, murder him like people are saying. Help me get into that house so I can start working on it. I can't pay you right up front but—"

"I'm not able to represent you," she said.

"I'll find the money pronto then."

"Trudy, I can't. It would be a conflict of interest. I represent Lyle's estate."

"But I own Lyle's estate."

"Not yet you don't," she said. "As beneficiary, you have a right to a copy of the will." She took the pages off the printer and handed them to me. "It's straightforward. He knew there would be protests to it, so it covers all bases of concern. The probate judge will need to address any challenges to its validity. If you as beneficiary and the personal representative have any disputes, the judge will settle them."

"What do you mean disputes?"

"They can range from perceived problems with how the personal representative administers the estate to disagreements on how certain estate assets should be handled." She pointed to the will. "Read it and let me know if you have questions. The entire value of Lyle's estate has been appraised at ten million."

Holy smoke! I was richer than rich. "Unbelievable."

"While Lyle and I covered all bases, I fully expect there to be a few nasty fights over your ownership," she said. "An estate that valuable usually brings out the worst behaviors."

"I'm not afraid of a fight."

"Is that right?" She sipped from a china cup and kept her eyes on me like I was a suspect of something. "Dwight informed me of Mark Riepe's visit to Lyle and his claim as rightful heir."

Wait a gosh darn minute. I was the one who told Dwight about that. Were those two in cahoots using me for information? I didn't like the idea of that chumminess one bit.

"The state of Minnesota, too, might protest, given they were beneficiaries before Lyle requested the change. They lost a huge asset when he changed his will and with the case ongoing... well. I'll send Mr. Riepe and the State of Minnesota copies of the will. That serves to limit their time frame for filing a protest."

"You think the state will fight me?"

"There is the question of the circumstances surrounding his death that might offer reason to fight. Your finding him dead presents a red flag. And there's also the matter of probate. Once a Last Will and Testament has been admitted to probate, it becomes a public record for anyone to see and read. In certain circumstances the beneficiaries can ask the judge to seal the court records to prevent the public from reading the will and other probate documents, but the judge will grant this request only in rare situations..."

It was hard for me to pay attention with the idea of ten million dollars floating in my head. I nodded and tried to understand what she was telling me.

"However, I don't see reason to petition for such a request." Her silver cuff bracelet clanked when she placed her arms on the table. I thought of the long arm of the law tapping my shoulder, cuffing my wrists.

"There's no red flag. I did not do it."

She leaned forward. "You need to obtain legal counsel."

"When can I start cleaning out the house?"

She looked surprised. "Did you not hear me?"

"Okay, I will but I'd like to know about the house." I needed work to focus on, take my mind off the law breathing down my neck.

"You're a bit eager." I didn't like the look she gave me.

"Do you doubt me?"

She didn't answer.

"Because if you do, I'm just going to tell you, I did not kill Lyle."

"Or assist in suicide?"

"Yeah, well, he never asked *me* to do it. And anyway, what if it was Lyle's last wish? Didn't he have a right to it?"

"Minnesota statutes for aiding suicide are clear. Up to 15 years in prison or a fine up to $30,000, or both."

"That's what life comes down to, time and money, which I do not have an excess of."

"Nevertheless, working on the house isn't possible. The BCI is in control of the crime scene. Best turn your attention to getting legal counsel. I'd recommend Patricia Irving; she's one of the best, but she's not taking new clients, as she'll soon be on maternity leave. Her partner, Joan Wakefield, is also one of the best—"

"Yeah, sure. I know who they are. How it is you came to be Lyle's lawyer anyway?"

"He and my father are friends from way back. In fact, one of my mother's last wishes was that Dad make amends with Lyle."

"Amends for what?"

She ignored my question. "As my father indicated, Lyle refused to accept the offer of friendship but then they ran into each other in the clinic waiting room, both under Edward Schemp's care. And well, Lyle had a change of heart, I guess."

"Change of heart, huh?"

"My father stole my mother away from Lyle which broke their friendship apart."

"Stole her?"

"I lived with this all my life. Mother's accusations against Father and his impatience with her bouts of sadness. She and Lyle were engaged at a time when her father was down on his luck without cash flow but with plenty of lumber land. My father's family used their wealth as leverage to…" She stopped talking when her father entered the kitchen.

I imagined Julianna in white wedding dresses that never made it to the altar. I wondered how much of her mother's sadness influenced her fleeing from marriage.

"Anything good in the mail, Dad?" she asked, sounding just as light as a feather.

8

It had been four weeks since Lyle's death when we met to release his ashes. He'd asked to be scattered on the property he loved so much. We stood where the land jutted out into the lake. Clouds were forming in the west but mostly the sky was clear blue.

Tom was too sick that morning to make it; but me, Father Stanislaus, Dwight, Julianna, and the hospice team of Lois and Caroline paid our respects. Birds were ape crazy for the place, darting in and out of the cottonwood trees while the priest recited, "The Lord is my shepherd, I shall not want…"

At the end of the Psalm, Lois worked up an emotional, "Amen."

The priest scattered some of Lyle in Emma Lake then invited us to partake in the ritual and say a few words. Dwight stepped to the urn, scooped out ashes, and dotted the shore with Lyle. The waves lapped up the ashes. "Peace," he said, choosing to be a man of few words that morning.

Caroline Woolover, hospice social worker, scattered ashes in the cattails. "Go now with the songbirds, Lyle."

Julianna faltered a bit when she moved toward the urn. Dwight grabbed her elbow, keeping his hand there even after she was steady. He then placed his arm around her waist like it had a right to be there, which is what it must've felt like to her because she leaned right into him. They lingered like that until the priest cleared his throat and broke up whatever was going on. Julianna stepped to the urn, gathered ashes, and scattered them along the sandy edge near the grasses. She stood beside Dwight, unfolded a slip of paper and read, "Ecclesiastes, 'The sun rises and the sun goes down and hastens to the place where it rises. The wind blows to the south and goes round to the north: round and round goes the wind, and on its circuits the wind returns.' We release your spirit." She put the paper in her skirt pocket and I heard her whisper to Dwight, "Mother loved that verse."

Lois stepped up to the urn. Sunshine hit the rhinestone brooch pinned to her jacket and reflected onto the priest. "It's hard for me to speak yet about this man, a soul once under my care..." She paused and looked up like she might find strength from the heavens. "Since his death, Lyle has appeared to me at the oddest times, even when I'm tending to another soul in my care. Weeding my gardens or knitting while listening to hymns, he is there." She cleared her throat as a blue jay shrieked. She was crying and the ashes were caking in her palm. I was sweating even in the shade. Lois raised her arm. "Goodbye gentle soul. Follow the Buteo." The ashes plunked into the water. Some stuck to her palm, which she brushed clean with a handkerchief.

I scattered the last of Lyle's ashes near the base of a cottonwood tree. "I'll always remember your smile, friend," I said.

The priest opened his Bible. "Let us—"

"But first." Lois reached into her oversized bag and pulled out sheets of paper. "I made copies for everyone." She handed them around and then lifted an iPad from the bag.

"All six verses?" Huntermeister asked.

"Indeed. He deserves nothing less."

"I understand, but I don't think he wanted..." Julianna stopped talking when Lois sighed. "Never mind," she said. "I'll try to stay in key."

"Okay, let's begin." Lois hit a button on her iPad and tinny piano music played. She began with enthusiasm and we stumbled in by the second line, "For all the saints, who from their labors rest, who thee by faith before the world confessed, thy name, O Jesus, be forever blest. Alleluia, Alleluia! ..."

By the time we got to the third verse, I was actually getting into it despite the sweat sliding down my spine. Knowing Lois, she probably imagined precious Bambi-like wildlife, waterfowl, and songbirds as back up choir praising Lois's lord for Lyle's goodness in providing this haven. "... the victor's crown of gold ..." By the sixth stanza, Lois's voice was almost broken as she soldiered on, "... through gates of pearls streams in the countless host ... Alleluia. Alleluia." The music stopped and we waited for Lois to get a grip, least that's how it seemed to me, we were all in sync on that thought.

"Let us pray," the priest finally said.

We were ready to leave when Lois felt faint. Julianna guided her to sit on a log. "I should have kept better control of his meds," she said. "Offered him more ..."

"More what?" I asked but she was too choked up to answer, or so it seemed. I felt for her. I missed him too. Reaching over to pat her shoulder, I wanted to offer comfort.

She pulled away.

"I didn't do it," I whispered.

Later that day, I got a letter from Meals-on-Wheels informing me that in light of the circumstances surrounding Lyle Staybler's death and due to the ongoing investigation, my services were no longer needed. I tossed the letter in the trash on my way to the freezer where a loyal pint of Neapolitan ice cream awaited. I was on the last spoonful when Iris called. She had a way of drawing junk out of me and I spilled the beans about that letter.

"It's their loss," she said. I called her my soul sister because she was the only black friend I ever had in my lily-white life. She called me an albatross around her neck. We got along real good.

Iris's story was right out of the movies: Young woman falls in love, gets pregnant, finds out her lover is married. Says goodbye to loved ones, flees Cobbers Creek, Virginia, with twin baby boys. Her Cancer the Crab water sign had her driving with the Atlantic Ocean in the rear view mirror and the Pacific Ocean on her radar. She stopped to study the Minnesota map and noted pure blue surrounding Luce. Said it might not be the ocean, but it was water, even if the moon didn't control it. She answered an ad to be caretaker of a home on Rush Lake. Within a month, Game Warden Nathan Buck was hot in pursuit. Four months later, she forgot about the ocean and crossed the lake to live with him.

When she talked about their sweet life, I filled with envy. In her words, people appear in our lives for a reason and Nathan's love was strong enough to quiet her desire to return to Cobbers Creek. Still I knew it wasn't easy, that a piece of her was still back there.

"Hello. Are you there?" Iris interrupted my thoughts. "I asked if you got a lawyer?"

I didn't say anything.

"Trudy, it's bad. Don't you get it? You need a lawyer."

"If I do that, it means it's real. It makes me look guilty enough to need a lawyer."

"Look, I know you're smarter than that. Innocent people need lawyers and you got to not care about how things appear to other people."

"You should see the nasty looks I get. People cross the street to avoid me."

"Ignore them."

"Easy for you to say."

Iris laughed. "Oh, yeah, real easy for a black woman living in this small town to ignore looks. I don't think so sister. Stop feeling sorry for yourself and get a lawyer."

When anxious, I'd sometimes do like Iris suggested: breathe deep, close my eyes, and imagine good things. Forcing myself to relax was hard for me. Iris was calm, never hurried herself or anyone else, not even her sons. She took chances but didn't fret.

"Do you ever feel sorry for yourself?" I asked.

Iris laughed.

"I mean, losing your parents when you were little, having to leave Washington, D.C., to live with your aunt, ending up in Luce."

"I did the grief work. No reason for self pity."

"I pity Martha."

"Don't think she'd want your pity."

"Well I suspect Randall is up to something criminal," I said.

"Ridiculous, Trudy. Don't say such a thing. Think about Martha."

"I do think about Martha. That's why someone should investigate whatever he's up to. He's shifty. Lyle caught him on his land one day."

"Doesn't mean anything. Nathan walks Lyle's land."

That took me completely by surprise. "What for?"

"To enjoy it. Why else?" she asked. Getting no reply she then said, "You suspect something otherwise?"

Maybe I did. Maybe I could imagine Nathan—who everyone knew loved Minnesota like he loved his own breath—scheming for a piece of pristine land. I wasn't dumb enough to say so to Iris, though. "Like I was saying, Lyle caught Randall on his land. Busted, Randall made up an excuse for being there, said he heard Lyle was sick and wondered if he could do anything for him. Lyle said, 'Sick? I heard I was dying. Can you do anything about that?' That's what Lyle told me."

"Wish I would've met him," Iris said.

"Did Nathan ever meet him?" I asked.

"Stands to reason."

"Oh yeah? Why would he?"

"Nathan's probably met most people in town," she said.

Of course, like Don, born and raised in Luce, Nathan knew everyone. "Anyway," I continued, "Lyle told me Randall said if Lyle was dying might as well leave the land with someone who'd put it to good use. And just because Randall didn't get it while Lyle was alive, doesn't mean he's going to accept he can't get his hands on that land now. Could be bent on causing trouble."

"Trudy, it doesn't do any good to point fingers without evidence. What has gotten into you?"

I wanted to spill the beans about Lyle leaving everything to me, make Iris understand why I was so concerned about Randall's obsession over the land, but I heard Huntermeister warning me to keep it to myself and I thought of those BCI guys and I didn't want to give any of them reason to come after me for being uncooperative or whatever the charge would be. "Lyle said Randall wanted to come inside, maybe see the deed, talk about buying some of the land if he wouldn't sell all of it, said he'd build land-friendly condos and name them Staybler Estates. Lyle told him that was a bunch of hooey he wasn't interested in. Randall shoved his card at Lyle, told him to give him a call."

"Did you tell Dwight?"

"Most of it. He's Randall's friend, you know?"

"He's yours, too."

"Not so sure."

"Friend or not, you should tell him."

"I don't trust him."

"He's doing his job."

"And a number on me."

"Trudy, for land's sake."

"My sake."

"Measure twice, cut once."

"What the heck is that..." Then I stopped and laughed. She had whipped out the phrase we women used to say to each other when one of us lost focus and tried to hurry on a project, risked making errors.

"Get yourself that lawyer," she said.

9

I was having nightmares about getting thrown in jail so I moved getting a lawyer to the top of my to-do list. I left a message at two law firms, neither of them recommended by Julianna. I wasn't sure I completely trusted her. She and Dwight acted way too chummy in a meeting I called to ask Dwight to have a patrol drive by Lyle's house more often. It was ripe for vandalism. They seemed uninterested in what I had to say and jabbered on about the best microbrews and wine selections in town. Whatever. It just seemed she held a whole heck of a lot of power in the scheme of things and my reputation was dirty laundry hanging on a line. Judgmental tongues moved faster than a plague of grasshoppers on a grapevine.

I read a text message from a volunteer: *Took on way too much. Bowing out of HFD.*

I called her cell but she didn't pick up. I left a message. "Whatever." She was the second one to quit Homes for Dwelling that week, one more fair weather friend, just like the customers who started avoiding me in the store. Courtney, too, had to deal with it, got in a fight after some kid said I sat on Lyle and suffocated him with my fat. The final straw was after Justine told Courtney her mother said to stay away from her. The acorn never falls far from the tree. *It blows to be your daughter*, Courtney yelled. I felt like calling Darcy and telling her to stop pestering Don for swim team photos. Get a man of her own, and while she was at it, teach her daughter some respect.

I had started locking our doors, which I did that morning before I left home. I double checked the lock, walked down the porch steps to the end of the sidewalk, and stopped to examine the turret where the paint had begun peeling. One more thing our house needed me to fix.

Our poor house: a Queen Anne built in 1899 by Joseph Dertinger owner of Luce Northern Pacific Brewery. He died in 1917, the same year the brewery was dismantled, though it had already fallen onto hard times in 1915 when the area was declared dry under an Indian Treaty. After his death, the house got passed around, the last buyer dividing it into apartments when zoning changes shifted. Don's parents finally rescued it and returned it to its original floor plan. A lot of houses of no particular style, minimal traditional houses, and ranch style houses, sprouted up around that jewel over the decades. I loved our house and had a hard time ignoring its needs.

I headed to the hardware store to talk to Don about scraping the clapboard and getting paint. Around the corner onto Main, I saw Bertha Hewitt, Meals-on-Wheels cook, walking toward me. You could spot her a mile away, really tall, like six-foot-two with bad hips and a humpback so she walked like someone was shoving her from behind. She belonged to a religious sect. Bible-thumpers that people called Two-by-Fours because when you opened your door, there would either be two or four of them waiting to save your soul. She looked up. I waved. She looked away and crossed at the middle of Main in front of an oncoming car that had to brake for her. Fool woman risking her life to avoid me.

It felt like my bruise had never disappeared and I was destined to wear it forever.

At the store, I found Don with Courtney taping gardening supplies sales posters to the wall beside the cash register. "HOT BUYS." The letters had flames surrounding them and I imagined Don and Courtney happily making the signs together. Don hadn't bothered to finish shelving the sacks of wild birdseed delivered that morning and I felt suddenly overwhelmed by the thought of lifting them. "Those sacks won't shelve themselves," I said. "And our peeling turret won't paint itself."

He turned and a sales banner fell to the ground. "Hello to you, too." He frowned when he saw my face. "What's wrong?"

"People," I said. "I wish they wouldn't think I'm—"

"Dad," Courtney said. "You let go." Just as well she interrupted. Why even begin talking about how crummy I felt? I watched her wait patiently for Don to hand her the banner. Don could easily charm Courtney, make her laugh and cement her love for him just by walking into the room. I usually felt like the third wheel on the bike and often saw that same look of admiration for Don on the faces of women who flirted with him. They'd give me a puzzled look like, 'how did you ever rate such eye candy?'

"So you were saying?" Don lifted another banner.

"Nothing important." I flipped through wallpaper samples; no one seemed to buy the stuff anymore but Don still kept updated offerings. I looked out the window, the traffic light turning from green to yellow. "It's just that it hurts my feelings that—"

"Dad!" Courtney squealed.

Don had draped the banner around her. "Let's put you up as special of the day."

"Don't be a dork." She laughed.

Clearly I wasn't needed. One reason I organized Homes for Dwelling was to give me something to focus on other than Don and the store after Courtney started kindergarten. Don said I had the bad habit of looking at people and seeing what I thought needed fixing rather than focusing on what was appealing. I got on his nerves redoing what he'd do or taking over a project he had planned to complete. He said I should go weed some other garden. Still, I wondered: if I had put more hours in at the store, would it have been thriving instead of dying?

"Banners look good!" I said cheerily, wanting to lose my bad mood. "How was practice?" I asked Courtney, unsure if she would speak to me. After I had asked her to pick up all the crap from her bedroom floor the night before, Courtney screamed that she wished she could live with Ericka and her parents.

"Sucks that coach put me in the medley for breaststroke," she replied. Midway down the ladder, she looked out the window and squealed, "Ericka!" She hurried down the rungs. "See you later." She raced out the door.

"Must not suck so bad after all," I said. Don taped a poster up while I held it in place. "People are avoiding me."

He laughed. "Honestly, Trudy."

"Don't say that and don't laugh. It's irritating."

"People act for reasons not connected to you. Don't assume anything."

"Nothing obvious in people crossing the street to avoid me. No, nothing at all," I said sarcastically.

"What?"

"Bertha did. Crossed the street when she saw me coming."

"People are like chickens."

"Meaning?"

"They cross the road to get to the other side." He laughed. He wanted me to laugh, too, so I faked it. "Try to let it go," he said. I hated it when he told me that. Five thousand residents in this town surrounded by one thousand lakes and the people who knew me had already taken a place on the jury. How could I just let it go?

"Easy for you to say."

"Nothing worth doing is ever easy." He stepped back to examine the poster, then caught me staring at him. "What?"

"How do you think it makes me feel being snubbed by someone like Bertha?" I said to remind him of my hurt feelings.

"Just let it go. You can't account for how people feel."

I hoisted sacks of birdseed onto the lower shelf. The extra baggage and movement killed my knees. Why even care about peeling paint when so much other stuff was deteriorating around me?

Lyle had been dead for seven weeks but it felt like a year with all the waiting and worry gnawing me. Second week of school, Courtney got into a fight with some kid who called me a killer. As punishment, she sentenced me to her silent treatment. In the meantime, I was going through our paltry bank accounts trying to find funds to pay for a lawyer when Julianna called.

"I've been meaning to let you know BCI completed their investigation at the house. Dwight thinks it advisable to board it up. He's concerned about vandals. I had a different take on the matter and mentioned the risk of losing the valuables within the house. Determined thieves would find a way to get in despite boards. So I talked to my father. As PR of the will and—"

"The what?" I asked.

"The personal representative."

"Isn't that you?"

"Trudy, did you read the will?"

I was embarrassed. "Started to but I—"

"Lyle contacted me to be his lawyer only after first asking my father to be the personal representative."

"Not to be rude, but your father is dying."

"What exactly is your point?"

"So your father is the boss of the will?"

"Don't worry, Trudy, he's not after Lyle's land."

"Who said I was worried?"

She had this really annoying habit of gliding right past hostility with a little laugh. "As I was saying, we have concerns."

"We?" I wanted to know if *we* was the trinity of her, her father, and Chief Huntermeister.

Again, that laugh. "I went before the probate judge and he granted you the right to clear out any valuables from the house and to haul away whatever is deemed debris. That's all. Just clean out the house. No other work is to be undertaken, no modifications made on the house, and by that I also mean the land."

"What am I supposed to do with everything?"

"My father offered his sheds. You can store valuables there until probate ends, then do as you wish."

"Oh yeah?" I wondered why she was bending over backwards to help clear the place out. Or was she planning to help herself out?

"Heed my words: you may not in any way alter the house or the land." She sounded like the boss lady I didn't need in my life. "Did Joan agree to represent you?"

"I'm waiting to hear back," I lied.

"No you are not because you never made the call."

"And just how do you know that?"

"I asked her."

"If you knew the answer, why'd you ask me in the first place?"

"To determine if I can trust what you say."

"How do I know I can trust what you say?"

"I represent the estate. It's imperative that I know it's moving in the right direction."

"I have 'call Joan' on my list of things to do." I wrote it on my list.

"Might I suggest you make it a top priority?"

"Sure thing." I wrote *#1* next to *call Joan.*

I hung up, angry and confused. What was it to her who I found to represent me? Why keep shoving Joan down my throat? Tom Mandle was right. His daughter was bossy.

Don came up from the basement where he'd been developing photos. The door scraped along the linoleum. "Who were you talking to?" He turned on the kitchen faucet and lathered up the soap.

"Julianna said I could clean stuff out of Lyle's house."

"And do what with it?"

I shrugged. "Maybe hold a huge estate sale, put the proceeds toward our bills, buy a new store van, pay cash for Courtney's braces." I was testing his anxiety over money, wanted to see if it was as high as mine.

"You can sell the stuff?" Don asked.

"I can do whatever I want," I lied. "It's my house."

"What about probate?"

"Household stuff isn't in probate."

"Is that what Julianna said?" Don dried his hands and stared at me. "Trudy?"

"Not in so many words."

"Judging by that look of yours, bet she said it in one word: *No.*"

"Yeah, well. What she doesn't know won't hurt her."

"Trudy. Do not do anything you'll regret."

I wanted the subject off me. "You need to take the van in. It doesn't shift right."

He got close to my face. "I'll put it on my list of things to do."

"What the heck, Honey. If only you had a list, mine could be shorter."

"Oh the burden of being Trudy."

"Got that right." I decided then and there that Don did not need to know everything that went on between me and Lyle's house.

"Did you ever call Joan?"

"For crap's sake. I wish people would stop asking me that."

"Then just do it," Don said.

I didn't want to be in the same room with him adding to the pressure. I was about to leave when Dwight knocked on the back door. He cast a tall shadow. I motioned him inside. "Need to talk to you, Trudy," he said looking all serious and concerned. He took off his hat and rubbed his head. "Don, you too."

"What now?" I asked. "If it's not one thing, it sure as heck is another."

"Hey, Trudy," Don said. "Calm down."

"You calm down." I glared at him until I saw the worry on his face. Then I got scared. What if Dwight had come to arrest me?

I patted his hand. "You're right. Look at me," I tried to lighten up. "Getting my tail feathers ruffled before I even know what's what. Maybe I won the lottery," I joked.

Don didn't lighten. Dwight looked grim.

We sat at the dining room table, the lace tablecloth damp under my sweating palms. "Trudy," Dwight said. "I don't like to have to ask you this, but I need you to be up front with me."

"Just ask already." I fingered a red silk rose in the centerpiece.

Dwight looked at Don. Frowning, he turned back to me. "Did you tell Bertha Hewitt you'd kill to get your hands on Lyle's house?"

I shook my head. "Oh for ridiculous. What did I ever do to her that she's got it out for me?" I laughed.

"Trudy?" Don said.

"No. Of course not. People use that expression all the time. I'd kill for …"

"Not all people are connected to Lyle's death," Dwight said. "Did you say it?"

"I don't know, maybe I did. But so what?"

"What a terrible thing to say," Don scolded.

"It's just a cliché," I defended myself. "It doesn't mean—"

"Lawyer up, Trudy," Dwight said. "BCI will be in touch again soon."

After Dwight left, I called Joan Wakefield's office and left a message, saying it was urgent. Don sat staring at me like I was an oddity. "What?" I said. "You suspect me too, now?"

"Sometimes if you'd just keep your thoughts to yourself, we'd all be better off."

"You don't have to be rude."

"And by the way, I need you to stop charging things to the store's account once and for all."

"The front gutter is—"

"As long as it's not falling down, there's no urgency."

I bit my tongue. When the porch ceiling flooded with rain again, rotted more, and fell on top of him, maybe then he'd care!

10

I called together what was left of the troops for a walk through Lyle's that morning to figure out what we should store in Tom's sheds. I was down to two volunteers, my friends, Martha and Iris. And then there was a third person, Greta Meinler, owner of a profitable floral and garden center, busted for growing marijuana in her greenhouses. She used her connections and money to get off with a not-large-enough fine and a slap on the wrist, six months of community service. Homes for Dwelling was the supposed winner. Took me one minute to realize she didn't know her elbow from her ass when it came to tools and repair work. Having her clean, pack, and haul instead of attempt to repair would be an advantage. I was stuck with her and decided to focus on her two hands, healthy knees, and strong back for heavy lifting.

I headed out early to enjoy the drive to Lyle's, tried to look around, see things as Iris would: with a desire to connect, I guess. The red light was blinking on top of Sunny's Dog Food Factory tower not far from St. Henry's Catholic Church steeple. That was the Luce skyline. I drove past the Municipal Cemetery and onto Highway 10 to see a thin line of light appearing in the east sandwiched between clouds and fields of corn. I sped past the big box stores, cell phone tower, and billboards.

One of the signs had a picture of a baby with the words: *Protect Life, Save the Unborn. Life begins at conception.* I thought of Lyle's *Do Not Resuscitate* orders, his right to choose death over life. Nothing was absolute and all issues carried the burden of decision. Absolute thinking allowed people to avoid hard decisions, dared anyone to cross their line. By my reasoning, life began with the first breath and ended after the last, as much about chance as it was choice. Like that home-made sign someone stuck up out past the old grain elevator: *Smile your mom was pro life.* But what if she wasn't? What if she just didn't have a choice, no other option? Lyle believed in his options, in his right to choose. Why else had he planned as he did, posted *Do Not Resuscitate* orders on his door?

I passed woods of poplars and oaks right before Sherman's Christmas Tree Farm fields. A slow-moving North Dakota oil train chugged along the tracks parallel to the highway. I drove the six miles to Lyle's house just west of the overpass where the tracks cross under Ten and keep heading East by Hiller's Farms with all their misery-stuffed turkeys. Then on past Wreck-A-Mended Auto Repair and the Handle Bar and Grill. By the time I reached Lyle's, the sun switched on its high beam and was heating the underside of the clouds with orange.

Pulling onto the frontage road, I saw litter from Wanderi's Mini-Mart stuck along the chicken wire fence. I wanted to walk over and tell Jerry to clean it up, but let it go. I knew he used to do things to purposely irritate Lyle, like leaning rusted signs against the back fence and playing loud music when working on old cars in his store's north shed. He's why Lyle painted his dining room windows black. "Keep him from my sight," he told me. Well, I could hardly wait to get that paint off those windows. No way I'd be tormented by Jerry.

Standing in the front yard, I gave the house an eyeball inspection. Clapboard needed sanding, T-lock shingles needed replacing, and chimney needed tuck-pointing. House needed a new roof for sure. I walked off the distance from the porch to where I'd set the Dumpster, far enough away from the house to leave room for us to park. I estimated half a year of work before it would be ready for its lucky inhabitant. I planned to devote all my Homes for Dwelling restoration resources to that house and that house alone. I'd put out a call for new volunteers. Oh Martha's sweet Jesus, I did not want to lose that house that needed me. Lyle would live on through his house.

I ripped the police tape from the porch and wound it into a ball. The rotted porch floor slanted. The *Do Not Resuscitate* orders greeted me like a still-powerful voice of authority. I ripped at the orange paper, but it didn't pull clean away. Pieces stuck to the door and I scratched with my bitten nails before using the house key as scraper. I got all of the middle off, but lines of orange remained like a picture frame around emptiness.

Inside, I tried to envision the room free of junk to get a better sense of the actual house, all 1,700 square feet of it. I imagined the train over a hundred years ago bringing the Sears kit to the railroad depot, Lyle's father raising people's ire for giving his business to outsiders.

I walked through various rooms and then out the back door to the porch where a decapitated crow lay on the top step. I kicked the crow off the porch. It landed in a galvanized tub sitting in the weeds. Then I saw the sign that had been beneath the crow: THIS PROPERTY IS CONDEMNED. Some idiot had scrawled it onto a sheet of notebook paper. I mulled over what it could possibly mean, deciding to ignore it while tending to that crow. With a rusted tin can, I dug a hole, tipped the crow into it, and covered it back up. I sat on Lyle's favorite rusted garden chair and propped my feet on the back porch railing with missing spindles. That's how it would be from then on, me noticing what needed to be done and feeling crazy for having to wait, just like my own house, needing me but having to wait. Focus on the positive, Iris would say. Okay then. It was a good back porch facing the west woods and a narrow clearing to Emma Lake.

"There you are," Martha soon called to me.

Iris followed her around to the back porch. "I am so anxious to get a look inside."

"I thought you were bringing Greta," I said, not really disappointed.

"She doesn't answer her cell and wasn't at her store," Martha said.

"Unreliable felon," I said.

"She's not a felon," Martha said. "That's a terrible thing to say."

"Okay. I'll try to keep that in mind," I said.

Martha's cell rang. "It's Greta." She answered the call. "Where are you?" Martha covered the phone. "She's on her way." She gave me a look like I'd better just be grateful she called and keep any rude comments to myself. After hanging up, Martha looked at her phone and shook her head. "Oh for stupid. Battery's almost dead. I can never remember to charge it before I leave home." She tucked it into her pants pocket. "Have you ever noticed how Greta always sounds out of breath like she's hurrying or has too much on her mind?"

I wanted to say she was probably hurrying around to cover her illegal doings but I kept my mouth shut. While we waited, I told Martha and Iris about the interrogation the day of Lyle's death. It still weighed heavy on me and I just wanted to get a few things off my chest, like the surprise of his leaving us the house. Tired of keeping a secret, I wanted to tell them about the land, but Greta breezed in to join us. I wasn't about to bring her into my confidence. We headed inside.

Stacks of newspapers lined the cellar steps. "What a cesspool," Greta said. "The stench is even worse down here." She breathed into the back of her hand. "Nauseating. How does anyone expect me to work in third world conditions?" She removed a silk scarf tied in her dark hair streaked with golden highlights, bunched it in her hand, held it to her face, and breathed in like her scent was salvation. Her skinny face got lost in that thick dark hair once the scarf no longer held it back.

"Get used to it," I suggested. I also wanted to tell her she could begin by dressing like a worker rather than a queen bee with her cropped black pants and silky black top. Maybe remove some of that glittery gold jewelry. I watched her examine a stack of flowerpots. She had sharp features: a long narrow nose, a pointy chin and prominent cheekbones; she was all bones and joints and sharp angles without any cushion; dark complexion and silky looking skin. A rock polished smooth to come out looking like a gem.

"What about health hazards?" she said. "Disease and contagion breed in places like this?" She brushed her hands together.

"Wear your work gloves," I said. "And a mask."

The damp cellar was full of mildew. Cobwebs streaked a grimy window. Planks formed a path along the dirt floor. A ringer washing machine was pushed against a wall where rusted steel leg-hold traps, mousetraps, and snowshoes hung.

"Stuff's scattered from hell to breakfast," Greta said.

"Hard to imagine how all this accumulated," Iris said. She turned the handle of a meat grinder screwed to a worktable.

"Harder to imagine getting rid of it," Martha said.

"Objects have lives." Iris brushed dust from a turquoise Mason jar. "They're witness to things. Like this jar. Imagine the hands that held it and what it once contained, maybe pickles or beets or green beans." Iris scratched her forehead and her bandanna slid back, exposing the fringe of her coarse dark hair cropped short because no one in Luce knew any other way to cut a black woman's hair. Iris was one of those focused people who got a lot of things done in a day and did it all quietly. I envied her for that. Didn't even follow a to-do list. Once I tried to go without a list but it made me nervous, like setting out on a trip without mapping my course. Iris had lots of courage, like a survivor.

"Thank God I only have a six-month sentence." Greta lifted a radio. "You'll be here cleaning all this junk out until kingdom come." She set the radio down hard next to a pile of skeleton keys.

"For crap's sake. Be careful," I said.

"Language, Trudy," Martha said.

"It's just an old radio." Greta looked at me like I was stupid.

"It could be Bakelite. That stuff's valuable." I stopped, as if I had just revealed where the jewels were hid. Greta noticed.

"I got busted for growing, not stealing," she said.

"Oh my," Iris said. "Look at these crocks. Auntie has some just like 'em." A dozen Red Wing crocks of various sizes lined the wall. "Not a single crack or chip. Can we buy any of his things?" I wondered if she believed having one of the crocks would give her a piece of Auntie right here in Luce. If so, she should have them all.

"Maybe later. For now don't want to give tongues more reason to wag."

"You talking about what Bertha said?" Martha asked.

I glared at her, didn't want my concerns known to Greta who smirked at me a lot.

"Like you say," Martha continued, "You were just joking when you said that. We all say stuff like that. 'I'm going to kill you if you don't stop—"

"Okay, Martha."

"I mean we all know the saying, you tell something to one person, you've told it to ten. No one can keep a—"

"Got it. Drop it." I walked the planks past shelves filled with corroded cans of food, Mason jars, and a bunch of promotional yardsticks bearing the names of local stores that had come and gone. A scrub board leaned inside a galvanized tub, a stiff rag over the edge. A cracked yellowed bar of soap sat in an aluminum pie plate. A clothesline drooped from the ceiling. I imagined Lyle hanging his clothes to dry.

Iris wiped her finger over the frame of a spinning wheel. "It's odd to see so much junk and then to spot valuable stuff, like everything was all the same to Lyle."

"We should call Jerome's Antiques," Martha said. "Don't want to accidentally get rid of something valuable. Haste makes waste, you know." She picked up a tall-stemmed milkshake glass imprinted with *Cree Me Dairy*. "Oh for charming." She examined the glass. "Oh say, did you see the sign for that new place Funky Junk? It says: *Create Instant Ancestors Out of Old Junk*. Like you can buy family memories that aren't real." She lifted a clothespin from the glass. "Here," she said, pretending to clasp it to Greta's nose. "This will keep the smell from bothering you."

"Need more than that," Greta said.

I sized them up and wondered when they'd become so buddy-buddy.

"You know, Trudy," Martha said, "All you have to do is take a lie detector test and prove that Bertha is making you out to be something you aren't, prove your innocence."

She was making me super nervous. "Let it go. Okay. Please?" I could hardly think for all the stuff around me and didn't need her to keep harping on batty Bertha. I'd stick to my story and be all right.

"If you say so." Martha tossed the clothespin back into the bucket and brushed hair away from her face. She had skinny wrists and long thin arms and legs. I wondered what it was like to be so delicate. Her boniness differed from Greta's. Martha had cushion and curves. Her neck was long and thin and her skin was smooth except for a worry crease between her eyes that seemed way too deep for someone who was only thirty-three. She wore loose, plain clothing like she was trying to hide the knockout figure her God blessed her with. And to add insult to a body she should've been proud to show off, she stood, sat, and walked with her shoulders hunched forward.

"I do say so." I tried to examine the condition of the walls behind all the junk. "Don't seem to be leaning in." I shined a flashlight toward a back room. "Cold storage in there. Stone walls. I'll get an inspector to come sign off on the foundation's integrity and then we can get to work, maybe whitewash down here." I pulled the chain hanging from a bare light bulb. Seeing the house as its owner rather than as a visitor, I understood its needs just like I understood my own house's needs. I was burning to get my tool belt slung around my hips and my hands on a hammer.

"Excuse me?" Greta wiped her hands with a tissue. "I believe the plan is to haul this junk out of here. I don't recall discussion of hard-to-imagine repair work on this dump."

"If you imagined a greenhouse full of marijuana, you should be able to imagine this dump restored," I said.

Greta grinned. "Touché." Nothing I said seemed to bother her. She pointed to a round tin and said, "How disgusting."

Iris read the label. "McNess Krestal Salve For Man or Beast."

"I mean, seriously," Greta said. "The idea that a human would put on his body something he'd put on an animal."

Iris opened the tin. "Ummm. Want to smell it?"

"Gross me out," Greta said.

Martha took the tin and replaced the lid. She read aloud. "A soothing first aid ointment for superficial burns, scalds, and cuts."

"Makes me shudder," Greta said.

Deciding to ratchet up Greta's discomfort, I lifted a box. "Bag Balm Dilutors. Fits all sizes of normal teats," I read aloud.

Greta said, "Let's try one out on you." She grinned. I shoved the box into her hand. She set it down. "Maybe later."

"Oh my gosh," Iris said. "This is strychnine. We'll have to call EPA before we can get rid of some of this stuff. You can't just haul this to the landfill or dump it on the land."

"So noted," I said.

When we got to the kitchen, I inspected the appliances, older than the hills and in worse condition than I'd realized. The porcelain sink was stained and the linoleum in front of it, torn. I lifted the flooring near the pantry door. "Looks like good wood plank underneath." I ran water in the sink. "Not much pressure. Probably need new pipes." I opened the cabinet beneath the sink and lifted scouring powder. Rust was thick along the lid's rim. Mouse droppings dotted a dishcloth. I pulled out a shredded brown paper nest, dead babies, victims of the poison I had spread for Lyle.

"Filthy," Greta said.

Utensils were crammed into drawers along with clippings, plastic containers, potholders, towels, and boxes of canning lids. Pens and pencils bearing the logos of long gone local businesses were bundled with rubber bands.

Iris picked at paint on the windowsill. "Got some serious wood rot."

I opened the jam closet. It was stuffed full. Wooden Land o' Lakes Pasteurized Blended American Cheese boxes filled with papers, receipts, jar lids, bottle caps, and mousetraps. Milk and pop bottles sat waiting to be returned for deposit. I would need two Dumpsters for the junk and a lot of research on what stuff was worth.

Soon we were digging around in the dining room. Iris moved boxes off the table and set them on chairs. "When do you think he last threw anything out?"

I opened a closet that was crammed from top to bottom. A black and orange cylinder with air vents hung from the rod. *No-Moth Solid. Kills Moths, Moth Eggs, Moth Larvae.*

"Look at this." Martha ran her hand over the edge of the oak buffet, opened and closed drawers. "Oh for beautiful." She lifted two tarnished silver candlesticks, moved aside a stack of old calendars, and placed the candlesticks on the table. She pulled a wooden box from another drawer. "It's full of clippings and photos."

We rummaged through the box. I pulled out several newspaper articles. *May 1906: Robert Kemper committed suicide by taking strychnine. Had domestic problems. October 1911:*

Tramps continue to find Luce a poor stopping place. Nine were given their walking papers. April 1912: Women arise! The ideal of a woman as weak, ignorant and inexperienced; a cross between an angel and an idiot, no longer fulfills any useful purpose. Why had someone bothered to clip and save that stuff? It was depressing me. I put the clippings back into the box.

Here's an obituary for Tilda Staybler Matz, died October 6, 1966," Iris read, "'*Preceded in death by her husband, Obed, and son, Martin, parents,*' etc., etc. '*Survived by brother Lyle Staybler of Luce.*'"

I riffled through the clippings. "This one's dated January 1958. Says '*Obed Matz and his son Martin were driving across Devil's Lake when their truck fell through the ice… Leaves behind widow and mother, Tilda Staybler Matz.*'"

"Here's a notice of auction and foreclosure on the Matz farm," Iris said. "Out on Luce Lake. Tom Mandle's land?"

"Here's Tilda's obituary. She died in—"

"Oh for sad. Bet she died of a broken heart," Martha said.

"People don't die of broken hearts," I said.

"Just a wives' tale," Greta said.

"Yes they do. I read that some part of the heart is linked to emotion. If you don't resolve painful things, it can throw your heart into an irregular and fatal beat."

"Geeze. Where do you find such—"

"Crying helps, though. Cuts emotional stress by *forty percent!*"

We looked at her and maybe Iris and Greta were wondering the same thing as me: Did she cry a lot? "Martha, we—"

"Now that I think about it, we're supposed to focus on virtue and praise to alleviate heartache. Maybe the brain needs to intercept negative junk. Turn it into edifying communication to minister grace unto the hearers, according to Ephesians. It seems—"

"Look at this," Greta interrupted. "An announcement of Ida Flautau's marriage to Tom Mandle, June 1943. Here's Ida

Flautau engaged to Lyle Staybler, April 1942." She whistled. "Skeletons in closets and bedroom affairs."

"Don't be ridiculous," I said. Spread out on the table, the obits and articles looked up at us like a storybook unfolding before our eyes. We were piecing together history that mattered to that place as we gazed at faces from long ago. Ida's short wavy hair was dark in contrast to her pale skin. She gazed at a handsome young Lyle who looked like he could hardly believe his good fortune sitting so close to Ida. Then in a different picture Tom, hair wild and thick, sat beside his new bride Ida, hands in his lap, looking off to the right as Ida held her bouquet and appeared none too pleased. The two pictures were separated by one year. I imagined tears and harsh words and the effect of it all over a lifetime. I thought maybe I had gotten sucked into the drama of a love triangle from over half a century ago and wondered if someday someone would look at my picture and connect me to them.

"Here's an obituary for Ida Mandle, wife of Thomas Mandle," Martha said. I grabbed it from her. "Hey, I was reading that," she protested.

My anxiety was getting the best of me. I apologized and handed it back to her. "We've spent enough time on this." I closed the box lid. "We don't have time to waste."

"You hurry, you worry," Martha said.

"That makes no sense," I said.

"Don't snap at me," Martha said.

"And don't grab," Greta said. "It's rude."

"She's right, Trudy," Iris said. "This is going to take a long time and if you're snapping on day one, what will you be like come day one hundred? Remember we always measure twice, cut once." She placed her hands on the blackened leaded glass windows. "Real shame he did this to such great windows."

Greta's cell phone rang and she got right on it. "I've been wondering if you'd call." Her voice rose high and happy. She walked out of the room. She always seemed up to something. Don told me she grew up poor, lived in the trailer park near the potato fields where her father worked on the line at the factory and in the summer supervised the migrant workers. Her mother ran the Handle Bar and Grill. The nastiest rumor was that Greta's real father was a migrant worker. She had a loose and daring way about her even back in high school. She was working at the potato chip factory and frequenting the casinos when she won big on the slot machines. Then she played the state lottery and won even bigger. Rumor had it at over a million. She bought a floral business from an elderly couple and changed her colors, so to speak, as a successful Luce businesswoman who paid dues to Rotary and Chamber of Commerce.

With her finally out of the room, it was safe to talk to my two remaining friends, confide in them and give reason for why I'd been snapping, how it felt to be accused. "What if I don't get to day one hundred? What if I lose?" I said anxiously. "I Googled 'assisted suicide.' It's a crime in Minnesota. They say a person who wants help killing themselves is crying for help, not for death. It said terminally ill people are depressed. And I thought no kidding, who wouldn't be? It said that in pain, they're not thinking clearly and need counseling. I didn't learn anything new. Fifteen frickin' years and a possible $30,000 fine. I don't have the money, well not yet, but I don't care about that. But doing time. Holy smoke. Being away from Courtney. I just can't stand the thought. Don would probably divorce me."

"Girl. Get that lawyer," Iris said.

Someone smacked me on the butt. "Come on, Trudy," Martha said. "No time to waste." She laughed, took me by the arm, and led me out of there.

Later we sat on the porch where the air was cool and the sun warm. Felt good to just sit, give my knees a rest, but my mind was always racing. "We need to make it seem like there are people here to keep vandals away," I said. "I'll put timer lights in some of the rooms."

"Seems a Band-Aid," Martha said.

"And don't talk about what we're doing here, not to anyone. One thing we don't want to do. Draw attention to ourselves."

"Not draw attention?" Greta said, "Seems a bit late, don't you think?"

"What do you mean?" Martha said.

"Just sit in Ebeling's and listen to the chatter about this place and Trudy finding—"

"Doesn't pay to listen to gossips," Iris said.

"Oh I agree, though I am grateful to you, Trudy," Greta said. "You took their focus off my little misadventure. You are something new to discuss."

I gave her a look but she'd turned away.

Martha sat up like she had spotted danger. "Shoot. Here comes Randall. I was supposed to call him when I was ready. Darn. I completely forgot."

Randall got out of his car. It was black, one of those expensive racy models. He wore a navy blue sports coat and a pair of jeans, fancier than most men's suits in this town. "Nothing else to do but hang out here?" he said. "I thought you were going to call?" He kissed Martha's cheek, obviously more for show than affection. "I took the kids to Cleone's. Ready to go?"

"Go?" I said.

"Minneapolis," Martha said. "Anniversary tomorrow. So we're celebrating there."

"Fourteen years of bliss," Randall said.

I leaned forward. "I think—"

Iris put her hand on my shoulder and eased me back. "Can I get those stained glass windows from the Pugmeyer place?" she asked Randall. She wanted them for the new workshop her and Nathan planned to build—a project Nathan probably hoped would take her mind off missing Cobbers Creek. Randall had promised the windows to her awhile back. Used to be he'd find it in himself to be thoughtful, offering something from an old house or building that we could use. But something shifted in him. He got greedier and less generous. Still it had been over a year since he offered them to Iris and she wasn't about to forget.

"Oh hey, Iris. Didn't I tell you? They got busted up." I knew he was lying because Martha told me they found asbestos at Pugmeyer's and demolition was on hold.

Iris grimaced. "Really? They were in perfect shape last time I checked. I could've come out and removed them."

Randall shrugged. "You know what they say about hindsight," he said. "Worthless."

I'd fill Iris in later about the windows, maybe try to come up with a plan to help her get them despite Randall's BS.

"Breaks my heart," Iris said. "They were gorgeous."

"Yeah, a real shame," he said then pointed at me. "Speaking of shame, heard something interesting about you."

"We should go now," Martha said uncomfortably.

He glared at her as if she had spoken without permission. The wind gusted and messed up his hair, shifted his focus off Martha as he smoothed it back into place. "Heard something about you telling people you'd kill for this old house. Interesting plan. Get Lyle to change his will and then pretend to find him dead. A bit transparent though, don't you think?" He laughed but I could tell he wasn't really joking.

"I'm not supposed to talk about it," I said.

"I bet you're not." He grinned.

I wanted to know if Randall was referring to the will in connection to just the house or if he had heard something about the land? A sinking feeling settled in my stomach. If he knew about the land, the whole town would soon find out.

"Change his will?" Martha said.

I looked at her but forced myself to keep quiet. Greta was

staring at me and Iris looked at me, waiting. I wanted to tell them about the land but not with Randall and Greta there. I needed to change the subject. "Heard there's asbestos in the Pugmeyer place."

His face reddened and he grabbed Martha's hand. "We should get on the road."

Martha pulled free and rubbed her hand. "You're hurting me."

He put his arm around her shoulder. "Just anxious to get on the road."

They drove off and Iris looked at me like I needed to tell her something important about the will. I kept my mouth shut in front of Greta.

Later, alone on the front porch, I left another message for Joan Wakefield, saying it was even more urgent. My name was Trudy Mud. To calm myself down, I was forming a plan for clearing out the house. I needed to focus on a project. We'd begin in the kitchen, then spread out across the main floor before hitting the upstairs. I was really getting into the plan when I saw a scrawny man cut across the Mini-Mart parking lot. His ill-fitting suit had a thrift store look about it, outdated, rumpled, and shiny. He waited for an odd-looking boy to catch up. Then they walked toward me. "Ma'am," the scrawny man said from the bottom of the steps. He had a stud pierced into his bottom lip. I figured they were Bible thumpers like Bertha, out of that same odd cut of cloth.

"Not interested in any scripture reading."

"That's not our thing." His wire-rim glasses slid down his nose. He pushed them back up and sniffed. "It's about dearly departed Mr. Staybler." He nodded toward the house then ran his finger along his mustache and scraggly goatee. After propping his foot on the bottom step, he placed a briefcase on his thigh and unfastened the latches. "I got this," he said. "It's official." He came onto the porch with a thick envelope wrapped in clear plastic.

I hesitated before taking what felt oddly cool.

"You've been notified."

"A summons?"

"Salvation of your soul."

He clicked the latch of his briefcase. "We'll be in touch."

"Who?"

Him and the boy hurried across the yard, around the chicken wire fence, past the front of the store, and disappeared.

I unwrapped the oversized envelope to see a piece of folded cardboard. It smelled rank. I hurled it to the ground. At the bottom of the steps, I kicked it. The cardboard opened. THE LORD STILL LOVES KILLER SCUM TRUDY PLUTH was written above a rotting walleye.

As Martha often said, her Lord worked in mysterious ways.

That night I asked Iris to meet me at the Cactus Corral for a drink and I spilled it to her about the entire will, told her Lyle's estate was all mine. She said, "Well, Trudy. I guess people'll be interested more than ever in you now." She swirled the stir stick around in her gin and tonic. "Guess that's better than a poke in the eye with a sharp stick." We leaned into each other and laughed. For that one moment, I felt like it would all be okay.

11

Just wanting to be left alone, I turned my phone off and sat in Ebeling's Café to prepare for an upcoming appointment with Joan Wakefield. Hunkered down, I documented my story, getting it right, noting all I needed to share. The back booth was quiet near the hallway leading to the bathrooms. An open doorway led straight through to Cleone's Gift Shop, so if I wanted to avoid someone in the café, I could make a clean escape. Cleone was Randall's sister, but she was a good person who asked fair prices. I ate eggs over easy. After mopping up the yolk with toast, I ordered two pieces of pie to go, banana cream and rhubarb, because cleaning work at Lyle's house gave me a huge appetite. The teenage waitress was humming when she brought the pie with my bill. She soon returned and took my money, still humming like the happiest little thing that morning. "I'll bring your change," she said.

"Keep it," I said, placing my silverware on the plate right before she lifted it. I knew the drudgery of waiting tables.

"Thanks and you have a super nice day." I wondered what it was like to be so cheerful, too blessed to be stressed, kind of effervescent. While finishing my coffee, I scanned the Fargo paper left behind in a nearby booth, horrified to see an article:

MILLIONAIRE RECLUSE'S DEATH:
MURDER OR ASSISTED SUICIDE?

"The on-going investigation into the death of Lyle Staybler continues in Luce, a town of five thousand … Several people have been interviewed, co-operated fully, they answered each question,"

Luce Police Chief Dwight Huntermeister said.

Detective Thomas Gabrielson said, "We gave them opportunity to explain the events. We've been very sensitive and have approached the case with an open mind. Our task is to continue to collate the information and offer it to the Attorney General. That will take months, not days or even weeks."

From over the top of the paper, I spotted Lois and Dwight at the front of the café talking. Had they come in together? Dwight motioned toward the booths and they headed my way. Thank the Methodist minister's God that the good reverend stopped to talk with Dwight, giving me a chance to grab my pie and scram into the gift shop. But when I saw a former volunteer who had ditched Homes for Dwelling, I turned and slipped into the hallway leading to the café bathrooms. Leaning against the wall near a coat rack and stacked plastic chairs, I heard the waitress seat Dwight and Lois down in the booth I had just vacated. She soon returned to take their order and I settled in to eavesdrop.

"So, what's on your mind?" Dwight asked.

"I've been contemplating your question," Lois said. "It's keeping me from getting a good night's sleep."

"Which question?"

"Did Lyle tell me anything that may have brought concerns? You know, separate from concerns about his health."

"And?"

"Well, he did say people had been bothering him."

"Give any names?"

"Randall Short for one."

"Anyone else?"

"What about the Mandle family rekindling their friendship with Lyle?"

"Did he say they were bothering him?"

"Well, no. It's just that, well, you read the will that morning. Why should Tom be personal representative when we know his history of preying on the financially weak? And then there's the love triangle we've all whispered about."

"Don't figure busted love is much involved and buying foreclosed land isn't illegal."

I found Lois's comments to be quite interesting. Why was she turning down the heat under me and adjusting the focus onto other people? I wondered what exactly she had to hide because as we all know, no one is perfect. Just then that ex-volunteer popped into view out of nowhere.

"Trudy!" She looked scared to see me. "I read, well ... it's just ..."

"Come back to work anytime," I said, trying to duck out that escape hall and through the gift shop but oh no.

"Trudy," Dwight was suddenly in front of me. "Why haven't you returned my calls?"

"Been busy," I said. "Judging by the news in the Fargo paper, you too."

"I didn't name you."

"Didn't have to," I said. Then I looked at Lois sipping her coffee and reading that article. "Thanks to her." I held tight to my pie, grabbed the paper out of her hands, and threw it on the floor. "You and your big mouth and suspicions."

She ignored my anger. "The guilty always show their true colors."

Dwight tried to shush us. "This isn't the place," he said.

I leaned in and kept my voice low, "I read about people who work with terminal patients wanting to relieve the pain as much as they—"

Lois slammed her palm onto the table. "I have been cleared of all suspicion. My fingerprints are not on the murder weapons."

"That's correct. Yours are all over in the house and how hard is it to wipe them off bottles?"

"A fortune did not fall into my lap; it fell into your big fat lap." She took a deep breath. "Alva Techmeier and Opal

Harvala said, in fact, that they were home that morning. I asked them."

"What, are you working on the case now Deputy Ur-Ho?"

"Who's the prosecutor in this case?" Lois asked Dwight.

"There is no court case yet, Lois. It's still under investigation. And about Alva and Opal, they told me they weren't home when I asked them on a subsequent visit. Alva's daughter said her mother sleeps a lot. And Opal . . . well she hardly knows what year it is let alone where she was on any recent day."

"Maybe," Lois said.

"I was good to Lyle," I said.

"I never said you weren't," Lois countered.

"Then why paint me as the bad guy?"

"I'm well aware that he looked forward to your visits."

I tried to wrap my mind around her shift; the kind remark made me feel relieved but still suspicious. Was she trying to trick me? I did what Martha often told me to do, returned a kindness. "Yeah, well, he said you were the best."

When the waitress asked if they wanted anything else, I made my getaway through the gift shop and out their front door. I noticed Wanda Laconda sitting in her car outside the café and for some reason, I considered going back in to give Dwight a heads up on her appearance; but I didn't know what was going on with that so why should I be concerned?

As soon as I got in my car, I turned on my phone to see I had missed calls from Huntermeister, Martha, and Iris. Then my phone rang. Julianna calling to tell me Mark Riepe was contesting the will. "It's more of an annoyance than a valid claim," she said. "Still, it slows the process."

"Why does this have to be so complicated?" I said. "I do something charitable and this is the thanks I get."

"Quite a quaint thought," she said. "By the way, Trudy. Has Edward Schemp's name come up anywhere in the house?"

"No one talked about him to me."

"No, I mean on documents, or did Lyle ever mention him?"

"Can't recall ... oh, wait. Schemp's professional card was in a pile of stuff. But wasn't Lyle under his care?"

"Keep your ears and eyes open. Don't mention it to your worker bee, Greta. Her vision is clouded when it comes to all things Dr. Edward Schemp."

"What's that supposed to mean?" I knew Julianna was in Suzie Schemp's social circle and maybe Suzie shared some dirt about Greta with Juliana. "Clouded how?"

"I have to take another call. I'll be in touch."

I dialed Joan Wakefield pronto and pleaded with her, said I needed to meet right away, couldn't wait for our appointment, and was relieved to hear that she could fit me in first thing the next morning. After hanging up, I pulled the plastic fork out of the bag and ate banana cream pie.

Still, I needed a friend so I called Iris. She didn't answer. Then I remembered she was with Nathan, Curtis, and Marcus for a day in Fargo. I called Martha, but she said she was busy. She and Greta were going to Sassy Spa. Since when did she go to Darcy's spa? She knew how much I despised that spa, built on land where the rust-colored brick shell of Joseph Dertinger's brewery used to serve as testament to Luce's history of brewing a celebrated lager beer. Money with an idea just came in one day, knocked it all down, and hauled it away. No sense of history left on that spot, not even one of those historical markers. "You should give it a try," Martha said. "You could use a massage after all the bad publicity in the Fargo paper. A facial, too," she added insult to injury. "There's daycare available."

"I don't need daycare," I said.

"Duh. No kidding, but I do."

I hung up feeling lower than low. To add further insult to injury, Don was out of town at one of Courtney's swim meets that I'd chosen not to attend. *Not on your list of things to do?* Don had sarcastically said. Courtney had been bringing home first place ribbons and Don took photos so I figured I had those tangibles to make it seem like I was there. Still, Don reminded me it was not the same as celebrating the actual moments at the meets with Courtney.

I drove to Lyle's and sat on his back porch. Just sat thinking about him, how he'd be rocking in his chair slurping melted ice cream and pain would grip him. I tried to teach him the calm breathing that Iris showed me, but he'd hold his breath and close his eyes and bear it until the pain eased up. Sometimes he tried to make it seem like the pain wasn't so bad but I could see it in his face and the way he held his body so stiff. He gave up trying to hide it altogether the week before he died. I thought of one of our last visits.

◆　◆　◆

"Not too hungry today," Lyle said. "Stomach's poorly." His voice was weaker and raspier.

"It's sauerkraut and sausage. Maybe not the best for you." I put the bag and aluminum container on the table beside his chair. "Try the potatoes."

"I used to garden. Raise chickens." He nibbled at the potatoes. "Goats, too."

"Maybe you want butter on those," I said. "Might taste better."

He shook his head.

With other clients, I delivered the food and went right back to my car, but I spent time with Lyle. Sometimes, I'd loop around to his house after my last delivery and visit a bit more before driving back to town. He seemed lonely, odd to think so of a recluse.

Lyle was poking at his potatoes when he dropped his fork. The pain hit him bad. When it ended he said, "Lois wants me to leave here."

"Nursing home?"

"Pain comes more. Brings Ida with it."

"Ida is she—"

"Ida passed on. Pain's getting worse."

"Do you need a pill?"

"Makes my stomach sick. Lois gives me the other stuff."

"Peppermint leaves?"

He shook his head. "The other stuff."

"How about ice cream? Won't take long for it to melt in this heat."

He waved his hand to dismiss the idea. "Used to be quiet on my front porch. Use to whittle out there."

"Oh yeah?"

"What is there at that nursing home? Walls and floors. No birds. No trees. What will I see out the windows? Nothing. Here's what's mine. My porch." His hands were shaking and his nose was running. "I'm not going there."

"No reason you should have to. The hospital bed is coming. That will—"

"Used to be panthers roamed this area," he said. "Wolves, too. Back in 1928, man claimed wolves ate his eight-year old boy. Claimed to come up on two wolves standing over the body. 'Course we got a lot of wolves in sheep clothing around here!" He smiled and wiped his nose.

◆　◆　◆

I unlocked the back door and stood in his kitchen. We'd spread stuff out all over the place, death-defying work. Place felt more cluttered than ever. We'd open a cabinet and an avalanche would come at us. Once, Iris laid her cell phone down and we couldn't find it for the longest time even after she dialed the number and we sniffed around like a pack of dogs trying to detect her chimes ringtone. Finally we heard it whimpering faintly where it had fallen behind boxes of jigsaw puzzles.

I got ice cream from the freezer and was digging for a spoon when I saw an old jar with a crusty cork stopper. The label said *NUSOLE: Saves Shoe Soles.* The directions read: *Clean off all loose dirt and apply with the dauber all over the sole. If applied at night, the shoe will be dry and ready to wear the next morning.* For some reason, of all the stuff packed into the house, that Nusole got to me. I imagined Lyle as a young man, sitting at the kitchen table applying it to his boots. I thought about his sadness, how it must have felt to lose the woman he loved and maybe that was the reason he became a recluse. Maybe putting that stuff on his boots helped him avoid walking into town for new ones. He wouldn't have to see anyone, wouldn't risk running into Ida or Tom or whoever else. I wondered if he got used to being a recluse. I wished I had asked him to tell me more about his life. I went back outside and sat on the front porch. For the first time I noticed the wood shavings lodged between the slats of the floorboards under my feet. I sat there a good long time, scooping ice cream onto my rhubarb pie and eating to keep from crying.

12

Julianna's sports car pulled out of the professional building parking lot as I drove in for my appointment with Joan Wakefield. Why was she there? Were they in cahoots? Talking about me in some scheme? I didn't need them to add to my fears. Then I saw Dwight's cruiser pull out from the back lot. Was I walking into a trap? My energy was lagging and it was hard for me to think straight.

A nasty call to our landline had woke me up early that morning. A man's voice, distant and disguised, "Woe unto those who covet." I slammed the receiver down. Don hit *69 but the number was blocked. Later when I called Iris, she said she got a call on her cell; the man called her a tar baby. Nathan wanted her to stop going to the house, said it wasn't safe. She said racism rears its ugly head once again. I tried to convince her otherwise, that it wasn't about race but about jackasses trying to scare us. Still, I knew the power of Nathan Buck in her life and if he was against the house, she could be convinced to be as well. I tried to get her to stick with me, said I got a call, too. She said it wasn't the same. Hate was ugly and it scared her. I told her not to let fear run her life. She sighed and said goodbye. Cranked my worries up to think of losing her.

I walked into the non-descript, two-story office building, checked the directory for Joan, took the elevator to the second floor, let the receptionist know I was there, sat and waited for way too long. "Ms. Wakefield is ready now." The receptionist was smiling really wide, maybe considered me just one more fool in need of counsel, given my name plastered in the news.

Joan was on her cell phone and waved me into her plush office. It was all leather and oak. She talked low, almost in a whisper. I settled down in a straight-back chair in front of her desk and smoothed my denim skirt as the waistband dug into my skin. The button had popped off that morning and I hoped the safety pin I used in place of the button wouldn't bust open and stick me. Martha thought it was odd that my passion for repair work didn't transfer to sewing. There's a huge difference between the heft of a hammer and the skinny of a needle.

Joan looked at me while listening to whoever was jabbering away on her phone. She held up her finger as if to say 'just one minute.' She wore a blousy blue top, maybe silk, with a scoop neck and short sleeves. Her blond hair was bouncy, one of those cuts where the back was shorter than the sides that curled toward her chin; bet it took more time to style than I'd ever want to spend on hair in a day. Her gold and pearl bracelet and ring looked expensive, like her legal services, and I thought she better not be charging me for minutes while I was sitting there with my gut cinched, watching her on the phone. I scanned the room; saw a picture of her daughter, Courtney's age. Joan was one of those hip mothers Courtney mentioned, letting her daughter get two piercings in each ear and wear shorts up to her butt. As Joan talked on the phone, I tried to gauge her trustworthiness. She certainly had good posture. Made me sit up straighter just looking at her.

She wrote in a small notebook, said goodbye, hung up, tossed the notebook into her purse, and put the purse in a drawer. She was most likely a woman who had a place for everything and kept everything in its place. After some small town chitchat about the new World War II Museum, we got down to business. "I talked with Julianna Mandle," she said.

"And Dwight," I said.

"No. Julianna and..." She stopped as if catching herself from leaking a secret, gave me a puzzled look and continued, "It's moving through probate but there is an on-going investigation and the property is in abeyance," she said.

"Think I'll lose it to Mark?"

"Highly unlikely. He is going for a long shot. Desperate men and their desperate measures. He got Leon Hopper to represent him. Leon generally takes cases no one else would consider. Still we have to address the matter. His filing is nothing more than an annoyance that wastes time and money."

"Don't have much of either. Which brings me to ... I can't pay you just yet."

"No?" She seemed to consider my value as she stared. "I'll treat you as pro bono until circumstances change."

"I'm a charity case?"

"Take it or leave it," she said but didn't wait for a reply. "I've been reviewing the investigation notes. Suspected assisted suicide, marijuana in Lyle's blood with the other drugs." She folded her hands and leaned forward. "I for one don't believe you'd be naive enough to have participated, given your free access to Lyle's house and your involvement with his care. Though why you submitted to that drug test is beyond me. Who cares if they found marijuana in that house? You have rights."

"I was clean. Proved it."

"Don't you know your rights?" I wasn't quite sure how to answer but she kept talking. "Well anyway, you turned up clean there. The state's case, if that's what one could even call it, will be circumstantial. Still I need to get you to understand a few things about the legality of ownership and probate. Need to be mindful of potential threats. The autopsy report reveals traces of marijuana as well as an entire cornucopia of pharmaceuticals. The prosecutors may make an issue of the marijuana in him and in the house, try to connect it to the recent bust of local marijuana growers, try to connect you to it, stack the suspicions against you. Given that medical marijuana was soon to be, but not yet legal in Minnesota at the time of Lyle's death, we need—"

"I don't know where he got the pot. Call Greta. She's the grower."

Joan raised an eyebrow. "Yes and ended up with you. Seems quite a coincidence."

"Look, I know nothing about the—"

"As for assisted suicide, if Lyle had convinced someone to help him die, I might think that person should be considered a saint, and not a criminal. Trouble is, the state of Minnesota doesn't see it that way and if you're formally charged—"

"Formally? Am I informally charged or something?"

"You're a suspect, Trudy. I don't know if I can say that any more clearly."

"I'm no saint. I can tell you that."

"There is absolutely no need to convince me of that."

"Only thing that keeps me from feeling crazy is work. So can we still clean out the house?"

"Yes, of course. By all means."

"What about my rights as owner of his possessions?"

"Julianna informed me she and her father offered storage space, so just be sure it all makes it into those sheds and is accounted for. You don't need any more accusations against you. The estate remains in probate court, so don't discard, distribute, or sell anything that could be claimed by someone else."

"How would anyone know?"

She frowned. I imagined her in court intimidating a witness. "You really don't want to take chances with that, now do you?" She waited for an answer.

"I suppose I don't."

"What about the locks on the house?" she asked.

"What about them?"

"Are they reliable?" She had a habit of pinching her bottom

lip and narrowing her eyes, like she was really taking in, not just what I said but how I said it, and how I looked when I said it, deciphering me and maybe gauging *my* trustworthiness.

"Sure are. Also boarded over the kitchen door window and cellar windows, too."

"Get a locksmith out there."

"What for?"

"Get new deadbolts."

"What good is that?"

"Precautionary measures. You don't know who else has a key."

"Oh, crap. Never thought of that. Shouldn't that point be raised in the investigation? Who else might've had access to the house?"

Joan cleared her throat. "Something else you should know." She didn't say anything and I got really nervous. She sighed and finally said, "About the circumstances surrounding Lyle's death. The woods—"

"They find anything leading to my attacker?"

"So many tracks out there, anyone could be a suspect."

"Yeah. I figured as much."

"You know those woods?"

I shrugged. "Some. Know to avoid poison ivy."

"Down by the pines bordering Old Settlers Homestead Farm, it's been a hang out for juveniles according to Dwight's report. Booze bottles, used condoms, wrappers, junk food containers."

"Guess I never ventured that far out on his land."

"So you aren't familiar with the woods?"

"Just what's around the granary and barn. It's a pigsty. Lyle burned trash out there."

"So you are familiar with the land?"

I suddenly felt like I shouldn't answer, but she was my lawyer and what the heck.

"Want me to answer again?"

She squinted. "Anything else I should know?"

"About the land?"

"About your familiarity with the land."

"Not really."

"If you think of anything, make sure you let me know."

"Will do."

"I'm serious," she said.

"Me too."

She was sizing me up, like she was trying to get some hidden read. "As I was saying, since there are suspicious circumstances surrounding Lyle's demise while he was under hospice care, there will be a formal meeting to discuss the matter of his death. Along with his hospice team and their counsel, you'll be asked to attend. I'll accompany you."

"Like a court of law?"

"Nothing of that nature."

"Do I have to go?"

"I don't know why you wouldn't want to cooperate."

"I'm tired of talking about it."

"Well it is unfortunate that you've grown weary of talking about it, given that I would like you to tell me a bit more about the day you found Mr. Staybler."

"Why not ask Dwight to share my story with you."

"He did and—"

"I knew it. He was here with her."

"Her?"

"Julianna. Those two are up to something."

Joan looked at me like I was hallucinating. Sticking to her point, she continued, "You'll be asked to tell the story again while recording it at the formal meeting."

"Oh for Pete's sake."

"For your sake, you need to make sure you have your story straight."

"What are you saying?"

"Dwight tells me you want to take a lie detector test."

"That's right. That's what I'd say to anyone in that room and that lie detecting needle would support my claim. I did not help Lyle die and I sure didn't kill him."

"So tell me about that day." She lifted a pen and set the point down on a legal pad.

For the next hour, I told her exactly what I told the investigators. "Knowing what I did about the shifty behavior of some people in this town, Lyle's unlocked door should've put me on alert." I ended with, "I didn't do it."

She finished writing, put down her pen, and let my declaration of innocence hang in the air.

A week later, I had to travel to the hospice main office, a forty-minute drive along mostly county roads bordering woods and lakeshore. Don told me a story he heard about a man who set out with his ox cart on that road. Caught in a blizzard, he killed the ox, gutted what he could, and climbed inside to keep from freezing to death. I never knew whether or not to believe such bizarre stories.

I arrived at the offices and waited in the lobby, watched people across the street mingle outside the Otter Tail County Historical Museum. Not but a minute after Joan arrived, a man who referred to himself as a mediator escorted me and her, all official like, into a conference room and said it was simply a meeting to gather information. He would file a formal report for hospice on the matter of Lyle Staybler's death. If it came to a court of law, he'd present his findings.

Joan and me sat across from him while he read a statement of fact, "Lyle Staybler was diagnosed with terminal pancreatic cancer and immediately placed under hospice care. His team was Carol Woolover and Lois Urho, who had recommended that he be moved to Luce Nursing Home—"

"Where, I might add, he did not want to go," I spoke up.

The man looked over his reading glasses at me and then down to his paper. "The hospice team feared for Mr.

Staybler's safety as he grew weaker and more vulnerable to outside influences—"

"Hey. Wait just one minute," I interrupted him. "Is that referring to me? Outside influences? Because I—"

"Trudy, please," Joan said.

"You are trying to pin this on me," I said. "Make Lois come out like a rose."

"Not at all." He patted my shoulder. "Impartiality ensures justice is served."

I was feeling kind of loopy. I wanted someone to say I shouldn't have to keep repeating my story but needed to keep quiet about how anxious I felt. Focus on what the man asked and tell him straight up what he needed to hear. I looked him in the eyes. "Knowing what I did about the shifty behavior of some people in this town— the real dangerous outside influences—Lyle's unlocked door should've put me on alert ..."

Afterward, on my way home, driving down that road, my life was a blizzard of a mess and I couldn't help but wish there was an ox I could climb into.

13

I was coming back from a service call in Gorman Township when the Pluth Hardware van broke down. I popped the hood but was pretty sure the tranny finally gave up the ghost. I was leaving Don a voice message when Dwight drove past. He turned around and offered to give me a lift. I locked the van and left it for a tow or to rust to kingdom come for all I cared.

I sat up front rather than in back because I sure as heck didn't want anyone thinking I'd been arrested. A red silk scarf was caught between my seat and the console. I lifted it and it released a real fine scent. Dwight got a funny look on his face, quickly taking it, and shoving it into his jacket pocket. "That's real pretty, Dwight. A good color for you."

"Trying to brighten up my khaki wardrobe," he said, offering a moment of lightness between us like in the old days.

"Scent's a little flowery, though. Might try something different." Then I just went for it. "What's with you and Wanda Laconda?"

"There's nothing with us," he said, but I didn't believe him.

We passed family farms, most of them dairy, profitable evident by the five or six Harvestore silos on their property.

The grasses along the Otter Tail River were dying back with the cooler early October weather. What was it Iris had said about October? "Heady little colorful autumn one day, skin-numbing Alberta Clipper winter the next." She had realized after her first full year in Luce that October could not be trusted. Even when dissing something, she sounded poetic. Like when she said Nathan lured her in the lusty heat of summer so that by the time harsh winter arrived, she was so mesmerized by him, she couldn't free herself from the weight of dark and cold. How he could love a season as brutal as Minnesota winter was beyond her.

It had rained the previous night. Before long it'd be snow falling. Summer tourists were long gone, good riddance. Duck hunters were blasting away at the sky. Round hay bales sat in fields across from the marsh. At the intersection, two bales with painted Jack-o-Lantern faces greeted us. The light in the sky had been the same shade of dismal all day long. I was craving sunshine. I once thought those light therapy boxes people use to combat so-called seasonal affective disorder was a bunch of hooey. But a week earlier, Iris showed me an article Nathan gave her when he suggested she use one to combat her winter blues. If it would help her endure Luce and winter, I told her, heck yes, she should buy one.

When we turned onto Honey Farm Lane, Dwight said, "Know what I like about this road?"

I shook my head.

"All the cattails." He smiled. "No one's destroyed the marsh."

"Yet," I said.

"I used to catch toads here when I was a boy. Didn't hurt 'em, just let 'em go. Used to pretend those cattails were cigars and 'smoke' 'em." He put air quotes around smoke like I wouldn't get that he didn't really smoke them.

"Great," I said. "Lyle told me there used to be cougars around here. Said wolves once killed and ate—"

"An eight-year old boy. That story's been around a long time. Then there's the one about the bear—"

"That fed children peanuts and abducted one. People said it was a Gypsy."

"Back in 1913. The father searched Gypsy camps for his son. Never found the boy."

I shook my head. "No wonder people believe Lyle killed dogs and held séances. People crave weird stories."

"The lore of the land."

At the bottom of a hill sat Lazy Acres Resort and a meadow lined with white pines. Farther down the road, the Mosquito Heights Resort owner had sold land to the city years back to expand the municipal golf course to eighteen holes.

"When I was a kid," Dwight said, "before this was a golf course, it was woods all the way to Luce Lake. We'd find arrowheads. My grandmother remembered Indian burial sites, said she was warned not to take anything. People did, though."

"Heard farmers let their cattle graze and the sites disappeared."

"Sadly true," he said.

"Ever wish you'd moved away from this town?"

"Maybe, but who doesn't second guess themselves after midlife hits, maybe want to go somewhere warm? But then we just never know what goodness is right under our noses waiting for us." He touched his pocket holding the red scarf.

"Yeah. Who knows?"

He turned onto the paved road where lake cabins had been razed to make way for huge houses that hog the lakeshore. How was it the DNR allowed people to erect 4,000-square-foot monsters and stress the land and the water? Chemically treated green lawns smack right up to the lake. Aquatic plants, whose purpose was to keep the lake healthy, had been dredged up. Three-stall garages, second floors, and eight-foot tall front-entry windows—death traps for migrating birds to smash into—stuck out like sore thumbs. Made no sense.

At the end of this long line of lake homes, we'd come to Martha's house abutting Tom's land. Dwight slowed down and said, "Something's wrong."

Then I saw Randall's sports car stuck in the ditch on the other side of the wooded lot. Martha's car was in the driveway but the driver's door was open. Dwight pulled in behind her car, parked, and cut the engine.

"Wait here," he said.

I followed him, stopping to look inside the car where grocery bags tipped over on the back seat. A couple of crafts and women's magazines sat on top of a box of Life cereal on the floor. A jar of peanut butter rolled against them.

He knocked and waited. I hung back just enough to not irritate him. He knocked again. "Hello?" he called.

Finally Martha came to the door carrying Grace, but stood back from the light as if trying to hide her face, the obvious truth that she'd been crying. Grace looked sleepy, sucking on a bottle, resting her head against her mother's chest as Martha stroked her blonde hair. I thought eighteen months was too old to still have a bottle, almost told her once but kept my mouth shut about it. Why bother? She was a good mother and protected her kids as best she could from Randall's rampages.

"Martha, what's going on?" Dwight asked.

"Are you okay?" I inched closer. Dwight gave me a stern look.

"Why are you with Dwight?" She looked at my hands. "Are you finally arrested?"

"Finally? What the—"

"Martha, what's going on?" Dwight repeated.

"What do you mean?"

"Randall's car's in the ditch. Your car door's wide open, groceries in the back seat."

She touched her forehead. "I forgot about the groceries." She laughed all nervous like wanting to make light of some situation she didn't feel like sharing. "I can be so scatterbrained," she said.

"Don't be hard on yourself," Dwight said. "Can happen to any of us, hurrying to get inside and maybe your hands were full of children."

"Yes, that's exactly it. In a hurry to come in and get the kids fed."

"Can I talk to Randall?" Dwight asked.

"He's not home."

"His car's right there in the ditch."

"He got a ride to town for a meeting."

"Why didn't he use your car?"

"Well, he couldn't. I got home after him."

I could tell she was lying. "Martha," I interrupted. "Why don't you and the kids come to my house?" I was worried about her.

Dwight motioned me to get back into his car. "Martha, let me come inside," he said.

She smiled but didn't budge. "I'll tell him to call you when he comes home."

"Let me just come inside for a moment."

"I really need to get back to the kids, change Grace's diaper."

Dwight seemed to consider his options. "You keep my cell phone number in your contacts, you hear? You call me if there's something you need to tell me."

"I'll just hang out here with Martha," I said to Dwight. "Don can pick me up."

"No," Martha said. I waited for her to explain why not. "I have to check on the children, make sure they're playing nicely." She shut the door.

Later that night, I called Martha. "Randall was inside wasn't he?"

"Passed out."

"Why didn't you tell Dwight? They're supposedly friends."

"And have Randall scream at me for letting *Dwight the Nag* in. That's what Randall calls him because Dwight's after him to return to AA."

"Where's Randall now?"

"I don't know." She blew her nose. "He sobered up, got his car out of the ditch, and drove off. His cell goes right to voice mail."

"I'm sorry he's drinking again."

"He won't listen to reason." She sniffled. "Trudy, I'm going to tell you something but you have to promise not to tell anyone. Not even Don."

"I promise."

"I checked Randall's laptop when he was passed out. I'm just sick with worry about him. He's so stressed; he's got a rash on his face. Said Dr. Schemp thinks it's a food allergy but I don't believe it. He doesn't tell me anything anymore unless it's lies like that. I typed in his password, the one he uses for everything: *Superman.* I checked his e-mail and scanned the usual subject lines from his employees, Rotary Club, Chamber of Commerce. Then I started seeing messages from sub-contractors. He's behind payment to some of them and they're threatening to take him to court. Court! It makes me weak to think about it so I just keep praying that whatever is going on will stop. Then I saw the subject line: *Staybler's land.* It was from Mark Riepe. *No go. Let me know what's next.* I checked the sent box, but didn't find a message from Randall to that address. I checked the history cache and saw that he visited sites about contesting wills, bankruptcy, and eminent domain. Then I found sites for hotels in Fargo, not the cheap motels off Interstate 94 that Randall owns. I logged onto our credit card accounts and found charges for hotels and expensive dinners in Fargo. He's closed some business bank accounts. What if he's having an affair?"

"No way," I said what she needed to hear.

"I read that fifty percent of men cheat on their women. Seriously. I will die."

"Martha. There's gotta be a legit reason for those charges, like for business, a meeting or something." I really wanted to know the date of that e-mail he got from Mark, maybe get a copy for Joan or Dwight.

"You think so?" Martha said. "Here let me just read something to you."

"Maybe not a good idea to do that right now because—"

"So listen," she said. "Are you listening?"

"Martha, I—"

"Listen!" She sounded like she was going to cry.

"Okay. Okay."

"So here's a Visa charge for last month. Dinner at Silver Moon in Fargo. And then—"

"What do you think you're doing?" Randall's voice came over the phone.

"Martha!" I said. "Martha?"

"I asked you what you think you're doing?" Randall said.

"I ... I got a call about an overdue—"

"You got nothing."

The phone went dead. I dialed her number and it went straight to voice message. My red flags were waving all over the place. I wanted to drive out to her house, get Martha and the children out of there. I called Dwight's cell and left a message telling him it was urgent. He should go to Martha's pronto.

After pacing with the phone and dialing Martha's number every ten minutes for over an hour—only to have it go right to voice mail—I needed to calm myself. We were out of ice cream, so I did that breathing thing Iris taught me. Inhale to the count of 1, 2, 3, Exhale to the count of 1, 2, 3, Inhale, 1, 2, 3 ... In the middle of an exhale, Don walked into the room. "Martha's on the phone." He handed me the portable.

"I didn't hear it ring."

"Came through when I was on the phone with Courtney."

I took the phone. "Where's Courtney?"

"Sleepover at Ericka's. Remember?" he asked with great irritation in his tone.

"Now I do."

He shook his head and left the room.

"Martha. I've been frantic. Should I come get you?"

She laughed. "No need. All's well. Randall's watching *Finding Nemo* with the kids.

"But I was afraid you—"

"All's well, I said, Trudy. For goodness sake. All is well."
She hung up.

I didn't believe her, but what could I do?

14

Last week of October and snow fell. It was a real pain in the butt to trudge through as I carried a busted up aluminum stepladder and parchment lampshade to toss on top of an already erupting volcano. Instead of wondering for the hundredth time why Lyle didn't just throw crap out, I figured I should've thought to place the Dumpster closer to the house.

At least we already hauled out tons of junk so the good stuff was starting to work its way to the surface inside the house. We'd been researching some of it on eBay. Iris said people were hot to buy salvaged wood and metals. Didn't want to throw any out and didn't want to haul it to storage. We should just sell it. I checked with Julianna but she forbade it, said to stick with the plan. As I was slogging my way back to the house, Martha drove up with her kids. "What the heck?" I called out to her.

She carried Grace. Ruthie and Michael trailed behind. "Meaning?"

"What's going on?" I tried to keep my voice even.

"Nothing to worry about. I'm fine."

"What're you doing with the children? Did you finally leave Randall?"

"Don't be silly," Martha said. "Randall can't watch them and my mother couldn't watch them either."

"Why didn't you tell me? Courtney could've come to your house?"

"No."

"What do you mean no?"

"I don't want a sitter to come there." She looked like she was trying to prevent some truth from coming forward.

"For the love of your sweet Jesus. Why not?" I waited for an answer but then she looked like she would cry, so I didn't push it. "Martha, this isn't a place for kids."

"Then I won't be able to work today," she said.

"Okay. Okay. We'll figure something out." Maybe I could bribe Courtney to give up Saturday morning laziness and watch them, or talk Don into driving out to get them, maybe shuttle them to our house. I could promise to fix the hardware store's back door in return for the favor. Fire trucks raced along the highway with their loud sirens and horns. The ambulance soon followed. The noise seemed to go on way too long.

I took Grace and the diaper bag while Martha held Michael's and Ruthie's hands. I unlocked the door. The rule was: Keep the door locked at all times. I had new locks installed and all of us, even Greta despite my better judgment, had keys. "Iris," I called out. "Martha's here."

Greta came from the dining room. "Why hello Martha and friends," she said. "I was down in the cellar going through—"

"This place stinks," Michael said. Ten years old and behaving rudely, but I wasn't surprised. I knew of Martha's concerns that he was picking on Ruthie more often lately. His teacher called Martha in to discuss his disruptive behaviors. Poor kid mirroring his father. "Where's Dad? I don't want to be here. I want to go to Aunt Cleone's, not here. P. U." He held his nose. His nervous habit of biting the skin around his fingertips had gotten worse. His thumb especially looked sore and red.

Greta held her nose and said, "P.U."

Ruthie held her nose. "P.U."

Ignoring such childishness, I asked, "Where's Iris?" Greta pointed overhead. "Iris," I called up the stairway.

"Be down in a sec," she shouted.

Ruthie said, "Greta, smell my hair. Mommy bought strawberry shampoo."

"Mmmm. Absolutely lovely. I wish this house smelled as good as you do." She picked up Ruthie and twirled her around. Ruthie, who looked just like her mother with dark brown hair and light complexion, wrapped her arms around Greta's neck and kissed her cheek. When had Greta stolen her affection? What the heck? I used to be the one Martha's kids laughed with. I was the one who built birdhouses with Michael and Ruthie to hang in their backyards. I was the one who had rocked colicky newborn Grace so Martha could nap. I was the one who could have been Grace's godmother if only—as Martha said to me—I would have professed my faith in her one true God.

Grace squirmed to get down. Just as soon as her feet hit the ground, she snatched up a rusty jar lid and put it in her mouth. Martha swooped her right back up. "Ish." She took it away.

A loud crash came from upstairs. Greta and Martha moved the kids toward the dining room door. I started up the stairway. "What are you doing up there? What broke?"

Iris rushed down the stairs. "Our window. Look what someone sent us." She held a fieldstone, at least two pounds, with the words **Get Out Now** written in black. "Came through the back bedroom window."

"Fools must be hiding in the woods, watching us."

"Shhh," Martha said, "You'll scare the children."

"They shouldn't even be here," I said.

"Don't snap at me," Martha said, keeping her children close.

"What say we close shop and call it a day?" Greta said.

"Nonsense. We'll keep the doors locked." I cleared junk from the mantle and set the stone next to two others that had been left on the back porch: **You Women Had Better Go   Get Out Now.**

"I don't like it here," Ruthie said.

"How about you go to my house and play with Courtney?" I said. Ruthie adored Courtney so I knew that was the perfect bait. She nodded and smiled.

Thirty minutes later, I was forty dollars in debt to Courtney who wasn't nearly as charitable as I thought she should be in naming her price, but she agreed to babysit and got Don to drive her to pick them up and take them back to our house.

I was glad Don hadn't come in. Didn't need anyone spilling it to him about rocks through windows. Martha held plywood over the window while I nailed it into place. The board hung crooked which seemed par for the course.

"It's chilly in here," Greta said.

"You ought to wear one of these." Martha pointed to her sweatshirt decorated with a waving snowman. "I created them for the Hunting Widow's Bazaar but they didn't sell."

I thought back to the year when she made them. Usually careful with her sewing, Martha hurried to meet the bazaar deadline and got sloppy. Ironed the patches on crooked and sewed sequins too far apart. The embroidered messages slanted and the stitching in the rickrack was hit or miss and some of it puckered. She had cried over her unsold inventory. I knew what that felt like to have to eat a loss, some of my efforts to save houses in rubble. When I suggested we wear them like uniforms for working on houses, she got all offended, but then warmed to the idea.

"There's a pile over there," she continued to try to win Greta's interest. "You should wear one to protect your clothes and keep you warm."

"Hmmm." Greta seemed amused by the shirts. "That's really sweet." She made a sweeping gesture across her black jeans and tee shirt. "I'm fine, though." Perhaps her usually dark attire made it easier to disappear into the shadows of the house, fitting for a marijuana grower.

I was just about to break up the chitchat when someone

banged on the front door. I opened it to find Randall. "What are you pounding for?"

"Can't you hear the bell?" Randall's shadow fell across the entryway floor.

"The bell's broken," Iris said.

"Well tack up a note saying so. Is that so hard to figure out? What're you doing in here that it takes," he counted, "four women to move so excruciatingly slow to the door?" His cologne was heavy and unpleasant. His boot prints tracked through the slushy snow on the porch. I tried not to stare at his rash-covered cheeks. Martha had said it was bad but I had no idea it was that bad; almost as red as a strawberry.

Martha laughed nervously. "Sorry. We were just—"

"Where's your cell?" Randall asked.

His question seemed to catch her off guard, like maybe she was unsure where it was. "I forgot to charge it."

"From now on, charge it, and keep it close so I don't have to drive out looking for you." He scanned the room. "Where are the children?"

"Courtney's watching them," Martha said.

"Go get them."

"At Trudy's house."

"Too bad. I was going to take them for ice cream." He opened his briefcase and removed a folder. "I need you to sign this."

"What is it?" I asked.

"Oh hey, I'll tell you what it is, Trudy. It's none of your business." He turned his briefcase sideways, set papers on top of it, and then waved Martha over.

"Sign this," he said.

"What's it for?"

"Nothing to concern your pretty little head. Just an inconsequential parcel of land. I told you about it," he said.

"I don't recall." Martha scanned the paper, perhaps for key words to make her believe him.

"Martha, please. I beg you for once in your life, don't be so slow. Just sign the thing. I need to get it to the bank before noon."

"That's not—" She dropped the pen and it rolled along the floor's slant behind a box. Randall huffed then searched for it, but before he could pick it up, Martha flipped a page to reveal to us: *Acreage, Parcel 25, Otter Tail County, Corliss Township.* So he wasn't lying.

He stood back up. "Tell your brain to tell your hand to hold on to this." He gave her the pen.

Martha signed quickly. "There. Satisfied?"

"Satisfied? That's right, Martha. That's exactly what I am."

"At least something satisfies you." She lifted her mug. When Randall turned, his elbow hit the mug, spilling coffee on his suit.

He stepped back, looked at the stain, then at her. "Christ, woman." He removed a handkerchief from his pants pocket and a one hundred dollar bill fell to the floor. Apparently unaware of it, he was busy dabbing his suit coat. Greta snatched the bill up and stuck it under a box. She winked at Martha. Randall put the papers in his briefcase. He opened the door and groaned. "Now what does he want?"

Chief Huntermeister got out of his cruiser and walked toward us. We all stepped onto the porch, the floor slick from melting snow.

"What brings you here?" Randall asked.

"Business. How about you?"

"Business."

"Oh yeah?" Dwight grinned. "Helping the women clean out the place?"

"Funny," Randall said. He looked at his ringing cell phone and frowned as he walked off toward his car without a goodbye to anyone—not even Martha.

Dwight turned to me. "Someone called in a complaint about—"

"The rock through the—"

I grabbed Iris's hand to stop her from saying more. I didn't need him telling us to leave the house because of a measly rock through the window.

"About flying debris." He nodded toward the Dumpster. "Look at that mess. You got to get that emptied."

"Who complained?" I asked.

"Not your concern, Trudy."

"Was it Jerry?" I said. "Litter blows around his place all the time."

"Just get it emptied and keep the lid down." Dwight was crankier than all get out.

"Geeze. Okay. Who poked you in the eye with a stick?"

"That'll keep the snow out of it, too," he said.

"Will do," I said.

"Appreciate it." He gave us all a wave but lingered on Martha, "Take care." He scanned the traffic along Highway 10, the frontage road, the Mini-Mart parking lot, like someone making sure it was all clear of danger before proceeding.

Back inside, Greta waved the one hundred dollar bill that had fallen from Randall's pocket. "You forgot this." She handed Martha the bill.

"Is this stealing?" Martha asked.

"Absolutely not," Greta interjected. "For richer and poorer. You married him; you married the money."

"Maybe it's like manna from Heaven," Martha said.

"Bitchin'," Greta laughed.

Funny how Martha didn't get indignant when Greta cussed.

Later someone knocked on the door. I looked through the living room window to see Tom Mandle on the porch. He didn't look too good. I opened the door.

"How's it?" he nodded.

"How's what?" Iris asked.

Tom stepped inside, removed his hat, and ran his hand

through thick white hair. His coloring was yellow, his skin waxy. It concerned me that he seemed to be going downhill fast. He gazed around the room, holding onto the door-frame while wiping his boots on the *Luce Bulletins*, tearing the papers with each swipe. He hurried to remove his coat like he was suddenly too hot then sat down hard in Lyle's rocking chair, working for breath. His coat fell to the floor with a thud.

"You don't look so good," I said. "Worse than the last time—"

"Saw Randall Short was out here earlier." Was Tom spying on the house? He looked out a window, then said, "That boy once had the gall to tell me to tear down my billboard and fences. Called my land weed infested. Poisoned my wildflowers. Chokecherries, too. He ought to tend to his own business. I hear what goes on over there. All the yelling at the wife and kids."

Iris gave me a puzzled look.

I shrugged, wanted him to keep his voice down so Martha, in the kitchen with Greta, didn't hear his comments. "Tom—"

"Wildflowers started dying, thistles and clover. Wild onion." Tom coughed really hard for a minute. He finally got his voice back and said, "Those people don't know neighborliness. Progress should make sense." Exhausted, he put his hand to his chest, labored for breath. "You need more help." He pulled a gun from his coat pocket.

"For crap's sake, Tom," I said.

"You take this and keep it here," he said, undeterred. "Use it for protection."

"We don't need a gun in—"

"Oh, go on. Take it. No bullets. Still, it'll do the trick."

Iris stuck the gun in the top drawer of an oak roll-top desk. "Good enough," she said.

He brushed the piano player keys with his fingertips. "Ida played piano."

"Don't know what I'll do with it. Weighs a ton." Wow, I thought, used to be Lyle talking about Ida to me and then it was Tom. She must've been quite the woman.

On the porch Tom mumbled something. Then he said, "Floor slants. You got rotten wood." He tapped a board with his foot. "That's why it slants, it's rotted. Remember, Lyle wants it fixed." On the bottom step, he coughed up phlegm and then spit. "Asking for too many favors to make up for the past." He pointed at me. "I do thank you."

"With all due respect, he seems a bit disoriented," Iris whispered.

"No kidding." I hoped he wouldn't make a habit of dropping in like we were friends or something. I had to stay focused.

Later Martha struggled to roll a forty-gallon Red Wing crock through the dining room door. "Geeze. Be careful." I grabbed hold of one side. She blew a bubble and popped it. "You know you can't chew gum and walk at the same time," I said, trying to be funny.

"Don't be rude." We set the crock near the wall. "Greta says these are valuable."

I examined the crock. "Any damage and they lose value."

"Duh." Martha had her hair tucked under a bandana, something she copied from Iris. When Iris wore a bandana, she looked like a hip artist, the potter that she was. Martha with her hair tied up in a red bandana looked sort of silly.

"Iris is interested in those. Said they remind her of her Auntie," I said.

"Lately everything seems to remind her of back home," Martha said. "When she's picking through all this stuff, she stops to say this or that about Auntie or Cobbers Creek."

I didn't like hearing that stuff there was pulling at her heartstrings. "Well. Let someone else carry them up, or at least ask for help," I suggested.

"Someone strong, I suppose you mean. Not weak like me." Martha sat on the floor and crossed her legs. Her chin was smudged. Her St. Patrick's Day sweatshirt was dirty. She could use some of that *Luck of The Irish* written across her chest. I dusted the crock's rim with the sleeve of the *Joyous Easter* sweatshirt I wore.

"I didn't say you weren't strong. Not what I meant. We all have stuff on our mind. It's distracting and ... well ... I mean ... we need to measure twice, cut once!"

She didn't respond to our saying, my attempt to cheer her up, just kept twisting that cleaning rag around her hand. "You are so obsessed with this place." Martha draped her arm along the rim of the crock. "Maybe you don't get enough niacin." I waited for the connection. "They say a lack of niacin in the diet can bring about personality changes."

"That must be it," I said.

"It's hard to talk to you anymore."

"You sound like Don," I said. "Besides, time is not on our side with this."

"Be still and know that I am God," Martha said. "That's the verse that soothes me when I'm anxious." She wound a cleaning rag around her finger. Her huge diamond ring glistened. She should've protected it with work gloves. "Randall deserved to buy this land."

"Lyle didn't think so," I said.

"I read an article about assisted suicide. It's a sin to take a life."

"Yeah, so they say. Even when the life is on its last leg and in pain. Get 'em born and keep 'em breathing, doesn't matter about the reality or curse of the life. "

"No one should play God." Martha slapped the rag against the floor, stirring up dust. That comment irritated me. "A person's right to choose ..." I stopped talking. Why bother? Might as well save my breath knowing my words on that subject went in one ear and out Martha's other.

Suddenly a rock slammed through the blackened dining room window and hit the wall across from me. Martha scrambled under the table. I dropped to the floor, hid my face in my hands. After a few minutes, it seemed safe again. Martha smoothed the bandana back from her forehead, then pointed to shards of black glass surrounding the stone with the message: **FIRE AWAY**.

Iris ran into the room. "What happened?" She sniffed the air. "I smell smoke."

We rushed into the kitchen as Greta came up the cellar steps. She put a crock down and then slid the mask away from her nose and mouth. "Do you smell smoke?"

From the back porch, Iris yelled. "Out here." She scooped snow onto the measly fire.

My hands shook as I dialed Dwight. Pushing the edge from my voice, I left a message. "Someone's setting fires at Lyle's. Whoever they are, they're stupid enough to try to burn green wood. Call me." I looked at Greta. "What were you doing down there?"

Her eyes were glazed. "Moving crocks." She looked like she was lying, but then she always looked like she was lying to me.

"Nathan's right. It's too dangerous here, Trudy," Iris said.

"Of course; he's always right since you look at him through a rosy hue."

"Hold on," she said. "This has nothing to do with my love for Nathan and everything to do with his concern for our safety."

"Our safety? He could care less about mine," I said.

Iris shook her head as if my self-pity was a drag.

"Iris is right," Greta said. "Place isn't safe."

I glared at her. "What were you doing in the cellar?"

"Short term memory going, Trudy? I told you. Moving crocks."

"Sounds like a crock to me," I said.

"Don't get your drift," Greta said.

"From now on stay close where I can keep my eye on you."

"Trudy!" Martha defended Greta.

Someone was banging on the front door. "For crap's sake. What are we holding, an open house today?" I said.

We traipsed into the living room. I carefully moved aside the curtain and looked out to see Tom again. I opened the door and he stepped inside. "Ladies." He tipped his hat. I really wished he'd stop acting as if he belonged in the house. He looked like death warmed over, a man whose affairs had better be in order because any day he would buy the farm.

"You need to go home. Where's Julianna?" I asked.

He shrugged and picked up a piece of Roseville pottery that Greta was chomping at the bit to buy. "It's the widowed sister's stuff. Lived with him after her husband and boy drowned, farm got foreclosed." He paused like he had traipsed all the way back to '58 and needed to rest before returning to the present. "I bought that place years ago."

"Does Julianna know you're here?" I asked.

"My own wife, Ida—dead now some years—was promised to him. Debt's owed and paid for me, now."

"Oh that's right; we saw those clippings," Martha said. "Remember?"

How could I forget? By now I felt like I was a key witness to that busted up old love triangle.

She turned to Tom. "Why'd Ida marry you and not Lyle?"

"You wouldn't know, you young people. Back then, Lutherans didn't marry Catholics. Ida knew I wasn't the better man, called me an atheist at heart. 'You supposed to be better than Lyle because he's a Catholic? In a pig's eye you are.' She knew." Tom coughed and braced himself against the wall. Martha soon guided him to a chair. He hacked up phlegm, pulled a handkerchief out of his pocket, and spit blood.

"Tom I better get you to—"

"Trudy." Dwight stepped inside, scared the bejesus out of me. "That door should be locked."

"Here's something of interest." I shoved the fieldstone into his hands. "Maybe you can find the culprit."

"Plus, they set a fire on the back porch, "Martha said.

"Catch sight of anyone?" Huntermeister asked.

"No." I placed the stone on the mantle at the end of the line of the others: **You Women   Had Better Go   Get Out Now   Fire Away**

"I insist you shut this down. Lock up and stay away. I don't have resources for additional patrol."

"Watch from over there." Tom pointed toward the Mini-Mart. "Juveniles and—"

"Dad?" Julianna stood in the entryway.

"It *is* an open house," I said. "Sure, why not?"

Julianna ignored me and focused on her father. "I told you to stopping driving out here alone."

"Julianna," Huntermeister said.

"Dwight." She nodded. It sure seemed like she wanted to say a whole lot more the way she raised her eyebrows and displayed a flirty little grin. Dwight was grinning, too, blushing all the way up to his forehead. He held out his hand like he wanted her to shake it. I'll be flummoxed if she didn't instead hug him. Whatever floats their boat, I thought and wondered if she'd been one of his conquests or he one of hers or why they seemed to want to be alone in the room. I noticed a scarf tied in her hair and wondered if it smelled like the scarf I last saw tucked in Dwight's pocket. "Good to see you," she said like it'd been years. I knew they talked because he told her things I said about Lyle and the house. Why the show?

"Hey Julianna," Greta said.

Holy Smoke did Julianna give Greta a hateful look. She folded her arms across her chest and said, "Ah Greta. So Judge Parla shifted a favor your way. And look at you standing here and not sitting pretty in jail."

Greta smiled. "Ah yes. Nothing like a shifting favor. You of all people should know."

I wanted them to continue because clearly there was no lost love between them and some festering feud going on, but Julianna turned her back to Greta. Maybe Martha could get Greta to tell her about it and she could tell me. Give me a one up on Greta.

"Seems my father just can't stay away," she said.

"What good's life if a man doesn't have free will?" he yelled at her.

"Okay. Sorry." She put her arm around him and surveyed the room. "You have certainly cleared a great deal out of here."

"Lyle wants his porch fixed." Tom pulled a photo from his coat pocket. "This is what it should look like." We passed around the black and white photo of Lyle's house. "Those are morning glories up that trellis there. Ida's favorite flowers," he said.

"Oh boy, do I ever want to fix his porch." I studied the photo.

"Then do it." He put his hat on and walked out the door.

"Dad, wait for me," Julianna called after him. "I'll follow you home." She turned to me. "Jerry Wanderi put a claim in against the estate for those five yards he insists are over his property line."

"He already lost that claim."

"He never went through the courts, just tried to get the city to take his side. Now he can either petition the personal representative, meaning Dad through me, or the court. If the claim is rejected, he has the right to file a lawsuit to attempt to prove the claim and collect money."

"How long will that take?" Iris asked.

"Depends. A lawsuit means the court treats the probate more formally. It may even allow the court to approve every transfer of every piece of property."

"Can we still clean out the house?" Iris asked.

Julianna hesitated and scanned the room. "It's overwhelming how much he stuffed into this place."

"For your own safety," Dwight said. "I suggest you lock the place up. Doesn't pay to push your luck with whoever has it out for you."

"They're just trying to scare us."

"You can't assume it's that simple," he said.

"Dwight is absolutely right," Julianna said while looking adoringly at him and then turning as if she remembered she was actually talking to me. "Dad's storage sheds are waiting. Haul as much out of here as you can and lock the house up."

"Whatever you say," I said. "You're the boss."

"Hmmm," she said, as if unconvinced that I meant it. "Two weeks seems enough time to figure out what's valuable, haul it out, and lock up."

"How about three?"

She gave me a stern look. "Two weeks, Trudy. And be careful." She walked to the door. Dwight caught up and placed his fingertip at the small of her back, gently guiding her from the house. I lingered at the open front door and heard Julianna say, "...keep it out of court if possible. Try to reason with ..." They had walked out of earshot and too far into the traffic noise for me to hear any more but left me wondering what exactly they were up to.

15

It had been just me and Iris working at the house. Martha was sick and Greta was a no show. It was dark when me and Iris left Lyle's and zoomed along Highway 10 past strip malls and chain store parking lots. Don was using my car since the van broke down so I had to hook a ride with Iris who had volunteered to pick up Martha's kids and take them to her place since Martha was sick with the flu and Randall was out of town.

That drive used to be full of beautiful maples that blazed out in autumn. Then it became all portable signs and neon lights. Past the Municipal Cemetery, we turned off Main onto County 8 where cornfields displayed signs, *For Sale: Commercial Lots.* The grain elevator used to be the sole business north of town along that stretch. Then, the International Harvester dealership got bought out by Tenneco and merged with Case. New corporation abandoned the original IH building on Main and relocated. Another turn, onto County 2, with its poplar windbreaks, fields, and barbed wire fences, and we were far from light litter.

"I love this time of night," Iris said. "Stars just coming out. Nathan knows all the constellations. Once he got lost on a back road. Said he found Orion, got his bearings, and was back on track."

"We should all be so lucky."

"Nathan asked me to marry him," Iris said.

"When?"

"Last night?"

"Did you say yes this time?" I was hopeful.

"I said living together is like being married. Marcus and Curtis love him so much. Don't need a piece of paper to tell me I love that man." Iris concentrated on the curving road.

"Sometimes it's not about just love," I said. "There are benefits, practical reasons."

"I asked if he could ever leave Minnesota and he said, 'Why would I? Everything and everyone I love is here.' I told him he was lucky he could say that. I wished everything and everyone I loved was here, too, but I truly don't need a piece of paper to tell me I love him. Then he said, 'What it seems you do need is to keep a way out of here open.' Didn't sit right with me to hear that but he looked mighty sad. Still, I thought of how he once said he had no interest in anything east of the Mississippi. I told him then he didn't have one hundred percent interest in me because a piece of me was east of the Mississippi."

I figured like last fall, the cold weather and growing darkness was pushing down on her, making her yearn for Virginia. Nathan's proposal apparently and her light therapy box hadn't helped soothe that one bit. "So your homesickness is bad again?"

Iris shrugged.

"On a scale of one to ten, ten being the worst of homesick blues, where are you?"

"Eight, maybe nine sometimes. Auntie warned me, said it would be a shock to my core to move so far from my roots. Then when I told her I wasn't going all the way to California but landed in Luce, she said it was a shame to raise my boys in the bleached out Midwest. She said race is not culture, but family is."

"No wonder Nathan's proposing," I said. "I bet those vibes are unsettling him."

"Could be part of it." Iris looked in the rearview mirror. "I do miss my community of familiar folk. Sometimes I could just scream for how much I miss it."

I couldn't imagine Iris ever screaming. "Why don't you visit?" I asked

"Afraid the boys and I wouldn't come back."

Oh man, I didn't like hearing that. I'd never seen Iris so sad and tense. I tried to think fast to counter her words, wanted her to think about something good. "I never told you this, but one time after you said I needed to loosen up, I laid down in the grass and watched butterflies until I felt calm."

She smiled. "No kidding. Isn't that something?" She looked in the rearview mirror and I turned around because headlights behind us seemed too bright.

"Maybe you should get back to your pottery studio," I said. "You know, bet you miss that part of you."

"You sound like Nathan." She fiddled with the rear view mirror. "Annoying car's been riding my tail for awhile." She slowed down to let it to pass, but it didn't.

"What a jerk," I said.

At the bottom of a hill, Iris turned onto the road along Tom's fallow fields on one side and a meadow on the other. The car followed, flashed its lights, and honked. The driver sped up and drove alongside us but didn't pass. Iris slowed and it slowed. She had to stop to keep from going off the road into the meadow. "I knew it," she said. "I should've listened to Nathan."

The other car stopped. "What the—" Someone wearing a ski mask jumped out and ran in front of us. Iris laid on the horn. The figure jumped back, covered his ears. She sped forward.

"Bitches," the guy yelled and tried to dive out of the way. I felt a bump. He screamed. I turned to see him lying on the road until a tall skinny figure helped him hobble along on one foot and get into the car.

Iris sped all the way to Martha's house, pulled into the driveway, and turned off the car. She dialed her cell phone. "Need to report an attempted assault," she said. "Out on

Mandle Road. We're okay. I'm at Martha and Randall Short's house." She gave the address, then hung up. "They're sending someone. Did you get the license?"

"No. But it was a four-door, maybe a Taurus. Silver for sure. You can tell silver in the dark." Then I said, "I think you hit him."

"Don't say that!" Iris threw her hands up and shook her head. She didn't say anything more and I thought maybe she was crying. I touched her shoulder but she pulled away. "I am officially done jeopardizing my safety for that house. It's too dangerous."

"What makes you think that had anything to do with Lyle's house?"

"I know you are not stupid, girl. And don't think you can be all about changing my mind. I should've listened to Nathan. With every rock through every window, I figured it was just some pranksters, some righteous SOB wanting you to pay for Lyle's death. But you know what? It's not okay! These people are seriously dangerous. And if you got any sense, you'll do as Julianna said and leave it until after the trial."

"What trial?"

"You know it's coming. You think it's going to somehow disappear? You are a suspect, Trudy. Assisted suicide, or worse. Land's sake. Hasn't that registered fully enough?"

"I haven't been arrested, have I? And so what if I am arrested or charged or whatever it is? Joan will prove I didn't do it."

"Girl, you repeat that often enough you think some magic will come your way and drop you down smack dab in the middle of the land of innocence? Like Dorothy tapping her ruby shoes, repeating 'There's no place like home,' waking from a dream."

"Maybe you got me confused with you. You're the one who needs the ruby slippers to get yourself back to Cobbers Creek."

She gasped. "If you put as much into proving yourself

innocent as you do on cleaning out that house, you might be less of a pain in my backside." Iris opened the car door. By the dome light I saw just how angry she was; whoa did she know how to give a person a killer look. She shook her head. "Hand me that bag so we can go see Martha and gather the children. When the police get here, I'm asking for an escort home to Nathan and my boys."

"Please don't bail on me now," I said. "I don't know what I'll do if you aren't there."

"Why shouldn't I bail? You being all mighty oblivious to what's stacked against you."

"I'm not. I swear it. It just doesn't do any good to sit around wringing my hands."

"Is that right? Maybe if you'd do a little hand wringing, people wouldn't feel like wringing your neck."

"That was rude," I said, and meant it. It stung.

Iris sighed. "Sorry, I didn't mean—"

"No, I got it; point taken. I swear I'll figure out some precautions. Hire someone to guard the house or something. I'll figure out a way to keep us safe until we have the rummage sale and—"

"No rummage sale, Trudy. I won't be a part of it."

I wasn't about to argue when I was pleading to begin with. "Okay, we'll get the valuables out and the doors locked. Please don't bail on me."

"Your so-called good fortune might be the ruin of you but I won't have it be the death of me. I got my boys to think about."

"And Nathan."

"Goes without saying."

"Are you going to tell him about tonight?"

"Why wouldn't I?"

I didn't answer.

16

I was tossing incontestable crap into the Dumpster when Lois Urho drove up. I hadn't seen her since that hospice meeting. She got out of her little yellow car and hesitated before walking through the snow toward me.

"I stopped to see if I might come in and look around before you lock it up."

I didn't reply ... or move.

She held a Tupperware container. "I made lemon bars for your crew. Recipe from the church cookbook." She closed the lid, burped it, and hugged the container close to her chest. "It's been weighing on my mind, some of the things I said about and to you. I do regret them. I keep thinking about Lyle. Maybe if you and I talk, we can piece together what happened between my leaving and your arrival."

I was flabbergasted by that complete turn around. "But I don't know what else to tell you. I didn't—" I stopped talking. Lois was crying. I shook my head and suggested she come in out of the cold, didn't need anyone seeing us like that on Lyle's porch.

"Now I'm not so sure I can go in."

"Try." I opened the door and stepped back for Lois to go first.

"The odor is practically gone," she said.

"Praise your lord for that."

"Oh my heavens. You uncovered the piano." She looked at me. "Do you mind if I—"

"Go ahead. The rolls are in that box." She put down the

lemon bars and rummaged through the player piano rolls. I turned up the electric space heater.

"Oh I love this one." She inserted the roll, clasped her hands, and sang. "Daisy. Daisy. Give me your answer do. I'm half crazy all for the love of you..." I figured she could go on until the cows came home. I could let her keep at it while I worked. Then the song ended. "Such a nice keepsake, this player piano," she said.

"Don't know how I'll move it out of here. It weighs a ton."

"I'm sorry, Trudy. I am truly sorry." She was all teary. "Have you found his woodcarvings?" she asked. "He used to whittle."

"He mentioned that once."

"I was wondering if I might have one."

"If I ever find them. Still got lots of stuff to go through."

"Just one." She sat in Lyle's rocking chair. She was crying again. "I keep returning to the last time I saw him," she said. "Trying to figure out if I had been remiss." I pulled a rickety folding chair over and sat across from her. She handed me the container of bars, so I ate a few while she talked.

"He was in bed when I arrived. The room was dark. I thought he was asleep."

"That's how he looked to me, too. Asleep," I said.

"I lifted the shade and he said, 'I made a mess.' I knew what he meant because the air was foul. I stopped him from getting out of bed knowing it would be easier to clean him up there. He told me he heard the cardinals that morning."

"He couldn't have," I said.

"Why not?"

"He stopped wearing his hearing aids. You know that."

"Just the same, he heard them in his mind. I got him cleaned up, and I—"

"Why are you telling me this?"

"Perhaps if we talk about that morning—just the two of us without any other influences—we'll remember something."

I ate another lemon bar. Did she think she'd get a confession out of me?

"He apologized for his accident. I tried to add levity by telling him at least we solved the problem of his constipation. After I cleaned him up, I approached the subject of protection from future accidents. 'A diaper, you mean?' he said. I told him it's not so bad but I could see his dignity battling the humiliation. Still, he said, 'Go on then.' I fastened the Depends into place and slipped clean pajamas on him. He was in such pain. I offered to light—" She stopped and bit her lip.

"Turn on a light?" I asked.

"I eased his pain as best as I could."

"Wonder if the diapers pushed him to the edge." As soon as I said it, I regretted it. "I mean..." I brushed crumbs off the front of my *God Bless America* sweatshirt. "Horrible pain," I said.

"He took his pill but would only sip Ensure. I put the cup on the nightstand and then helped him to the chair where he sat while I put clean sheets on the bed. Back in bed, he said, 'I'm leaving this.' I thought he was referring to the cup and said that was fine. 'I mean this place, my home,' he said. I told him yes, for a heavenly home, as we all will." She then gave me a look that suggested, *well, as some of us will.* I checked his pulse, listened to his heart, noted his vitals. His weight was down to one hundred and forty."

"Skin and bones," I said. "And pain. Barely existing. Not really life, now is it?"

"He then said the oddest thing. 'My porch. I called in a favor.' I asked him what he meant. He said, 'I want to sleep now, Ida.' He had been saying her name more often, so sad. Well, anyway, that was just before eight. I made a note to check on the hospital bed's delivery and on the volunteer who would start sitting with him between the team visits until we could get him into the nursing home. I told him I'd be back at four. Knew you'd be coming with lunch later. I pulled the shade against the sun and turned the fan to low. I soon left the house. I just ..." She could not finish her sentence and sat there balling like she had lost her mother. "I should have convinced him to move to the home."

"Lois," I said softly. "He wasn't about to leave his house. No matter what."

"I know I locked his door when I left that morning. I know I did."

"I believe you." I waited for her to say she believed me, but she didn't.

"Just wanted you to know that I was not careless that morning."

"Hard to know what to trust," I said, brushing crumbs off the crooked Stars and Stripes applique on my sweatshirt.

17

I talked Iris into not bailing on me and she talked me into buying Mace for all of us. I kept my canister in my tool belt. I was emptying the buffet drawers so we could move it when someone knocked on the door. I parted the ratty drapes to see a person standing on the porch facing the highway. He turned, saw me looking at him, and gawked through the dirty window. "Whoever you are, what're you sneaking around on the porch for?"

"I've been ringing the bell. Can't you hear the bell?"

"Bell's broken."

"So I waited, then I like finally knocked."

"No trespassing!"

"Gotta deliver this pizza." He held up a box. "Stewart's Pizza and we deliver."

"No one ordered a pizza." Iris came up behind me and placed her hands on my shoulders, an attempt to calm me down, I suspected.

"It's cold out here."

"Like I said, no one ordered a pizza," I repeated.

"Greta Meinler," the boy yelled. "Phone number's right here on the ticket."

I unlocked and opened the door. The boy smiled. "Well, come in," I said. "Shut the door. Stomp the snow off your boots."

"You oughta do something about that Dumpster. All kinds of stuff flying out of it." He looked at Iris. "It's like totally windy out and all."

"It wasn't blowing around earlier," I said.

"Whatever." He seemed to size up the room. "Heard the old guy died."

"You ought to be more respectful," Iris said.

"Hey, you know Jackie Chase?" he asked Iris.

"Name's not familiar."

"She's black. Plays basketball for Effington. Top scorer—"

"I don't play basketball," Iris said.

"But you're black and I—"

"Sweetie," Iris said, "You need to get out more."

"I don't follow."

"Do you know all skinny white guys like yourself?"

"Huh?"

Iris shook her head and let it go.

I was not about to pay for Greta's pizza. I dialed her cell phone and heard it ringing behind me on a windowsill.

"I'll go get her." Iris walked upstairs and returned with Martha and Greta.

"Tony!" Greta shrieked. "You're already here?"

He stood with his mouth open and stared at Greta. "Special delivery." When he whipped the strap of his carrier bag over his head, his baseball cap came off. For Pete's sake his hair was green and red. His eyebrows, also tinted red, seemed like slices of candied fruit. He looked like a clown; oddest sight, this boy standing in the middle of us women with our Martha-created sweatshirts.

Martha's was decorated with an appliquéd Christmas tree and plaid bows; glitter flaked off around the crooked message: *Give the Gift of Love.* Iris had firecrackers exploding on a striped red, white, and blue sweatshirt with *Keep America Beautiful.* I wore a sequined red valentine on a pink sweatshirt stating *The Greatest of These is Love.* Greta still refused to wear one of Martha's rejects. With the little effort she put into cleaning, no way she'd get her fancy black sweater messy anyhow.

"How much is it?" Greta asked.

"There's the ticket." Tony unzipped the warming carrier and pulled out the box. "I made it myself," he said. "I'm like in training as a cook. Got two new employees to train, too. They're lost or something from some country in Africa."

"Sudan," Iris said.

"Huh?"

"They're Lost Boys from Sudan."

"They go to your high school," Martha said. "They lost their parents."

"And their country and their culture," Iris said.

"Right," Tony said. "I know. Just forgot. You must know them," he said to Iris.

"I'm not from Sudan. I'm from Virginia."

He looked like he was struggling with a geography lesson. "Right." He removed napkins from his jacket pocket and handed them to Greta. Mother have mercy but that pizza smelled good.

"Here you go." She handed him two twenties.

"That's way too much."

"Don't be silly. Keep it." Greta closed his hand around the bills.

"Ballin'." He shoved the money into his pocket.

"Buy something from iTunes."

"Cool." He tucked the insulated bag under his arm and seemed suddenly nervous, shifting his weight from one foot to the other, scanning the room. He pointed to the mounted deer. "Find any dead dogs?"

"What dogs?" Greta said.

"The ones the old guy sacrificed?"

"Never happened," I said.

"Sure it did. My friend said his dog disappeared and he saw—"

"Your friend is full of it," I said. "Never happened."

"Don't get all salty on me. I'm just telling you what Arnold—"

"Thanks for the delivery." Iris guided the boy out the door.

"You didn't have to yell at him," Greta said. "He's sweet."

"Sweet?" I said.

"His mom's the one who got me busted. Snoop that she is. All the employees know to stay out of the small, private greenhouse, but not her. Busy body. Her older son gave me growing tips, though, so she did that much right. A real hunk of a young man, I might add."

"Flirting with boys." I gripped a screwdriver poking up from my tool belt. "You must be, what, thirty-five?"

"Oh, how sweet," Greta said. "Close but not quite. Thirty-eight. And you?" She held up her hand. "Wait. Don't tell me." I waited. "It's hard to tell when someone has a fuller face like yours." She smiled. "Forty-four?"

"Off by three years."

"Forty-seven! Wow, Sweet Don really does like older women."

Little snot.

"Funny," I said. "You went three years in the wrong direction, kind of like you in general."

"Enough sniping," Martha said, "Let's eat."

"We don't have time for a break," I said.

Greta checked her watch. "The thing about time, Trudy, there is always more the next day." They walked toward the kitchen.

Iris turned. "Are you coming?"

"Do I look like I'm coming?"

"Don't you like pizza?" Greta said. "I could have ordered something else for you. A salad maybe with lite dressing."

"Greta, why be rude?" Iris said.

"Trudy, just come with," Martha said.

"I'm busy." I picked up a lamp and dusted the ceramic base.

Iris shrugged. "Suit yourself."

After they left, I felt six years old, the country girl not invited into town for Janet Hudson's party, imagining girls blowing paper horns, wearing party hats, and eating fancy bakery cake. My grandmother let me help myself to the cookie jar to stuff away my hurt feelings. But my grandfather coaxed me away from sadness to help him build a chicken coop. Lyle reminded me of an eccentric and sloppy version of my grandfather who owned a dairy herd and collected old farm tools and machinery that he'd let me tinker with. Helped me fall in love with the heft of tools and the power of what you can do with them.

Iris returned and stood with her hands on her hips. "You shouldn't let her get to you. She loves to irritate you and you feed into it. Just let her be."

"You don't have to stay out here because you feel sorry for me," I pouted.

"I don't feel sorry for you. I just don't like pizza with fake crab."

"Take it off, then."

"The fake flavor oozes into the cheese."

"Kind of like people," I said.

Iris looked at me, then laughed. "Know what I'd really like?"

"What?"

"Some of Sugar Nymph's incredible pan fried shad roe with bacon and mushrooms. Nothing fake about it." She handed me a cold glass of something. "Drink this. It will perk you up." I stared at her. "I mixed a batch of Auntie's ginger beer fruit punch. Tastes just like home. I can see Auntie now, hanging at Sugar Nymph's, ordering tomato and hominy casserole, a side of succotash and barbequed chicken. 'Shagla,' Sugar'd likely say to Auntie, 'I never saw a woman eat so much and be so skinny.'"

"She wouldn't say that to me," I said, jokingly.

"No, 'spose not."

I wanted to head her off at the homesick pass. "We ought to go to Pugmeyer's place and get those stained glass windows."

"I'm not about to steal windows," she said.

"They're not destroyed, you know."

"Indeed I do know it."

"You do?"

"Drove past the place after Randall told me I couldn't have them. Was a huge relief to realize my instincts were right about him lying."

"We could snatch them out from under Randall's nose and set them aside for that studio of yours."

"Studio can wait," she said.

I didn't like her lack of enthusiasm and the thought of Iris leaving Luce made me feel low. The ginger beer seemed like a magic elixir, though, and I went back for seconds. Even swallowed my pride along with a slice of pizza.

18

At Lyle's house early the next morning Iris announced, "I want to cleanse this place."

"What do you think we've been doing?" I said.

"Not clean. Cleanse of bad spirits."

"So, open a window."

"I'm serious."

"What the heck, Iris." But I didn't say more. Let her do whatever she wanted. She lit a bundle of some kind of dried herb. "What is that?"

"Sage," she said. "It has cleansing qualities."

"So does bleach."

"Not quite the same." She fanned the sage and the smoke practically choked me. "Follow along if you like."

"Will I have to chant?"

"Only if you'd like." We went from room to room, waving smoke in every corner. Lingering in Lyle's bedroom, I choked up more from the memory of seeing him dead than from the smoke. Back in the kitchen, she placed the sage in the sink where a line of smoke rose in front of the window frosted with geometric designs. I got to admit, it did smell good once I got used to it. We were going to cleanse the cellar but something stopped Iris in her tracks when she looked out the window. "There's a dog out there," she said. "A large dog."

"Where?" I didn't see anything in the dusky light.

"Off to the right of the path. There, see, it just moved."

Sure enough, a dog was looking toward the house. It paced a few feet back and forth. Iris grabbed her jacket.

"I'm checking it out."

"Are you nuts?" I said. "It could be mean."

"Guess I'll soon find out."

I then added, "Someone could be lurking out there." She stopped and seemed to ponder my words of caution.

"The dog needs help." She lifted her Mace from the table and got leftover pizza from the refrigerator. I put on my coat, grabbed my phone and Mace and then a flashlight to illuminate the edge of the shadowed woods.

"This is crazy," I whispered, following behind her.

Iris walked toward the dog and then slowed down as she held the pizza out to it. "Hey there," she called. "It's okay." She whistled low and soothing to put the dog under her charming spell, but I was still nervous.

I held back. "For crap's sake, Iris. Don't get so close."

The dog whimpered and sat down. It was some kind of mix, black lab maybe, some kind of cattle dog; dappled chest, golden eyebrows, and a freckled muzzle. "Hey, boy. Hey. It's okay." She dropped the pizza. The dog wolfed it down. "His tail's in a trap!" she yelled.

I shined light on the leg-hold trap clamped high on the dog's tail near its rump. Iris tracked the light along the chain nailed to a dead tree. She kept her gloves on and offered the dog her hand, palm down. The dog sniffed. "Good boy. Good." It let her stroke its head and massage its scruff. She reached for the trap. The dog yelped and cowered. "Okay, boy. It's okay." She pulled out her cell phone.

"Who are you calling?"

"Nathan."

"Make sure you tell him coming out to the woods to rescue this dog was your doing, not mine!"

She talked into her phone. "Hey Babe. Call me as soon as you can. Nothing to worry about, just need some advice." She sat on the log by the dog.

"Now what?"

"Go get a hammer," she said. "Need to get the nails out of the tree."

I returned with a hammer and another flashlight. Iris distracted the dog while I removed three nails from the tree. What thanks did we get from the dog? It ran into the woods, the trap still attached high on its tail and Iris all upset about it being in pain. She whistled but the dog didn't return.

"Let him go," I said.

"No way." We traipsed the narrow path through the woods, mostly cedar elm and burr oak. Iris pulled her knit cap down around her ears. We walked deeper into the woods. I kept one hand on the Mace in my pocket and the other shielding my face from prickly ash thorns. We came upon a board nailed at eye level to a poplar. *Buried here: Scout 1999.* Sawdust sprinkled the ground around the tree.

"That's a new cut." Iris pointed to a limb. She moved the beam of light around. More limbs had been cut from various trees. A stack of firewood and large stones held a blue tarp in place. I lifted it to find a shallow pit littered with charred beer cans and pizza boxes.

"Listen," Iris said. "Did you hear that?"

I gripped the Mace. "Is it the dog?" Something was running toward us. I held up my Mace, ready to spray.

A doe raced by.

"Holy crap," I said. My heart beat so hard, I thought I'd choke.

"We need to get out of here," Iris said.

"Oh you think so?" The dog was barking and I worried—oh Martha's sweet Jesus—that Iris might go deeper into the woods for that mutt. The dog barked like it was really agitated and then after what sounded like a car door slamming, it yelped. I grabbed the back of Iris's jacket to keep her from running in that direction. The dog raced out from the underbrush, past us, and onto the path out of the woods towards the house. Iris ran after it. I tried to run, but my knee went into a spasm and slowed me down. I hobbled along as fast as I could. The dog ran up the porch steps, the chain clanging behind. Iris opened the door. The dog ran into the kitchen. She waited for me and once I was through the door, she slammed it, turned the deadbolt, and jammed a chair beneath the doorknob for safe measure. Then she pulled out her phone.

"You calling the shelter?"

She held up her hand. "Nathan, call me back. I'm okay. Just call me back."

"Gotta get this dog to the shelter," I said.

"No way, sister. He is not going there." The dog sat by her legs like it knew she was the sucker in the room and I was not to be trusted. Iris rubbed the dog behind his ears. "Be still so I can check you out," she said. The leg-hold trap clung to the top of its tail, blood crusted on the fur. The dog jumped when Iris touched the trap. "He's still bleeding!"

"Maybe you should let it be," I said.

She ignored me. "If we could just spring it somehow." The dog wouldn't let her touch its tail. I knew I could've sprung it but wasn't about to try under the threat of a dog bite.

While she was thinking about that, I noticed an open box beside the cellar door. We had tossed dozens of old traps into that box to take to the county historical museum. Did someone get into the house and steal a trap? I crouched lower to examine the trap on the dog's tail, see if it was like any of them in the box. Iris leaned in close, soothing the dog. Her cell phone rang. Scared the Bejesus out of us.

"Nathan. Baby. No I'm okay. We found a dog. It's got a trap on its tail." She waited for a moment then said. "No. He's a stray. Wandered into Lyle's yard with a trap on its tail." The dog barked loud like it heard something disturbing. It stood and stared at the back door. "I need to get it off. It's nasty with rust. He's bleeding."

I appreciated that she didn't' tell him the chain had been nailed to a tree, made this seem like no big deal, just a stray dog. All the more reason not to mention that open box of traps by the cellar door and the pretty good possibility that someone broke in and got one. But how? I needed to better secure the place.

"Ask him about tetanus," I said.

"Can animals get tetanus?" Iris asked. She nodded. "Yes, Baby. I know they can carry rabies. Okay we'll put him in another room until you get here."

She didn't.

The dog licked her face and she laughed, talking sweet and low. I thought of Martha's comment when Iris first joined our group, talking with that southern lilt; Martha imagined magnolia trees and honeysuckle bushes. Even though Martha had never seen either, she said she knew they were sweet and grew in Virginia, just like Iris and her accent.

When Nathan arrived, the dog let him pet it. Nathan gave me a stern look like the dog's misfortune was my fault, just like everything else since the day Lyle died. He was clearly in a bad mood, not even bothering to soothe Iris when she said she was afraid the dog was in pain.

"If I had my way, you'd be out of this house. Don't know what Dwight's thinking allowing you to still be in here with all the vandalism and threats. It's asinine."

"Baby, can you just—"

"And you can't tell me those men who came after you on Mandle Road have just given up and gone home."

"I didn't call you out here to be upset with me," Iris said. "Please just help the dog."

Iris stroked the dog's neck while Nathan checked its tail. "This thing's a relic. Who'd be setting this out anymore?" I wasn't about to mention that box of traps. "And why on this dog's tail?"

"Please," Iris said, "Just get it off."

"You're lucky it didn't bite you."

"I'm not stupid."

"Stubborn." Nathan rummaged around in an emergency medical kit.

"You talking about me or the trap?" she joked.

"Just hold him around the neck. Put some gloves and your coat on first. Keep your face away from his, for Christ's sake."

"What should I do?" I asked.

"You should get your head examined."

"Nathan!" Iris said.

He inspected the trap. The dog flinched. Using pliers on the springs, Nathan pried the trap's jaws apart. The dog whined and busted free from Iris. I wanted to say that I could've sprung the trap, too, if it hadn't been attached to an animal in pain. "Let him settle down before I clean the wound." Nathan rummaged through the medical kit and pulled out gauze. Iris got the dog to lie on the floor. Nathan poured peroxide on the wound and the dog flinched. "When you take him to the shelter—"

"No way!"

Nathan shook his head. "At least put a notice in the paper."

"Maybe the owner doesn't deserve him."

"Try to find the owner," Nathan said.

"Of course," Iris said.

Nathan didn't look convinced. "Promise me you'll take it to the vet for a check-up and shots before you let it around the boys."

"Of course, Baby," Iris said. She patted the dog and kissed Nathan's cheek.

His bad mood was melting away as he watched Iris loving up that dog. "Lucky he found you," he said, then smiled and pulled her bandana down over her eyes. I wondered if he thought it was luck that had brought him Iris. Was luck the same thing as chance? Take a chance. Try your luck. How then did Martha's belief in predestination come to play in any of this? If her god had already predetermined our fate, as Martha told me, what chance did any of us have to try our luck? Were we all just pawns? I found myself short of breath thinking of all of that. Then I heard Iris laugh.

"Hey," she said. Still laughing, she yanked at his cap. He pulled her in for a hug.

I figured their mush could go on for a while and left the room before it got too thick. The dog had no interest in following me. He just sat there gazing at Iris.

19

A few nights later, I knocked on Iris and Nathan's front door. I get that it's rude to show up unannounced, but I was worried that Nathan was putting the pressure on Iris to ditch the house and I needed to snoop it out. Nathan, dressed in his game warden uniform, answered the door. He held a *National Geographic* magazine and I could tell he wasn't happy to see me. He kept his reading glasses low on his nose, peering over them, eyes narrowed. A chicken pox mark was smack in the center of his left cheek and his chin had a deep dimple, which I knew, Iris found incredibly sexy.

"Sorry to just drop in," I said. "Need to get something from Iris." I hoped he wouldn't ask me what.

"She's throwing pots."

"Whew, glad she's throwing and not growing," I laughed.

"Don't get you," he said.

"Iris is throwing pots. Greta was growing pot."

"Clever." He kept a straight face. "Focusing on her art for a change. About time, too. She's been neglecting what's important."

"Hate to be a bother," I said, wondering if he meant himself or her art as neglected, surely not her twin boys who ran up and offered high-fives to me. Marcus was slightly taller and less shy than Curtis, otherwise it'd be hard to tell the identical twins apart. Best behaved three-year olds ever. Once I asked Iris if they looked anything like their father. She said they got his little golden specks in their brown eyes but nothing more. But I wondered if she'd blocked out their father's features so fully, she couldn't see what I saw. They both had her Cupid's bow mouth and round eyes but someone else's nose. Nubian was the word for it; Iris had corrected me after I said big. I saw pictures of her parents, a good-looking couple, and detected both of them in Iris, who definitely had her mother's long neck and prominent collarbones.

Nathan tapped Marcus' head with his rolled up magazine. "No bother, right boys?" He pointed toward the kitchen. "Just made coffee. Help yourself."

"Where's Courtney?" Marcus asked.

"Swimming."

"She's a fish," Curtis said.

Nathan opened the basement door. "Come on boys. Let's get Mommy." They took off after Nathan. I considered the coffee, but didn't want night jitters. I sat at the kitchen table feeling calmed by Iris's home in the way that I often felt calmed in her presence. Her pottery sat on shelves I helped build to showcase her creations. I also installed the bay window over the sink where herbs were thriving. Dried flowers from her summer garden hung upside down from a board nailed across the top of the doorframe. A wreath made of dried hydrangeas and lavender hung on the wall. Whatever was simmering on the stove smelled really good. A ceramic turkey candy jar sat on the middle of the table. I lifted the lid and grabbed a handful of candy corn.

Iris had kept the dog—no surprise there—and named him Cobber. He ran into the kitchen ahead of Iris, her hair covered with a bandana. She wore a tank top and had the most incredibly beautiful arms, all length and muscle. The dog jumped up and put its paws in my lap.

Iris clapped and said, "Cobber. Off." He got down and went to her.

"Needs more training," Nathan said. "But he's a good dog."

"What's up?" Iris asked, a bit coolly it seemed to me. She picked at the clay around her fingernails.

"Nothing in particular," I said.

"Oh, I thought Nathan said you needed—"

"Just checking to see how Cobber was doing," I lied.

"Real good." She nodded toward the kitchen corner where the boys sat on the floor, tugging on a pull toy with Cobber.

"Back to your pottery, I hear."

"Walked down there and looked at my wheel, the buckets of glazes, bisque pieces, trying to remember what I had planned for them, gas or wood firing, what color glazes. It was like stepping back in time."

"Oh," I said. If it felt good to step back in time, that's how it might be for her to see Cobbers Creek again. "And that felt good? Not going backwards?"

"Backwards? To return to the familiar? Felt incredibly good."

"Sure. Okay. I get that."

"Want to stay for dinner?" she asked. Nathan cleared his throat. Iris looked at him. She turned back to me. "Venison chili. I know you love it."

"Thanks, but I have to pick Courtney up."

Nathan stirred the chili. "Does it need more cumin?"

Iris sampled it. "And some hot sauce."

"You're my hot sauce."

"She's Mommy." Marcus pulled crust off a piece of bread and gave it to Cobber.

"Honey. No, please don't give Cobber food from the table. You'll turn him into a beggar," Iris said.

"Can I have toast?" Curtis asked.

"Both of you wash your hands and then sit at the table." They took turns standing on a stool as Nathan helped them wash up.

"Oh hey, what do you think of my latest piece?" Iris removed a raku bowl from the shelf.

"Never seen one like this before."

"I did a primitive firing, spread sawdust in the bottom

of the pit, added dried leaves and pine branches, arranged it with three other pieces, some facing up, some down, so colors would flash off each piece. I spread copper carbonate and salt on them and a bit of sawdust at the base to blacken. Then I lit the fire made of birch and popple, added oak to sustain it. Filled me with happiness to get this one done."

"Gorgeous," I said.

"Magnificent," Nathan said. "That's what you need to focus on, your art. Ground your mind."

"Really Nathan," Iris said. "My mind is in question now?" I wondered why she jabbed at him for saying that.

"Show us, Mommy," Marcus said.

She placed the bowl on the table. The boys ran their fingers over it.

"It's pretty," Marcus said.

"Shiny," Curtis said.

She handed it to Nathan. "It's a love bowl because I pressed walleye scales and bones into the clay. See the indentations where they fired out? Finally tried my hand with copper edging." She touched the wire along the rim. "This place that connects us: the fish, the water, the land. Those are the very same bones from the walleye you caught and brought to the boys and me that day you introduced yourself."

"Get out," I said, but no one looked at me.

"Baby you are the best catch ever," Nathan said.

I'm not too good at reading emotions, but something seemed kind of fake, like he had something on his mind and was trying too hard to avoid it. And why was she making a love bowl of all things?

"Yes indeed, you reeled me in."

"Took me a few weeks to get up the nerve."

"Pulled up to the dock and asked if my babies and I wanted to share a meal of just-caught walleye."

"Then you said, 'Only fish my babies eat is what they get through my breast milk.'" He smiled. "I was smart enough to know a good thing when I saw you," he said.

"Eyes wide open." They were putting on a show for me. Why?

"Okay," I interrupted. "I'll see you tomorrow. Just wanted to remind you we ought to get those Pugmeyer windows for your new studio."

They looked at each other like I had said something wrong. "Not now," Iris said.

"Well, I just thought—"

"Apparently a new studio and any other future plans are on hold," Nathan said.

Iris glared at him, hands on her hips, and I figured I better just keep my mouth shut. "Not the time," Iris said. She pointed at the boys coloring in their books at the table, waiting for supper, such good boys, so patient. Just like their mother.

I stepped closer to the door. "Marcus and Curtis are waiting for supper. I should—"

"Iris, all I'm asking is for you to be reasonable," Nathan said.

"We talked about this."

"No, we didn't because you're all over the place on it and—"

"Yes. We did. You'd never in a million years leave Minnesota for me, but you want me to stay for you. Virginia has as much beauty."

"My work is here. This is the land I know how to protect. I know about freshwater lakes, not saltwater tributaries."

"Exactly. Here is not there."

"I know it's not the same. I get that, so go visit. Bring Auntie here. Do something but don't keep holding it over my head that you might leave."

They were facing off and I wanted a trap door to open, remove me from that kitchen. The tension was tighter than the muscles in my hands after working at Lyle's all day. Marcus and Curtis looked worried. "Okay well, maybe we can get them when we—"

Nathan turned and gave me a look like I'd said something hateful to his woman. "Haven't you done enough damage?" he said. "Putting your friends at risk when you're the only one benefitting."

"Nathan!" Iris said.

"I'm not saying anything that others haven't thought."

"I'm not putting anyone at risk," I said.

"I beg to differ," he said. "Set to inherit millions of dollars worth of land, suspected of assisted suicide or worse. People after you on lake roads and starting fires at the house, rocks through windows. Could it be that people hate you?"

That made my eyes sting.

"Nathan!"

There was no holding him back. "You're lucky you haven't been locked up yet."

"Nathan. What has got into you?" Iris said.

"If you had any sense you would've just left that house alone. But no, you pull your friends into it, causing us to fight for all the stress and worry Iris carries. Giving her reason to want to get out of town."

I looked at Iris but she didn't look my way, as if I was guilty of something and she was ashamed of me.

"More stress here, the better Cobbers Creek looks to her," Nathan said

"Easier to blame me, I guess than to … " I bit my tongue against accusing him of showing no interest in ever even visiting Cobbers Creek with her, thinking the only land worth putting his footprints down on was land that he loved.

"Nothing's easy when it comes to you," he said.

"Stop it, Nathan," Iris said. "I mean it. You're being a bully."

"Me? Isn't that what you called Trudy?"

"Nathan, I really need you to slam the brakes on your mouth," Iris yelled.

"Oh oh, Mommy's mad," Marcus said.

"Mommy's not mad," Nathan said. "We're just talking."

"Trudy, just go. It's bad timing, that's all. Nothing more."
Iris stepped close to me but I stepped away. "Nothing said
that can't be unsaid. You caught us on a bad night."

"This is the thanks I get. Come over here concerned about
you and—"

"I distinctly recall you saying you stopped by to get something," Nathan said.

"Never said that."

"See," he said to Iris. "Don't know what you can trust. Say
one thing, deny one thing."

I slid out of that kitchen feeling lower than a dog chained
to a tree. What else were my friends saying about me behind
my back?

20

My nerves were still raw when I pulled into the Luce High School parking lot and watched for Courtney to come out. To beat back my blues, I basked in the glory of the two-story school, built in 1925. The only Art Deco building in town: smooth stucco walls, zigzag chevrons and geometric motifs. Sure the building had major repair and maintenance expenses, an inefficient cooling and heating system; but voters approved bonds, and year after year the building was upgraded. Neighboring town of Effington was losing population and there was talk of voting for consolidation. I was okay with Luce-Effington School District as long as it didn't threaten that gorgeous building with the best indoor pool in town.

Courtney got in the car and slammed the door. I was about to apologize for being late when she said, "It blows that you're always totally late." She fastened her seatbelt.

"Are you sure it doesn't suck?"

"Whatever."

"Is it worse if something blows or sucks?"

"Look it up. It's in the dictionary."

"I'm going to bet it's worse if something sucks."

The silence between us as I drove home made me sad but I didn't know what to say or how to ease the burden she'd come to carry as my daughter. She sat with cell phone in hand checking who knew what that connected her to friends. I parked in our back alley beside the dead store van. The back yard light illuminated the patio I had laid with red bricks salvaged from the St. Paul Hospital rubble years ago. After Randall had that building razed, I got wind that the Repurpose Store was interested in the bricks, so I figured I had better get what I could before they finalized a deal with Randall's company. I hauled them away at night, two dozen or so at a time, over many weeks to make sure the old hospital would live on in my own backyard. To make up for taking the bricks, I donated a great claw foot tub to the Repurpose Store. Fair's fair.

"You should dry your hair before you come out to the car. It's too cold to—"

"I'd care about my hair if I had a permanent."

"Answer is still no."

"Ericka's mom let her get a permanent," Courtney said.

"Slippery slope, first a permanent then you'll want nose piercings."

"A permanent, Mom. Duh, don't you ever listen?"

"The answer is still no." I got out of the car.

"No sucks." She slammed the door.

"That's how you communicate your anger?"

"Why not? You slam stuff a bazillion times a day." She started for the back porch.

"Get your backpack," I said. She sighed like I had asked her to do some monumental chore. At the bottom of the back porch steps, I paused and rubbed my aching knee.

Courtney ran right into me. "Come on, Mom. Move it." She was through the door and out of sight in the blink of an eye. Oh to be young and nimble.

I wanted to check for the mail, so I went around to the front of the house. I liked to stand outside and look in, left the curtains open and the lights set on timers to offer the beauty of our house to passersby. The dining room bay window showed off the round oak table, caned-back chairs, and leaded front-glass hutch. But when I walked around the house, I found all the curtains drawn and the lights off. Even the porch light was off. No mail either.

In the kitchen, I defrosted hamburger patties and poured

frozen corn into a pot. The basement door opened, rubbing against the linoleum and my nerves. Don stepped into the kitchen.

"Why are all the lights off and the curtains closed?"

"Don't need anyone looking inside our house."

I wanted to ask why he'd come to care about such a thing but kept the question to myself, didn't really want to know the answer.

Courtney came into the kitchen. "Mom was totally later than ever," she said.

Don kissed Courtney's head and then ran his newly grown bushy beard along her cheek. She laughed. He didn't hunt but grew a beard for deer hunting opener as if it would make him feel part of that crowd. Don lifted her damp hair from her neck. "Your hair's wet."

"If I had a permanent, I'd care about my hair."

"Don't start," I said.

"Who needs a permanent with form like this?" Don held a photo. "Look at that perfect back stroke. Look how straight those arms are."

"Cool," Courtney said.

"See how I framed it? The frame's the beginning of the photo's geometry."

"Geometry sucks. Ericka says her brother hates it."

"Well, he's not you. Maybe you'll end up a math whiz like me," Don said.

"No way I want to be a math geek," Courtney teased.

"Hey, you hurt my feelings." Don pretended to pout and this game could have continued but Courtney's attention got diverted when her cell phone dinged a text message. Her little thumbs responded right away.

"Where were you?" Don asked.

"Stopped at Pugmeyer's to look at stained glass windows with Iris," I lied. Why bother trying to explain Iris and Nathan and my fear that I'd lose my seemingly one remaining friend? I mean Martha was clinging to Greta like they were twins in heat for Sassy Spa. Don just might agree with Nathan, anyway; everything wrong was my fault.

"In the dark?"

"Wasn't dark when I got there."

"Maybe you should stay away from places that don't belong to you for awhile."

"Maybe you should mind your own business."

He leaned against the edge of the counter, stretched his legs, and crossed one ankle over the other. "Well," he said, bending close and talking low, "Unfortunately a wife suspected of swindling and killing an old man is a husband's business."

"Poor Don."

"From now on, I'll pick Courtney up. Cross that off your list of things to do."

"Fine by me. Better get the van fixed, then."

"I'll take the car."

"What am I supposed to do?"

"You always manage to get by with a little help from your friends."

"What friends?"

"Care to tell me why you think it's okay to charge new locks and the locksmith's work at Lyle's house to the store account?"

"No other way to pay." Humming, I removed the broiler pan from the oven.

"Care to tell me why Tom Mandle would call looking for you?"

"Never called me. Don't know what you're talking about."

"Called the store looking for you."

"Why didn't you ask him what he wanted?"

"I did. He said to ask you."

"Well that's just crazy. He's not acting right lately."

"Do we have pickles?" Courtney asked.

Glad for the intrusion, I quickly said, "Yes. Get the ketch-up and mustard too." I put the burgers on the broiler pan and slid it into the oven.

Courtney set the condiments on the counter and opened a jar of pickles. "I like the other kind better."

"What other kind?"

"The sweet ones." She looked at me and then said to her father. "Someone's been throwing rocks through windows at Lyle's house." Don stared at me. "They write stuff on the—"

"Okay. Thanks, Courtney," I interrupted.

"Martha told Ericka's mom someone set the back porch—"

"Great," I said. "Thanks."

"...on fire." Courtney reached across the counter for her cell phone and accidentally knocked off the pickle jar. It shattered. Brine and pickles spread across the floor.

"Geeze, Courtney!" I yelled.

"Chill out," Courtney said.

"What?" I said. "What did you just say?"

"Okay. Enough," Don said. "Courtney, clean this mess up." He lifted pieces of glass, put them into the trash, and said, "Don't cut yourself."

"I'm sorry," Courtney said. "Mom's so emo."

"Careful," Don said.

"She is. Bet she doesn't act like that when she has to clean up broken windows at that gross house."

I wondered if other mothers ever wished they could wave a hand and mute their child until adulthood. "It might be gross to you but to me it's a house in need."

"Maybe this is a house in need, too," Don said.

"You think I don't know that? Which thing on my list for this house should we start with?"

"Don't mean the actual house, more like those in it." Don motioned toward Courtney and that really got to me. Was he saying I neglected my own daughter? Accusing me of being a bad mother?

I couldn't go there or else I'd get weepy. Instead I stayed safe in my anger and said, "I know, let's start with that warped door that scraps the linoleum every time you open it to go down and play photographer in your dark room. Or how about—"

"Something's burning," Courtney said.

I opened the oven and smoke poured out. I turned on the vent. When I pulled out the broiler pan, sizzling grease burned my hand. The smoke detector went off. Courtney covered her ears. Don just stood there watching like he was amused. I got a chair and reached the detector to remove the battery. The chair wobbled as I stepped down. I slammed the battery on the counter and glared at Don. "Guess we can eat now." I lifted the lid from the pan and burned my fingers. "Ow. Ow."

"Being accident prone is a sign of anger," Don said. "Who you angry at?"

"You," I said.

"Other than the obvious, who you mad at?" He narrowed his eyes and clenched his jaw. I could see I was pushing him close to the edge of something, knew for sure who he was mad at, flames shooting out of his eyes right at me.

"You name it, I'm mad at it," I said, though it made no sense.

"Ericka's mom laughs a lot," Courtney said. "She sings, too."

"That's just great. Good for her," I said.

Don leaned in close and whispered. "I'm not the one who is a suspect in this town. You had better think more clearly about the mess you're in and do as Julianna says. Lock that house up and walk away."

"I never wanted his fortune."

"Well, Trudy. You got it and you got yourself in deep and if you had any sense, you'd think about—"

"Dinner's ready," I said.

"Actually," Don said, "I'm not hungry." He opened the basement door and it scraped against the linoleum. His anger was always controlled, which made it more powerful and accurately conveyed than my own messy anger ever could be.

"Stop concentrating on me and do something constructive," I yelled. "Get your nose out of those developing chemicals and fix the damn door."

Don smiled, stood above the fray.

"Daddy, wait." Courtney slapped two charred burgers on buns and set them on plates. She squirted ketchup on the burgers, spooned corn on the plates, grabbed forks, and hurried after Don like she could not get to him fast enough or get away from me fast enough. "Let's listen to your dorky music while we eat."

"Dorky music? That is classic rock you are hearing." They went downstairs to eat their dinner together.

In the dining room, I lifted a bag of peanut M&Ms, the colors of fall, poured them into a dish on the buffet, scooped up a handful, and sat on the window seat. The red water tower light was blinking. Stretching my legs across the window seat eased the ache in my knees. Eating candy, I imagined having my own television show, Bob Vila watching me in action. He'd call me to say I was so incredibly good at renovation work he'd like to do a special segment on the homes I had saved. Bob Vila, now there was a man who knew the difference between a block plane and a bench plane. Don could hardly tell one from the other. Oh boy was he ever mad at me now. I got to thinking about his comment that people inside our house needed tending to. Why hadn't I agreed when he said that? Why had I killed that moment to talk about our family? I got teary wondering how many moments, chances, in my life I had killed rather than tended to. I was through half the bag of candy when my phone rang.

"Trudy, it's Joan. Jerry Wanderi has filed a formal lawsuit against Lyle's estate."

"What does that mean?"

"It prolongs waiting for ownership to transfer to you."

"In the meantime some jerk is breaking the windows and trying to scare us away, but I have no power over anything. Maybe I should go over to the Mini-Mart and shoplift, maybe do some damage to the women's room toilet, clog the pipes and flood the place. Go out to Mark Riepe's dump of a place and throw some rocks through his windows."

"Did someone flood the house?"

"No!"

"Oh I thought you said—"

"Forget it." I leaned my forehead against the wall while Joan advised me not to say such threatening things to anyone else and not to do anything rash.

That night I lay in bed, Don snoring away without a care in the world. I got to thinking about Iris, reminding myself of what all she had been through. Ten when her parents died in a car accident, she had to leave Washington, D.C., to live in Cobbers Creek with her Auntie. Years later, desperate to distance herself from the married man who got her pregnant, she drew from her inheritance, bought a car, packed up her twin babies, kissed Auntie goodbye, and ended up in Luce in love with Nathan but yearning for Virginia. *Torn between two lovers, like that 70s song,* she once said to me. What bridge could she build between two places to save herself? I wondered what was wrong with me that I didn't miss my childhood home, but then why should I? No one there to visit. My parents, eventually living in Florida, never knew how to deal with me as a rebellious teenager. They were always too tired after working at the meatpacking plant to worry about me failing middle school. Took my grandfather to get me back on track. Chores on a dairy farm were no picnic, let me tell you, but I learned at his side the value of hard work and good tools. Day he died, I felt orphaned. Even my grandmother lost interest in me and the farm after he was gone.

Maybe I could sort of relate to Iris's confusion of place. She got pregnant, had her boys, and fled. I got pregnant, had Courtney, and got anchored. Neither of us planned to stay in Luce. What kept us from leaving?

21

Soon after that eruption in her kitchen, I called Iris, said no hard feelings. Why hold a grudge? It didn't do anyone any good. We made amends and she came back to work, bringing Cobber with her. The shorter days were eating away at the light. I psyched myself into getting right with the people still left to help me. I stopped caring about Greta's shenanigans after she called Martha to say she wasn't feeling good, wouldn't be able to come to the house. Feeling good? Was anyone feeling good those days? Anyway, me, Iris, and Martha worked longer than we should've at the house and it was getting dark by the time we left. We were all on alert and mad at ourselves for losing track of time.

Iris—the only one with a car since Don was using mine and Randall had borrowed Martha's for some lame reason—was driving and going on about dislodging spirits within Lyle's house by burning more sage and hanging rosemary. She said we had to push back the dark with all our might, be like the embers of sun setting on the gray horizon. It unsettled me to sense that she was out of whack.

"There's a dead doe." Martha pointed to the side of the road. "You're not supposed to look at road kill."

"Hard not to look at what you're trying to avoid," Iris said.

I was in back, Cobber next to me. Seemed fitting.

"No. Really. They say it raises your anxiety level," Martha said.

"Okay then," Iris said. "I won't look." Cobber put his front paws on the back of Iris's seat like he wanted to be up front with her. Iris patted its head as she turned off Highway 10 onto Main, passing Coast-to-Coast, Cleone's Gift Shop, Ebeling's Café, Luce Bakery, Service Food, all intact brick buildings dating back to the late 1800s, all businesses that somehow continued to turn a profit even as chains out on Highway 10 stole customers. The cupola on City Hall was decorated with red, white, and green Christmas lights. "City should wait to turn those on," Martha said. "It's too early."

"I miss summer," Iris said. "This cold undermines my energy."

"People can't even wait for Thanksgiving to pass before they're rushing to Christmas," Martha said. "Some stores plan to open on Thanksgiving now. It's terrible."

"Thanksgivings with Auntie are the best," Iris said.

"Thanksgiving is old school," I said, using one of Courtney's terms. "People care more about Black Friday."

"That's an awful thing to say," Martha said. "We need a day set aside to give thanks."

"And watch football and drink beer," I said not interested in sentimentalizing a holiday, like May Day and its flagpole, that was running its course in America.

"And don't forget the turkeys," Iris said. "I read something like 204 million pounds of turkey meat ends up in the garbage after the holiday feast. All that misery turkeys endure in factory farms. Senseless. We ought to rethink these customs." Iris put her blinker on at the four-way stop sign, started to go, then slammed on the brakes to avoid getting t-boned by some jerk who ran the sign and sped past.

"They tried to hit us," Martha said.

"No they didn't," I quickly said not wanting that idea to take hold and fester.

"You ought to get police protection until the trial," Martha said.

"What trial? Do you know something I don't know?" I asked. "Because I haven't heard anything about—"

"They need a light here," Iris said. "That's all. They just need to put up a light." I could hear she was on edge and wanted to tell her to do that deep breathing but it didn't seem like the right time. Iris turned off Main and drove past the Luce Clinic.

At the stop sign, Martha pointed at a white sports car sitting in a far corner of the clinic's back parking lot; the running lights were on. "That's Greta's car," she said.

"Oh, yeah. So it is," Iris said. "Hard to see it behind the clinic's *Care A Van*."

"Well, beep hello," I said. "Let her know we're glad she made a miraculous recovery."

"Maybe she had a doctor's appointment. Don't sound so suspicious," Martha said.

I checked my watch. "After-hours appointment."

"Maybe she doesn't want to be seen, so—"

"Well look at that," I interrupted Iris. "She's not alone."

Dr. Schemp got out of the car and hurried into the clinic. "Oh for stupid. She should know better than that," Martha said.

"What do you know about it?" I asked.

"He's going to leave his wife for Greta." Martha put her hand over her mouth. "Forget I said that. I shouldn't have said that."

"No way. They rarely leave their wives," Iris said with great authority.

"So, I guess Greta was in bed today after all," I said. "Just not sick."

"Lovesick," Martha said.

"Wait 'til I see her."

"Let it go, Trudy," Iris said.

Martha gave me a stern look. "Before you judge her, keep in mind sometimes people falter. Hate the sin, not the sinner. *Do no unrighteousness in judgment*, we're warned. You of all people should understand that."

"Am I having an affair?" I said.

"Greta brings out the part of Dr. Schemp buried under his demanding wife," Martha said. "And all those patients needing him."

"Oh for the love of…" I didn't know what to say about such nonsense.

"You don't see the good side of Greta, Trudy."

"Maybe she doesn't show it," I countered.

"She built that floral business up practically from scratch."

"I heard she took advantage of the elderly couple who owned it."

"She did no such thing. Bought it when it was failing and they were in the nursing home."

"Whatever."

"You sound like a child when you say that," Martha said.

I ignored the comment.

"Greta spent all her days and nights working to expand the greenhouses and the retail shop. That's why she can afford down time now. She earned it."

I didn't feel like hearing Martha go on about Greta's success in building a dying business given that Pluth Hardware was struggling to keep from going down the drain. "Yeah well, I heard she grew up poor and wild," I said.

"Doesn't matter. Did you know she bought her parents that real nice little house after she won the lottery? Moved them out of the trailer court. She even joined that Adult Children of Alcoholics group to help her forgive and understand her mother."

"How do you know all this?" Iris asked.

"Friends confide in friends," Martha said.

"I'm your friend," I countered. I also wondered if she connected any of that Adult Children of Alcoholics talk to what it would be like for her kids someday in dealing with their daddy's addiction.

"So then, go ahead and tell me something," Martha said.

I just let that sit. I stopped telling her things awhile back anyway; only way to keep my business to myself. "How's Randall these days?" I asked. "Still got that face rash?"

"Yes and I'd rather not talk about Randall. A wife shouldn't discuss her husband's business with others. As Paul says in the letter to Ephesians, *We wrestle not against flesh and blood but against principalities … against the darkness.*"

I leaned back and tried to read between whatever lines she had just offered, but decided to do as Don had been telling me and let it go. I imagined opening my palm and just letting it all go, feel tension leave my spine, just let it go from the mind and the fists unclench, the jaw relaxes. Just let it go and sit back in the seat. "Anyway. That's too bad about his rash." I think I meant it, too.

"Almost forgot," Martha said. "Can I keep this? It was in a stack of junk. I meant to ask you back at the house." She handed me a two-inch square block of wood.

"Can't read it. Turn on the dome light," I said. With the light from above, I looked down and read the fancy script: *Prayer Changes Things.* "Sure, Martha. You can keep it."

22

The temperature dipped way below freezing; as my grand-father used to say, *not enough chance for the blood to thick-en*. My skin, however, was a different story. Shifting rumors about me had made it as thick as my waist. Thanksgiving Day came and went and our time with the house was growing to a close. I brought in three space heaters against the chill. We had the good stuff lined up to haul to Tom's storage sheds and some set aside on the slim chance I could figure out how to have a rummage sale on the sly.

In the dining room, I found Martha polishing silverware. "It's just going to tarnish sitting in storage," I said.

"I like polishing silver." She buffed a knife. "There are eight forks and knives but only six spoons." She looked oddly tan.

"You planning a dinner party?" I said.

Martha laughed. "Why not? We practically live here." It was good to see her happy. I should have left it at that.

"Why are you tan?" I had to ask.

"Spa tanning. Greta suggested it. Brightens my spirit."

I nodded. Didn't feel like preaching about the negative effects of fake baking.

"Help me move this table to the living room," Iris called. She stood with hands on hips. Her copper wire and doo-dad gems bracelet jangled loose around the cuff of her work glove. She'd been wearing some kind of crystal necklace and rubbing it a lot like it was a worry stone. It made me jittery to see calm Iris nervous, her Mace always on the ready. I do think she believed Martha was right, that whoever ran that stop sign on

Main had her as a target, because after that her and Nathan drove each other's cars.

"You should take those dangling traps off." I tapped her bracelet.

"They bring me energy." She patted Cobber. The adoration that dog had for her kind of picked up where Nathan left off, so to speak.

We finished setting the table down near the entry when the front door opened. Mark Riepe stepped in with a blast of cold air. Seeing him standing in the doorway raised my hackles, but his appearance really agitated Cobber. He growled like he smelled a rat. Mark stepped back. "Whoa."

"How'd you get in?" I said.

"Door's open."

"It was locked."

"Appears we got a different opinion on that," he said. "Like we got on this house."

"You got your claim in against probate," I replied. "No reason to show up here now."

Iris grabbed Cobber's collar. "Shhhh Boy. Shhhh."

"Got yourself a dog, I see." Mark held out his hand. "Hi, Boy."

Cobber growled and lurched forward. Iris held him back.

"Shit man." Mark pulled his hand away. He was a scrawny man hidden under a stocking cap and bulky jacket. For someone brazen enough to enter the house, he sure was nervous, scanning the room. He seemed unable to look at anything long enough to really see it and he sure didn't look me or Iris in the eye. Don felt pity for him, said Mark's toxic mother made him the mess he was, but maybe that was just Mark's cop-out, an excuse to be a lowlife jerk.

"I'm calling Dwight," I said. "Get you out of here."

Cobber bared his teeth. "That dog's not right," Mark said.

"Seems he thinks you're not right." Iris attached the leash to his collar. Staying close to Iris and growling, Cobber kept

Mark in his sights. Mark stepped into the living room. Cobber lunged. Iris pulled him back.

"Get out." I pulled Mace from my shirt pocket.

"Whoa. You don't need no assault charge on top of murder pending against you. All you girls spend time in here and it's still a junk heap." He fingered the brass light switch. "This stuff isn't legally yours to sell. Family's what matters."

"Who said I'm selling anything?"

"Heard you was, is all."

"Yeah, well. You heard wrong," I said. Then got to wondering. No one but we women knew about a rummage sale idea that got shot down. How would he have heard? Had Martha told Randall then Randall told him? "Randall Short send you?" I asked.

"Why would he?"

"Doing his dirty work?"

"Ha. That's a good one," Mark said. "Hear stuff like that, you oughta check it out, let other people—interested parties so to speak—know about it. Like I heard about you selling stuff that's rightfully mine."

"No sale and nothing's rightfully your anything," I yelled.

"Difference of opinion is all."

"Are you calling Dwight?" Iris asked. "Or should I?"

A knock on the door got Cobber all stirred up again. Mark sneered. "Wonder who that could that be?" He opened the door and then said, "Arnold. What'd I tell you?"

The boy shrugged.

"I told you to wait, Boy."

"I gotta bounce."

"All right, then. Walk."

"That blows."

"Since you interrupted, get your ass inside."

He stepped in, a weaselly kid, looked unhealthy with a stud in his nostril, a stocking cap pulled down over his eyebrows. Cobber lunged, tugged the leash away from Iris, and made a beeline for him. The kid ran out and slammed the door.

"Your dog don't care much for my boy."

"A good judge of character." Iris pulled Cobber away from the door and handed me the leash. "Hold this."

"You got some things of interest to me." Mark gripped the back of Lyle's rocking chair. "Them's family heirlooms." He nodded toward china and crystal waiting to be packed up and hauled away. "Willing to get past my own grandmother getting the short end of the stick when they said she wasn't blood."

"This might interest you." Iris pointed Tom's gun at Mark. "Now leave!"

"Look at the little lady." He sneered.

"I'll shoot you." She cocked the trigger. "Trespasser."

He raised his arms. "Whoa. That's a serious offense."

"You're a serious offense," Iris said. "Get out."

"You'll regret this. I got my sights on you now, girl," he pointed at Iris. "I know about you uppity people."

Martha walked into the room. "Greta just called and ..." She stopped dead in her tracks. "Oh my dear Lord." She raised her hand to her mouth and stood perfectly still.

Mark opened the door. "Ought not to have done that, girl."

Iris kept her aim on him. "Done what?"

"Bunch of crazy females."

After he left, we heaved a huge sigh of relief and sat on the stairway. "Geeze Iris. What got into you?" Martha asked.

Iris shrugged. "I'm tired of it all."

"This place will undo us yet," Martha said.

"Nathan's right," Iris said.

"About what?" I asked.

"Everything."

She wouldn't say any more, just sat there petting Cobber, lost in thought like she was concentrating on one-way tickets out of Luce.

23

G reta was late as usual when she swept in carrying a bright red poinsettia. "Oh for beautiful." Martha reached beneath the plastic to admire it.

"Thought I'd bring a few over to cheer everyone up," Greta said. "They just came in." Cobber sniffed at the plant. "Don't whiz on that, boy," she warned.

"Auntie and I always picked holly for Christmas." Iris patted Cobber. "Made beautiful wreaths."

"I've got holly at the store. And now, it has your name on it," Greta said. I glared at her, first buying Martha's friendship with favors and then trying to win the affections of Iris. Greta removed the plastic from the poinsettia with great fanfare. Floorboards creaked beneath her. I felt like doing something worthwhile, wanted to go to the cellar and drive a wooden wedge between the bottom of the floorboard and the top of the supporting joist. Silence the noise. Greta set the plant on top of a box and leaned next to it in that pose used by women who display prizes on television game shows.

"We have work to do." I slid on gloves, ready to get down to the last of the mess. Then we heard a snowmobile out front.

"Now what?" Martha said.

We looked through the window to see a snowmobile zoom around in front of the house then idle by Greta's delivery truck: *Meinler's Floral.*

Greta shrugged.

I went on the porch. Whoever it was drove way. Gas fumes in the cold air mixed with the smell of strawberry and cooking oil from the town's licorice and potato chip factories. When the wind was right, those scents traveled for miles.

Martha rubbed her arms. "Just shut the door and lock it. Brace a chair against it."

"If you're so worried, get out of sight," Greta said to me.

Back inside, I glared at Greta. She raised her eyebrows and smiled. I closed the door.

She opened it right back. "What the … ?"

"Need to get the other two poinsettias from my truck. They're very cheery little fellows and I brought one for each of you."

"Red is a bold color," Martha said. "You should wear red."

"No. It's a better color for you," Greta said.

"When you're done, maybe you can haul boxes of stuff for storage into your van."

"My van?"

"For the love of Martha's Jesus. You said we could use it to haul stuff to Tom's."

"Right. Right. Of course I did. So much to keep track of these days, but it's full of flowers. My driver called in sick, so I need to do the delivery run. I didn't plan to stay here."

I bit my tongue and left the room.

Iris followed me into the kitchen, crossed her arms, un-crossed them, then crossed them again, as if she didn't know whether to keep to herself whatever was bugging her or let it go. "She's being difficult," she said. "We can rent a truck."

"I don't have money for that."

"Put it on credit."

"She was supposed to borrow us the van."

"Just work around her."

"She knows who was on that snowmobile."

"You need a rest, girlfriend." Iris scowled at me, hands on her hips.

"Rest is for the dead."

Iris said, "Ummm humm. If you're not banging your

head against a wall, you're looking for one to bust through. Like Auntie would say, 'self-pity is one awful destructive point of view.'"

"Whatever that means." I noticed the vintage Jadeite dishes on the table. "Who was supposed to pack these up? Time's a wasting. For the love of Martha's Jesus, I have to do everything." I lifted a bowl. "Do you know how valuable this stuff is? After Martha Stewart showcased it years ago, the value skyrocketed."

"I think I'll leave you to your misery and let you haul yourself and this stuff out of here alone," Iris said. "And stop saying 'For the love of Martha's Jesus.' That upsets her."

"It does?" I was dumbfounded by that idea. Iris shook her head as if disgusted with me. "Wait. I'm ..." Clearly not caring what I had to say, she left the room. I sat thinking about Jesus, then stared at the Jadeite dishes and thought about the power of Martha Stewart. How at the right time, she took what county extension offices and rural women had been doing for decades and capitalized on it, made it trendy to be old fashioned. Very smart woman. What was it she had to do jail time for? I had to stop thinking of that; it felt too close to home.

Greta and Martha entered the kitchen. I felt like banging a sledgehammer into a wall. Get this renovation going. Standing beside the buzzing refrigerator, I hummed and focused on the light flickering over the sink. If I couldn't release my pent-up anger, at least I could keep my mouth shut.

Greta rubbed her arms. "It's just as cold in here. Can't you turn up the heat?"

"Slip one of these on." Martha lifted a sweatshirt from the pile on a rickety card table. I expected Greta to laugh at that suggestion.

"Good idea."

"This one suits you."

Greta unfolded it. "Oh, for funny." She slipped on the

bright red sweatshirt. It was startling to see her wearing color. *There's no Man Like a Snowman* danced across her chest as a smiling snowman waved, and sparkling snowflakes fell around him.

Martha slipped on a white sweatshirt emblazoned with *Jesus is the Reason for the Season.* She looked at me, "Something wrong?"

"No," I said and went back to working on a list.

I thought about what Iris said about me hurting Martha's feelings with Jesus and figured I should apologize but not in front of Greta. "Martha maybe later, me and you—"

"So." Greta lifted a pop bottle from a wooden crate and shook it. "Guess it's too late to get the deposit back." She laughed.

"Poor thing." Martha stared at the mouse skeleton rattling inside.

"That's what happens when you search for a little sugar in tight places," Greta said.

"Guess you'd know," I said.

"What's that supposed to mean?"

"Who was on that snowmobile?" I demanded. "Someone who breaks windows and sets fires because of you?"

"Me?" Greta shrugged. "No broken windows. No fires. Just you being difficult."

I turned on Martha. "Was it Randall?"

"Why on earth would it be Randall?" Martha asked.

"Why not?" I said. "Up to no good, sending e-mails to Mark and—"

"I never should have told you about that," Martha said.

"He's been surly ever since he didn't get what he wanted."

"Trudy." Iris set a box down hard on the table. I hadn't even realized she was in the kitchen. "Enough."

"Enough?" I repeated. "No one's even said out loud what we've all been thinking."

"How would you know what I've been thinking?" Greta said.

"True. Hard to read liars," I said.

"You are acting a fool," Iris said.

"Randall wants this land and he'd do whatever it takes to get it from me," I said. "He's rude and obnoxious and you even said he's moodier than usual, Martha. Taking it out on you and the kids. A rash on his face. Right?"

"Stop," Iris said. "Just stop now, Trudy. Give it a rest."

"Are you saying my husband would actually do such things to destroy this place while we're inside and could be harmed?"

"He's smarter than that," I said.

"Meaning?" Martha said.

"His money can hire someone to do it for him."

Martha pounded the kitchen table; the Jadeite dishes rattled. "How dare you. Of all that he is or has been, he would not do such a thing."

"Hard to say."

"Would it be hard to say whether or not you'd kill Lyle to get his fortune?" Martha said. "Randall would never kill anyone or do anything to this place for some reason only you can imagine. As far as I know he's not a suspect in any of this."

It felt like she had taken a board to the back of my head. But worse, it felt like I deserved it.

Iris reached for Martha; she pulled away.

"You're hateful," Martha said to me. "Why on earth are we bending over backwards for you? Just to be friends, not abandon you when everyone else has? As far as I'm concerned, I'm done. Right now. As of this minute, you're on your own, lady."

"Maybe we should just take a few breaths and calm down," Iris said.

"She's lucky we stayed working here while people in town trash talk about her," Martha said as if I had left the room. "To think I defend her when people call her murderer."

Wow, were my eyes stinging from that.

"We're all a little tense." Greta moved toward Martha.

"I'm out of here." Martha stomped from the kitchen.

"Way to go, Trudy." Greta followed after her.

"You were looking for a fight. Well, you got it, girl." Iris left the room.

Let them go. Good riddance, I thought as I sat at the kitchen table all those nasty words echoing around me. I got busy boxing up more stuff. There was nothing else to do. I was packing up the Jadeite when I saw a cell phone lying between two boxes full of extension cords and chewing tobacco tins. I pressed the button and saw *one missed call. Voice Mail. View.* I pressed that button and saw. *Edward.* I pressed *Voice Mail,* relieved not to need the password. I pressed 1 and listened: "Why didn't you come out of that house? I was tempted to go in after you. I'm sorry about what I said. Please, Greta. I need to see you. I'm tied up most of the day, but we could meet for an hour at your place. Four? Let me make it up to you, help you relocate the stash."

I dialed Martha's number on my phone and it went to voice mail. "Tell your friend Greta, she left her phone here."

I was working to calm down, just keep packing when Joan Wakefield called. "What's this about you taking a gun to Mark Riepe?"

"Where'd you hear that?"

"Doesn't matter," she said. "What exactly are you doing, Trudy? You will invite more trouble. Get that stuff out of there and into storage. Now! Today."

"That was my plan before tomfoolery showed up."

I hung up and sat there madder than a hornet. I was so sick of the mess Lyle left me, going through all those boxes and finding one piece of junk after another. I felt like hauling it all out to the Dumpster, not even bother figuring out what was valuable. Who hoards so much junk in a lifetime? Why couldn't Lyle have been one of those people who hid cash under his mattress? I paced the room, stopped long enough to kick a flimsy corrugated cardboard chest Iris had hauled up from the cellar. Pieces of wood went flying. Then I realized not just any wood. They were carvings. I picked up the figure of a man, about twelve inches tall. Hands in his pockets, a paddle tucked beneath his arm. An old guy with a beard and a round belly. He wore a sea captain's cap. His coat had half-inch nails for buttons. The box held other figures: ducks, roosters, cows, pigs, and geese; a man sitting in a rocking chair, a man polishing his boots, a man holding a hoe, and a man sitting on a horse. There was only one woman; she sat in a rocking chair holding a bouquet of flowers. Some of the carvings were painted. I turned the sea captain upside down and saw *LS 1960*.

I cleared the kitchen table and set thirty carvings down. I stared at beautiful folk art. I was so happy, standing there gazing at them. "Iris!" I called out. "Iris, come see..." I then remembered; everyone had left.

24

News about the gun pulled on Mark spread faster than the rash on Randall's face, but word was that I pulled it on him. Don didn't believe me when I told him Iris did it. He actually said Iris would never do such a thing! For crap's sake!

I left the house without breakfast or even coffee. I hated to give Jerry the business but I walked into the Mini-Mart, just wanted to fill a cup, get out of there, and get through the last day at the house. No one was behind the counter. I cleared my throat and finally Nunda Ward came around the corner. She held up a finger to instruct me to wait because, obviously, she was busy on her cell phone. I took a sip. Then another. By the time she hung up, I had refilled my cup.

"How's it going?" she said.

"How's it going with you?" I handed her my money.

"Mr. Wanderi's running a special on pet food."

"I don't own a pet."

"That's okay. You don't need a pet to get the special deal," she said sounding very assured of her reasoning. I looked at her. She handed me the change. "Here you go, Ma'am."

I counted it to make sure she didn't short me. "There's no milk back there," I said.

"I'll get you some skim."

"I don't like skim milk."

"It's got less calories."

"Whole," I said, vowing to ignore her insult.

"Yes Ma'am." She slid two half and half mini containers across the counter. "We carry these now." I dumped them in my coffee and headed for the door. "You have a real sweet treat of a day," she called after me. "And thanks for stopping in. Pet food special runs all week."

I opened the door and stepped back to allow two women to walk through. "Hey Darcy," I said, "Haven't had a chance to talk to you at the swim meets lately."

She ignored me. "They're forecasting more snow," she said to the other woman.

"Darcy?"

She looked at me, scowled, and kept walking. Near the display advertising the pet food specials, she put her hand to her mouth and leaned toward the other woman, no doubt sharing some morsel about me because the other woman then glanced my way and shook her head.

Iris agreed to work at the house but said Nathan was coming with her. Fine, I said, we can use the extra help. I called Martha and left a pleading I'm-so-sorry message. Then I dialed Greta's number.

"Where are you?"

"What's it to you?" she said.

"Just wanted to apologize and ask you to help haul stuff out. Last day."

"I had to go back there for my phone. Gave me chance to look around the place, really see it for the pit it is. Your apology isn't enough to bring me back to your fold."

"I'll ask Julianna to get your sentence reduced."

"As if I need anything from that snob," Greta laughed.

"Why's there bad blood between you two?"

"Honey, you don't want to know."

"Yes I do."

"Well the point is, I don't need any favors from Julianna who resents my climbing up from the bottom to irritate her social circle. Well at least from the fringe of it."

"Come with your truck and I'll say you're still working with us on the next house even if you're not. Then your last month will be easy street. Just help me get that stuff hauled out."

"You assume there will be another house after this."

"By the way, did you lock up after you left Lyle's with your phone?"

"I always do."

"Always? How often do you go there alone?"

"Bye for now."

After she hung up, I needed to think about something good, like the land. When I got enough money, I'd buy a four-wheeler and explore every acre. Ride all the way to the pines abutting the fallow fields where Lyle posted *No Trespassing* and *No Hunting* signs. I'd patch up Lyle's canoe and take it all the way across Emma Lake and just sit there doing nothing, maybe enjoy squandering time. In the meantime, I had to focus on the last day at the house.

Not long after arriving with Iris, Nathan got a call to investigate reported poachers by Rush Lake near Effington. Before leaving, he gave us a lecture on precautions. Time was slipping away and I wanted him to just go, let us get on with it. Finally, me and Iris stacked boxes to load in the truck. "What if Martha and Greta don't show up?" I said. "We'll never get all this hauled out today?"

"They will," Iris said.

"I apologized, you know. To both of them."

"They'll be here. Patience." Iris wore a light blue sweatshirt that said *Call of the Wild*. A loon swam across her chest.

I wore a sweatshirt decorated with a lily and *Jesus is Risen*. "I still say it's possible that Greta could be a spy."

"No she isn't," Iris said. "She's got no reason to be."

"Maybe for someone interested in the land, or the house, or drug money."

We heard car doors slam. Iris looked through the window. "They're here and it's better than her van."

Greta was backing a U-Haul truck toward the porch steps. Martha parked Greta's van on the other side and soon stood by the porch waving Greta back with one hand, holding Grace with the other. They waltzed in and didn't seem to harbor ill will over our spat. Martha unbundled Grace from her coat, hat, and mittens. "Stop glaring at me," Martha said to me. "I couldn't get a sitter."

"Hey. It's all cool," I said, sounding more like Courtney than me, even as I wondered why Iris was always able to get a sitter but Martha was not.

"We packing or just loading boxes?" Greta asked.

"Most of the packing's done—"

"Yeah, Iris took care of that! Packing heat while you get to take the heat for it," Greta laughed.

"So it's mostly loading," I said, ignoring her attempt to goad me. "Maybe start with the dining room."

"We're on it." Greta carried Grace, who seemed bewildered by her surroundings. Martha trailed after Greta.

"I liked it better when Martha followed you around," I said to Iris.

"They are strange bedfellows," she said. "Still, can't help notice that Martha seems a bit lighter when she's with Greta."

"Just a show."

"Are you jealous?"

"No I am not," I lied.

"It's okay," Iris said. "Shows you're human." She left me to think about that.

Later I went in search of Iris but didn't find her upstairs. I went into the dining room and overheard Greta and Martha talking in the kitchen. "Ever notice how when she works, she purses her lips real tight?" Greta said.

"She's concentrating," Martha said.

"Except when she's bossing everyone around. And oh

those hands on her hips when she gives a person a piece of her mind."

"Randall feels sorry for Don being married to her."

It felt like a two-by-four whacked me upside the head. I tiptoed away and stepped onto the porch. Sorry for Don? Randall? Of all things. All the time I spent feeling sorry for Martha while Randall was feeling sorry for Don. It ate at me as I wondered what specific reasons he could ever find for feeling sorry for Don? Then I thought of one, my impatience, and then another, my crankiness, and another, my sarcasm. I had to make myself not think about any more reasons. Breathe it away. I leaned on the porch column and counted cars moving along Highway 10, plowed after yesterday's snow. The Sven Viborg farm across the highway was for sale. Next door at the Lubitz farm, two children ducked behind snow-covered hay bales and threw snowballs at each other. A pair of stuffed jeans and boots protruded from the side of one bale as if someone got rolled up inside it.

"There you are," Iris said, coming up from behind.

"I can't believe Viborg is selling out," I said. "Lubitz will be next, no doubt."

"Hard to say no to a life made easier by a wealthy developer's offer. Still, land will always hold the ghosts of what used to be."

"Do you feel sorry for Don?" I asked.

Iris gave me a funny look. "Is there some reason why I should?"

We worked our butts off loading that truck and I was grateful that Greta had rented it, told her so, too. Later we took a break and Martha sat in Lyle's rocking chair humming to Grace. I saw Grace's pacifier on the floor. I reached for it but lost my balance and knocked into the rocker. It lurched forward and Martha had to brace her foot to keep from tipping.

"Stop pushing me," Martha said.

"I'm sorry," I said. "I tripped."

Grace was wide-awake and fussing. Martha stood, supporting Grace's head against her chest, and faced me. "Just stop," she said, testily.

"I tripped!"

"Now shut up while I rock Grace for as long as I want to." She swayed back and forth to soothe Grace and slowly disappeared through the swinging dining room door.

I stood there stunned. She told me to shut up. I'd never ever heard her say that before to anyone. I was feeling sad, looking at my reflection in an oak-framed mirror, when Greta's face appeared within it. She was staring me down. I turned around. "What?" I yelled.

"Randall's bankrupted them," Greta said. "And he got arrested for disorderly conduct at some motel in Fargo." She stood there rocking the chair with her hand.

"No way! Martha would've told me," I said waiting to be let in on the joke. Nothing. "He in jail?" I said finally.

"She posted bail."

"Maybe jail's a good place for him. Should've left him there."

"And you wonder why she didn't tell you. Don't go ragging on her. She already feels low enough." Greta left the room.

I waited all day for Martha to tell me about Randall but she didn't. The truck was loaded so we finally took a late lunch break. Sitting at the dining room table, we sorted through photos, clippings, and documents while we ate sub sandwiches from Boedigheimer's Deli. I had two space heaters going even though I was afraid we'd blow a fuse. That old fuse box was one of the first things I'd get rid of in that house to help bring it up to code. "So many clippings," Martha said. "And seed packets." She shook them like a rattle for Grace sitting on Greta's lap. That kept her interest for all of a minute before she tried to tear into the clippings. Greta gave her clothespins and a bucket and Grace got busy dropping them in and taking them out, then dropping them in again and taking them out.

"I took a box of stuff home," I said. "Maybe we should each take one home, go through it for anything of value. You like going through things like this, Martha, right?" I was trying to make up to her but she was reading intently. She held a piece of yellowed newspaper.

"Listen to this," she said, coming out of her trance. "It's dated 1899. *The Platt Brothers have a novel attraction in the show window of their general store. A large box contains six ordinary live mice. In the box are also inclined revolving stands, which the mice revolve by the hour. It is the most amusing sight and attracts a good deal of attention.*"

"Weird," Greta said.

"Life was simpler back then," Martha said.

"Apparently so were the people," I said trying to get a laugh from someone, but got nothing. "Wonder if that would attract customers to our store." Again, nothing.

"Someone wrote *MICKEY Mouse* on here," Martha said.

"Listen to this," Iris said. "From 1887. *Two carloads of cows, enroute for Helena, Montana, were unloaded in Luce, being unable to proceed farther without a rest. They were well cared for and reloaded after a rest of 24 hours.* Imagine that," she said.

"Here's a picture of some boy playing an accordion in front of a Christmas tree. No name or date," Greta said.

I leafed through a binder full of brittle clippings. "I'd hate my life to come down to people going through my stuff." I thought Martha would jump on that. She used to love to go on and on about ideas that didn't really matter but she stood up and left the room. Greta, still holding Grace, followed after her.

I waited for Iris to leave, but she stayed in the room. "Randall got picked up for disorderly conduct."

"I know. A disturbance at a Fargo motel," she said.

"Was it in the paper?"

"Martha told me."

"Why didn't you tell me?"

"I just did even though she asked me not to tell anyone."

"Why didn't she tell me?"

"Maybe because you suspect he's causing trouble. Why give you fuel against him?"

"No one tells me anything anymore."

25

We hauled it all out to Tom's where Julianna met us. She said her father was feeling too ill to come out. Dwight was with her and Nathan also came to help. Those two did most of the heavy lifting, which was a huge relief to my aching knees. Don said he couldn't leave the store to help. Whatever. Julianna soon double-locked the shed and we all parted ways. I couldn't shake feeling low about giving up the ghost on Lyle's house. Then I figured I should get another box of clippings to go through, give me something to do. Besides, no one else had followed my suggestion that they take one. So I went in the house, grabbed two boxes, and put them in my car.

Before locking up the house, I decided to do one last walk through and noticed light down in the cellar. My knees were killing me, but I hobbled down the steps to find the light on in the cold storage area. Why had anyone even been back there? There was a burnt and kind of skunky odor. The ceiling light chain was caught on something. I opened a rickety wooden folding chair, stepped up while bracing myself against the wall, and reached for the chain. A black arrow drawn on the wall pointed up toward a split fieldstone jutting out like a ledge. I repositioned the chair and held onto the stone for support. My fingertips brushed against something. I lifted the object, surprised to see a tin Mickey Mouse toy. I steadied myself on the wobbly chair and turned to get down. The chair slats broke. My foot went straight through and slammed to the floor. The full impact on my left knee brought fierce pain.

I could hardly breathe. I got the damn chair off my leg and screamed to keep from passing out. I lay there holding my knee and moaning.

I heard footsteps overhead and then hurrying down the stairs, kicking into Mason jars that rolled along the planks.

"I have a gun," I called out. "Who's there?"

"It's me, Greta."

I opened my eyes enough to see her and some other figure behind her. "Who's with you? Someone's with you?"

"Edward." By the dim light, I could barely make out his face.

"What for?" Then pain hit me and I closed my eyes real tight.

"To help you."

I knew that made no sense but I was in so much pain, I didn't care. Lying on my side, facing the wall, I moaned.

"Let me examine you." Dr. Schemp got between me and the wall and probed my knee.

I screamed and wanted to punch his lights out.

"Could be a fractured patella," he said.

"I'm blacking out," I moaned.

"Breathe. Keep breathing," Dr. Schemp said.

I breathed. It hurt.

"Good, good. Again. Breathe deeply. Okay good. Keep breathing."

"Oh mother have mercy!" I felt like I was in the delivery room again but the only cries were from me. "I'm blacking out!" I yelled.

Then did.

26

I dreamed I was walking along a never-ending sidewalk to a house that had been razed. The sidewalk just kept going on and on and I had to keep walking it as punishment for losing that house. Bob Vila appeared and told me to remember the shame of sidewalks leading nowhere that once led to houses. I must not let that happen to Lyle's house. A stairway appeared but I couldn't climb because something held my knees down. Pigweed and thistle overtook peonies, hollyhocks, and daisies. The weeds tried to wrap around me and then turned to morning glories. "You can do it, girl," Bob said. He complimented my expert handling of a keyhole saw I was using to cut down poison ivy. Said I moved it for maximum control and smoothness of cut, as good as the guys on his crew. He suggested we get together to saw some boards, clucked his tongue, elbowed me in the side, and grinned.

Suddenly, Bob's soothing voice morphed into what sounded like Chief Huntermeister's.

"She awake yet?" it said.

I heard myself say, "Need the block plane, Bob?"

Someone said, "Hey, you awake?" It wasn't Bob.

I opened my eyes and looked straight at Greta who smiled like I was an amusement.

She touched my shoulder. "Still with Bob, huh." She winked, placed her hand to the side of her mouth, and whispered, "It's the Demerol. Pretty good stuff."

"You're sure she fell from a chair?" Dwight asked.

"Busted it up completely."

"No one else around when she fell?"

"Not a single soul." Greta said. "Good thing I went back searching for my phone because there she was screaming in pain on the cellar floor."

"When she comes out of it, tell her I stopped by," he said.

I wanted to tell Dwight that something was fishy, that Dr. Schemp had been there, too, that Greta had already got her phone out of the house; but then I didn't really care one way or the other. I was really sleepy. It then dawned on me that I didn't hear Don in the room. Where was Don?

Greta poked me. "So you are awake?"

"What?"

"You asked where Don is."

"No I didn't."

"Should be here pronto. Tracked him down at a swim meet."

Oh crap. I forgot about the swim meet. A pillow was tucked under my knee and a cloth splint crossed my kneecap. I remember the nurse telling me that I was going to get something through the needle poked into my hand. Must be why I didn't feel the pain. A white curtain surrounded the head of the bed. Greta turned off the overhead fluorescent light and the room was more bearable with light only from the wall fixture behind me.

Greta leaned close to my ear. "Who's Bob, anyway?"

"What?"

"Who's Bob? You've been talking to him."

I ignored the question. "I can't stand lying flat on my back like this," I said.

"Don't think you have a choice."

"Can you raise the head?" I asked. Greta pushed a button. The foot of the bed went up. The movement sent a shot of pain to my knee. "For the love of Martha's ... for Pete's sake," I said.

"Sorry." She pressed the next button to elevate my head. "Maybe you're supposed to lie flat." She drummed her fingers against the arm of the chair, upholstered vinyl the color of a Granny Smith apple.

"I'd like to get out of here before Christmas," I yelled. I looked into the glass-front cabinet filled with sponges, gauze, towels, basins, tendon repair trays, and suture trays. The air vents were humming and the wheels of carts clacked by. Greta poked her fingertip into a hollow metal tube near the foot of the bed and had to tug hard to free her finger.

"What the heck are you doing?" I asked.

"This must be for the suturing tray."

"Do I care?"

"They just got this bed. Remember the dance? Raised the money through that dance last year. Did you go? I didn't. There was a photo of Edward and his wife dancing to promote the fundraiser. Guess they figured that would actually attract people. She looked out of step if you ask me. Course she usually looks that way."

"Now how could I possibly care?"

"Funny thing is, now with the Fargo hospital set to take over, Luce Hospital will have so much money, they can expand, build out on Highway 10 by the ..." She stopped talking, looked surprised at what she had just shared.

"What are you talking about? What Fargo deal? How would you know about a—"

"Is your Demerol wearing off? Maybe you'd like more." Greta laughed. "Anyway, just thought you'd know about the bed. And the dance," she said. "Don't forget the dance. I like to dance. Do you like to dance, Trudy? Slow and easy or fast and furious?" I ignored the question. Greta removed a stethoscope from a hook, placed the earpiece in her ears and the diaphragm bell to her chest. "The heart is a very resilient organ," she said.

"Not according to Martha."

"Edward said the heart has its own memory." She seemed all dreamy like she was thinking about how that stethoscope was lucky enough to sometimes hang around Dr. Schemp's neck.

"Where is he? They took x-rays decades ago." I punched the pillow.

My outburst seemed to amuse Greta. She put her colossal purse on the bed, opened it, and lifted a tin Mickey Mouse toy. After smoothing the sheet, she put the toy on the bed.

"How'd you get that?"

"Picking up after you, my dear. Just think, this little thing is why you got knocked on your ass." It had rat-like teeth behind a freaky exaggerated smile. "Why'd the old guy put a toy in such an out-of-the-way place? Senility maybe?" Greta turned Mickey Mouse around and examined his hind end, feet, and hands. "Quaint little thing."

"A real charmer," I said, staring at it. Mickey's torso was attached to a square that rose from the platform. A crank protruded from another square that had *Mickey Mouse Slate Dancer* printed on it. Hinge screws secured Mickey's legs, knees, and elbows, allowing the joints to dangle.

"I bet it has sentimental value." She turned the crank and the mouse danced. "Probably painted the arrow on the wall so he'd remember where he put the thing, knowing the value of sentiment—" Greta stopped talking when we heard Dr. Schemp's voice in the hallway. I closed my eyes. "So anyway, I think he put … Are you sleeping again?" I didn't answer and she said, "Hope Bob returns to your dreams." She rose from the bed.

I opened my eyes and saw her standing behind the partially open door. When Dr. Schemp walked in, she pulled him over to the side out of view of anyone in the hallway. "Is Trudy sleeping?" he asked.

"Knocked out," she said. I closed my eyes quick in case he looked over at me. It was quiet and I wondered what it felt like to see someone in public that you could only put your hands on in private. I bet Greta loved moments when he appeared to her, like maybe they were sly and daring, desiring private time even in a crowd. I imagined she longed to act in public like she did in private with him, maybe hugging and kissing hello. I snuck a peek at them standing close like two pieces of a puzzle trying to fit. The earpiece of his stethoscope touched his neck where his light brown hair was shaggy, too busy to get a trim, maybe. The way Greta was staring at him, touching his tie, I imagined she wanted to kiss him. Maybe she wanted to run her skinny fingers through his wavy hair. Put her head on his broad chest. He was several inches taller than her and about ten years older. Maybe he looked like pleasure and pain tumbled all together in a white lab coat and a gold wedding band. For crap's sake, I scolded myself. Where were all those thoughts coming from?

"Who's there?" I finally said.

Dr. Schemp held a clipboard. He tilted his head as if contemplating something significant and walked toward me. Greta followed and fingered the bell of that stethoscope slung around her neck. He looked from the stethoscope to her. "I was listening to my heart," she said.

"What's it doing?"

"Beating faster."

"Let me hear it." He placed the bell of his stethoscope beneath her shirt collar and moved downward.

"Like what you hear?" Greta asked.

"Love it," he said.

"Hello," I said. "Who's the patient here?"

He turned as if surprised that I was in the room. "I thought Don would have shown up by now," he said.

I tried to sit up and that hurt like a son of a gun.

Dr. Schemp noted something on the clipboard. "Took a pretty bad fall, Trudy."

"Tell me something I don't know," I said.

He pointed to a computer screen. "The x-rays reveal a simple fracture of the patella. See the crack through the kneecap?"

He turned the monitor toward me and pointed to the image of my knee. "See the dark line running through your knee-cap? It could have been worse, considering your history of knee trouble. You'll need to ice it for at least twenty-four hours. Keep the swelling down. Stay in bed until the pain subsides. You don't want to bend the knee. Keep the weight off." He looked at me and I nodded. "I'll fit you with a knee immobilizer. The main thing is, don't bend your knee even as the pain subsides. Crutches will keep pressure off."

"And how do I keep pressure off my back?" I said.

Dr. Schemp sat on the bed and leaned in close. "I'm not sure I understand. Did you injure your back?" He placed his hands in his lap, pressed his forefingers and thumbs together to form a tent and looked at me, waiting for a reply. I didn't have anything to say.

"Have your knees been bothering you a lot before this?" he asked.

"They're the same. I'm fat, so they're overburdened. Isn't that basically what you told me last year?"

"If you lost just thirty pounds—forty would be better—you'd alleviate pressure on your knees. Even five pounds would be good. You'd decrease the risk of other complications from extra weight such as high blood pressure, diabetes, heart disease. If you—"

"Tell me," I interrupted the good doctor as my face reddened. "How does a person *just* lose thirty to forty pounds?"

"Self-control." He aimed his pen toward my knee. "It may swell. Keep it iced and don't bend it."

A nurse entered the room. She brushed against Dr. Schemp as she handed him a teal-colored device from which four straps hung down. Greta glared at the nurse who then turned and left the room. Dr. Schemp ripped the straps apart one at a time, staring at Greta as if he wanted to say something to her but had to focus on me. He unwrapped the splint, lifted my leg, removed the pillow, and placed the device beneath my leg.

"Keep your leg elevated, no pressure or weight on the knee whatsoever. I'll give you a week's supply of Darvocet. After that take ibuprofen for pain." He secured the device then nodded toward Mickey. "Pretty old toy."

"Just put it away," I said to Greta.

A repetitive beep interrupted Dr. Schemp. "When Don shows up, I'd like to talk to him."

"Me too," I said.

Greta hurried after the doctor, left me alone to watch the clock until fifteen minutes later she returned. I couldn't tell if the flush on her face was from happiness or sadness. "I'm heading out," she said. "Don should be here momentarily."

"You don't sound as happy as you did when he was in the room."

"He has nice hands," Greta said. "You should count it as a blessing that you got to feel his smooth hands on your knee. And to look into those golden brown eyes."

"I suddenly feel sick to my stomach."

"I'll get a nurse."

"Here's one for you. What's the difference between God and a doctor?"

"What are you talking about?"

"God doesn't think he's a doctor."

"That's not funny," Greta said. "He doesn't act like that."

"You two might want to try being less obvious," I said.

"I don't know what you're talking about."

"You'll end up the bad woman who tried to break up a happy home and his wife will remain the saint that she thinks she is. Keep your eye on that nurse, too, licking her lips over your lover."

"Wow, Trudy." She walked to the doorway, stopped, and then turned. "By the way, Martha and I are going to Sassy Spa tonight. We signed up for a cross fit class. Then we'll take the kids for burgers. She could use a friend. She's going through a really rough time. Maybe you don't know that. Oh, that's right; you didn't know until I told you."

"Hey girls." Don entered the room. "I got here as soon as I could. What happened?"

Greta stood too close to Don. "Hello handsome," she said. "And good luck."

27

Three days after my fall, I hobbled downstairs. I sat in the recliner, pushing the footrest out to support my knees. The Mickey Mouse toy sat on the coffee table. I stared at it, wondered why Lyle had put it where he did? Was it because that particular stone ledge had nothing on it, so why not fill up an empty place?

Don came into the room. "Need anything?"

"A glass of water." Last night he came home late smelling of perfume and whiskey but I wasn't about to call him on it. Who had energy these days for confrontation?

He returned with the water and sat on the couch. "Take a look. I entered it in the newspaper contest."

I examined the photo. "It's good."

"Pay attention to the edge—the frame—and let your eye follow along it and then look inward to what attracts your eye."

"Oh yeah?"

"It's the birch grove on the slope of Lyle's land by the Indian Mounds."

"When were you out there?"

"Snowshoed out. I've been taking Courtney on shoots."

"Oh really?" Dad and daughter photo shoots. Who knew? No one told me anything anymore. I felt weepy.

Courtney came into the room, hesitated, and seemed unsure like maybe I'd be in a bad mood. "Here's the paper. Check the swim meet results. We rock." I set the paper, thick with holiday shopping inserts, aside. She lifted Mickey

Mouse. "This old thing is kind of cool." She turned the crank and Mickey Mouse danced. "Can I have it?" Courtney asked.

"By all means, take it away," I said.

"Awesome." Courtney smiled. "Ericka's mom's giving me a ride to practice."

"Get your things together," Don said. "Don't want to make her wait."

"She's never late." Courtney turned the crank as she left the room. Don followed.

Darvocet sat in my bathrobe pocket like a new friend. I took one and thought of Lyle swallowing all his meds. I thought of Dr. Schemp's comment about "just" losing thirty pounds and considered becoming a woman who concentrated on one thing at a time, like uncovering my collarbone. I wondered what kind of a woman I'd be if I did things like going to a spa instead of eating when stressed. Maybe I'd be less cranky with two good knees and a happy marriage.

28

While in bed going through a box of clippings from Lyle's, I sat straight up when one dated August 1984 caught my eye: "*MICKEY MOUSE A Hot Item.*" It was from the "Ask Jerome's Antiques" column. Beneath the photo a caption read: *A Mickey Mouse Slate Dancer sold at an auction in Maine for $29,500, the record for a comic-character toy. Notice the teeth and five-finger hands.*

"What the heck?"

I continued to read. *Dear Antiques Guy: here is a photograph of a toy my mother had. Please tell me what you know about it. Signed L. S. of Luce.*

I kept reading, feeling more excited with each word from Antiques Guy. "*Mickey Mouse collectibles have long been collectors' favorites. The early Mickey toys are especially desirable. The colorful graphics are decorative and Mickey brings memories of childhood fun. Mickey Mouse had rat-like teeth and five fingers from 1928, his birth date, to 1932. Last month, a Mickey Mouse Slate Dancer toy sold at auction for $29,500, setting a record for a comic toy. It is one of the most sought after comic-character toys. It was made by Johann Distler of Nuremberg, about 1931. Made of lithographed tin, Mickey moves when the crank is turned. If you are interested in selling, please give me a call.*"

"Unbelievable," I said. "Thank you Lyle." All the things I could use that money toward: a new van, porch ceiling, Joan's retainer, Courtney's braces. I could hardly wait for her to get home and give me back that toy. To quiet my mind and my knee pain, I took two Darvocet.

I woke up in a fog, could hardly open my eyes and my mouth was dryer than sawdust. I heard Don's voice calling up the stairs. "Are you ever going to get up today?"

I grabbed the bedside clock. After one? What day was it? I hobbled downstairs. "Where's Courtney?"

"Hanging out with friends."

"Where?" I yelled.

"You want something to eat?" He ignored my question as if he wanted to punish me for not knowing where our daughter was.

"Where's the toy?" I asked.

Don shrugged.

Which is exactly what Courtney did after I asked her three hours later when she finally came home. "I don't remember where I put it."

Down payment on a shop van?

"Well, think for a second."

"I don't remember."

Joan's retainer fee?

"Take your time."

New porch roof?

"I don't know, Mom…."

"Well, go find it!"

"Why are you yelling?"

Courtney's braces?

"You gave it to her," Don said.

"That doesn't mean she had to go and lose it."

"I didn't lose it. I just don't remember what I did with it after I took it to practice."

"I really need to see that toy." I was shaking.

"We stopped at Ericka's house after, then we went for pizza, then we—"

"Go find it!"

"WTF?" she said.

"Don't you dare talk like that!"

"Courtney," Don said, "Apologize for saying that and then get your coat. We'll retrace your steps."

29

The next evening I sat in the living room watching my grandfather's taped episodes of *This Old House*. The fire Don built needed another log. I didn't care; let it go out. Don carried a paper bag into the room. "Dinner." He removed the take-out containers. "Caesar salad with grilled chicken." He placed it on the TV tray with a knife and fork.

"I really want that toy," I said.

"It'll turn up," he said.

"Thanks for getting dinner." I didn't know what kind of mood I was in; the painkillers were messing with me. I did know whenever I thought about that lost Mickey Mouse toy, my anxiety soared through the roof. I drummed my fingers on the arm of the recliner and then smoothed my blue flannel robe, tapped my pocket holding the Darvocet.

"Man, it's cold tonight." Don threw his jacket and scarf over the back of a chair. He placed a gift-wrapped box on the cluttered coffee table next to the paper I still hadn't bothered to read. He handed me a napkin and moved the TV tray closer.

"Supposed to get more snow, according to the news." I lifted the plastic bubble lid covering the salad and sprinkled half the Parmesan cheese into the bowl. I added only six croutons and squeezed only a tablespoon of dressing onto the salad. I wondered what the gift-wrapped box contained but wasn't about to ask. What I was really burning to know was where he had been that night he came home smelling of perfume and whiskey.

"Fire's almost out." Don opened the screen, poked the embers, and stoked the fire. He added two logs and crumpled newspaper. Sparks shot up. "Want the tree lights on?" He was trying too hard. I felt his pity.

"Suit yourself," I said. He turned on the tree lights and the colors did brighten the room. He unwrapped his pita sandwich and picked up the paper.

I wasn't as hungry as I thought. I'd cut back on the pain pills, but my appetite was still low. I put the lid on my salad. "This is for you." Don put down the paper and handed me the gift. "Greta dropped it off at the store."

"Greta?" I tore the wrapping paper and opened the box. Two silver balls nested in red silk. *Healthyballs.*

Don read the instructions, "To strengthen hand muscles and relax you."

I lifted the balls. "They're cold." I squeezed the balls that jingled.

He continued reading, "The musical tones help soothe you. It says the fingers are connected through channels to the body's vital organs, like the brain, heart, liver, lungs, so the balls massage acupuncture hand points. You get better blood circulation, improved muscle tone, and clearer thinking."

I moved the clinking metal around in my palm, was feeling kindly toward Don as he looked through mail stacked on the coffee table. I put the balls in my lap and lifted the Luce newspaper to read a headline: *Area Businesses Busy with Lots of Special Holiday Gatherings and Lots of Spending.* The editor's favorite adjective was *lots.* People were dancing in the photo. The caption read: *Cactus Corral was extra busy with lots of Luce Clinic and Hospital employees celebrating the holiday season. They danced to the music of the Johnny Holms Band.* I scanned the faces in the crowd and landed on Greta. The man dancing with her looked like Don. I brought the paper closer. It *was* Don. One hand rested on Greta's waist. I imagined his other hand on her skinny butt. I held the paper out to him. "You look ridiculous," I said.

"Excuse me?"

"That's where you were, out dancing." I held up the paper and pointed at the photo. The Healthyballs jingled in my lap.

"It's no big deal," Don said.

"It is to me." I jabbed the photo. "How did it feel to have your arms around her skinny butt?"

"They were not around her butt."

"Just leave. That's all. Go!" I motioned toward the door.

"I'm not done with my dinner." He took a bite, chewed, and stared at me. I understood that he would not tie into my jealousy. He was, as always, above the fray. "You see a photo and assume I'd do something to hurt you."

"Don't tell me what I assume." I shook my fist and the balls jingled. "I asked you to leave. Go hang out with Greta. Smoke her dope."

"Suit yourself." Don walked to the foyer. He pulled on his boots, came back for his jacket and scarf, which he angrily put on. He opened the door.

I stood and threw a pillow at him. "You're not just going to walk out feeling all dignified while I'm fuming. Aren't I worth a fight?"

"*You*, dear Trudy, are always up for a fight, whether it's worth one or not." He gently closed the door. That really got my goat.

I hobbled after him, turned on the porch lights, opened the door, and walked outside, ducking under evergreen garland Don had hung for the season. From the top step, I yelled, "Take Greta's Merry Christmas balls with you." I threw a ball. It zoomed past Don.

He turned around. "Please control yourself."

"Where are you going?"

"For a walk."

I threw the other ball and like a hammer dead set on a nail;

it traveled in a perfectly straight line, hit Don in the back of the head, and knocked him down.

"Oh crap!" I made it down the steps and limped along the sidewalk. I sat in the snow, my immobilized leg sticking straight out. "Don!" I rubbed his cheeks and felt his head. No blood. Good. The streetlight illuminated us. I put snow on his head to prevent swelling.

Don sat up, grabbed my hands, squeezed, and then shoved them away. "What is wrong with you?"

"Nothing. Something. I don't know."

Don formed a snowball and held it to his head. "I'm going to have a splitting headache." He tried to stand up. "Whoa."

"You're dizzy."

"Trudy. What is wrong with you?"

"I don't want you to leave while you're angry."

"You wanted me to leave."

"I thought I wanted you to leave." I felt suddenly cold and sorry and miserable on the sidewalk and I wouldn't have blamed Don if he did just go, leave, take Courtney and abandon me like I abandoned Lyle's house. I was a disaster, had made a mess of everything.

"Go inside," Don said. He slowly stood and helped me up.

"Are you going to the store?"

"You know. I bring you dinner. Stoke the fire. Turn the tree lights on. Deliver a gift. Sit down to talk with you. And look what you did." He rubbed his head. "How hard would it be to relax and get over yourself?" He brushed snow from his coat sleeves. "I'm tired of fighting with you, Trudy. Tired of feeling tense in my own home. You see that photo but you don't see the photo that matters to me."

I was freezing and my teeth were chattering. "What?"

"My birch grove photo took first place. See. That matters to me and it was in the paper tonight, too, but you only saw what you wanted to."

I felt lower than low. I wanted to say congratulations but I had already ruined that moment so what good was it to say it after what I had done to him?

Don picked the ball out of the snow and tossed it to me. "Something has to change," he said. "I won't be home to-night."

"What about Courtney?"

"She's spending the night at Ericka's. Maybe you haven't noticed but she's been doing that more and more lately."

Two nights later, he still had not come home and Courtney refused to talk to me even as I tried to help her stop crying. "Don. Please call me back," I said into his voice mail. "Please. Courtney misses you, too. I'm sorry." Courtney slammed the door on her way out to meet Ericka and her mother waiting in their car.

In Courtney's room, I sat on the bed. Maybe I should learn to appreciate that she was my teenage daughter with such a crazy busy life that the mess of her room could not possibly matter to her. What mattered was what went on in her life outside of that. And hadn't I lost track? What was wrong with me? I lifted a blanket from the floor, noticed plates and glasses shoved beneath her desk. I used my crutch to pull them out toward me. A tray was shoved back against the wall. I managed to pull that forward. Courtney's damp pool towel came with it. I lifted the mildewed towel and shook it out. Something fell and clinked against the plates.

Mickey Mouse stared up at me.

"Martha's Jesus, Joseph, and Mary," I said, "Am I ever happy to see you. Merry Christmas Mother Lode."

I hid the toy in the back of my top dresser drawer and got busy researching how to sell stuff on ebay. I was going to be in the money and my mind shifted to full speed ahead on what to do with it. Within hours, I got Mickey Mouse up and posted and two days later, an antiques dealer in Michigan contacted me. Boom, just like that, in the wink of an eye, I made a deal to sell Mickey to the man for twenty thousand dollars. I could've wrangled around for more, knowing it was worth it; but when he said he was buying it from me at current top value, I let it go at that. He'd send someone to Luce to pick it up.

I was feeling happier than a pig in mud until Don came home and said he was getting some of his things. He made the apartment above the hardware store livable and would stay there for as long as it took him to see things more clearly.

"But it's going to get better," I said. "The money will be coming in after probate, maybe even before then, and it won't be so bad."

"Money?" He stopped shoving socks and underwear into his duffle bag. "You think money matters in this?" He looked at me like I was the biggest fool he'd ever laid eyes on. "You know, I was thinking about who you were that night you pulled over to help me by the side of the road all those years ago."

"Yeah," I laughed, tried to sound light. "You didn't even know how to change a flat."

"Oh but I did know how. I had forgotten to put the jack back in the trunk; otherwise I wouldn't have had to flag for help. When you stopped all assured and eager to do the work, I figured what the heck. Might as well let you. I found myself moved by how passionately you worked. Green eyes, red hair, freckles. Then you dropped the jack on your foot and seemed vulnerable, trying to hide that you wanted to cry. You were funny and open and interested in me. You liked sex back then. What I want to know, Trudy." He looked at me with narrowed eyes. "When did your wit turn to sarcasm and your keen senses zoom in on all my faults, real or imagined? When did you start wanting to kill the things in me you used to love?"

I didn't know what to say. I was struck dumb. My mouth hung open. After an excruciatingly long silence, I said, "I found Mickey Mouse. He's worth—"

"Great," Don said. He lifted his suitcase. "Now you can stop riding Courtney over it."

"But I just needed to tell you something important."

"I asked her to stay the weekend with me. I'll get her Friday after school. I'm borrowing a car from Nathan."

"I don't like being alone," I said, surprising myself.

"Well. Well," Don said. "Look at you testing out your vulnerable side."

That night before going to bed, I opened and closed the basement door to hear it scrape across the floor, imagined Don coming up the steps with some photo to show me.

The next day, I was tired, on edge, and wanted a Darvocet. I was contemplating calling Schemp for more when Iris stopped by.

"It's unbearably cold and looks like it'll snow any minute now." She put a jar on the kitchen table. "I brought some of Nancy's clover honey."

"From a traitor?"

"Traitor? Me?"

"She quit after Lyle's death. Gone just like that." I snapped my fingers.

"I figured you'd be crankier than usual." Iris loosened her scarf, took off her coat, and removed her knitted cap like she planned to stay awhile.

"What'd you do to your hair?" It was shorter than ever.

"Easier to take care of."

I thought of something Martha read in one of those women's magazines. A woman frustrated with her life rearranges the furniture. She also changes her hairstyle.

"I'm leaving now," Iris said. "I have plans. I wanted to tell you before I—"

"You just got here," I protested, suspecting I wasn't cheerful enough for her to want to stay. "No one cares about me. Look how long it took you to visit me, the poor shut in."

"I have nothing to say in response to your self-pity."

"Since we're barred from the house, what's there to say to you anyway?" I retaliated. "Just go." I waved my hand through the air to dismiss her. Wait. Hadn't I said those same words to Don and look what happened? "I didn't mean—"

She put on her cap and coat. "I'll be on my way. You have your misery to get along with." She stopped at the doorway. "I'll always appreciate that Lyle's place brought me Cobber. Will store other good memories in the corners of my mind if I need them later."

"What's that supposed to mean?" I asked; but she left without explanation.

30

I felt lower than ever all week. I missed Don and Courtney. Iris wouldn't return my calls and Martha hadn't talked to me for ages. I popped in a *This Old House* tape, but with Don gone, I felt sad rather than interested. I called Martha again. To my surprise, she picked up.

She sounded frantic. I could barely understand but heard, "Randall's out of control. I've never seen him like this."

"I'll be right there," I assured her.

"No don't come," she said. "Someone else is coming."

"Let me at least come get the children." No answer. "Hello?" We were disconnected.

I dialed Dwight's cell and left a message, "Get to Martha's pronto." I put on my coat, got my crutches, and left the house. Snow covered the sidewalk. For the first time, I appreciated that Don had always been the one to snow blow and shovel the walk and driveway. He never put it on a to-do list or complained; he just quietly did it.

I managed to drive without any problem, my left leg stretched out as far as it could and the pressure off. The roads were slick, so I took my time even though I wanted to speed. I got there to see Dwight's cruiser parked in Martha's driveway. I hobbled to the front door. Locked. I didn't know what was going on in there, so I didn't ring the bell. Plus I didn't want Dwight to tell me to go home. I found the garage door unlocked. I went in and turned the knob to the side door leading into the mudroom. I slowly opened that door and got a pretty good view into the kitchen. Files and papers were scattered around the floor and stacked on the counter. Looked like two bottles of Jack on the table. Randall's back was to the door but Martha saw me. Her eyes got real wide. She shook her head and frowned. Dwight focused on Randall, who looked out the windows to the lake. It was dusk and the kitchen lights cast a glare on his profile.

My cell phone indicated a text message from Martha: *U should go. Kids r next door with Julianna. I M OK.*

Then I heard Martha yell, "Randall. Don't say that." He turned very slowly and I had to keep from gasping when I saw his face. He had a black eye and a bandage over his left cheek. The rash seemed less severe. His white shirt was rumpled and the tail stuck out from the waistband of his pants. One of the shirt cuffs was unbuttoned and it flapped as he rubbed his forehead.

"I've been..." He stopped, cleared his throat, and then coughed. "I've been trying to put order to this, Martha. Trying to figure out how to show you just how bad it is. What I've done."

"Like I said, all you have to do is just tell me, Randall." Martha stepped closer, reached for him, then crossed her arms over her chest like maybe she wanted to touch him but forced herself not to. "Just tell me," she said.

He gestured around the room, kicked a stack of papers, and scattered them. "I should have listened." He lifted his tie, tugged it as if it were a noose.

"Randall. Don't do that!"

He collapsed into a chair. "I invested in a scheme. Smart businessman undone by his own greed. Wiped us out. How could I have been such a fool?" He pressed hard and rubbed his forehead. "Then I thought I could make up for losing millions by investing in more land. Hoped for that Staybler land. Foolish long shot. I should've known better, but..." He laughed. "What does it matter now?"

Martha gripped the back of a chair. "We have other pieces, the Fargo properties."

"There's a lien. They'll be foreclosed on. Should've burned them down when I had the chance. Insurance, that's the ticket. Me. The properties. The car. That's the ticket."

"That's not the ticket," Martha said.

"I could've hired an arsonist. I considered it." He lifted a piece of paper. "But this," he said. "This here's a sure million for you and the kids." He handed her the document. "Me dead leaves you with one million clear."

"Randall, don't say such a thing. Don't!"

"Why not? People do it all the time. You think it would matter to anyone if I was dead?"

"Stop! People have bad fortune all the time. People recover. We can too."

"You might think differently when we lose the house," he said.

"It doesn't matter. It's just a house."

"Homeless." He leaned over and bent his elbows on his knees, his face cradled in his palms. He shook his head. "I thought it was a sure thing, the best deal possible. One of those deals only a fool would pass up."

"We won't lose our house, Randall. I'll get a job. We'll sell other assets. We'll cut back. We'll make it."

"No. I'd rather give you a million. Better cash in before I lose that, too." He stood up, flung papers off the counter and began to pace. "I have this hot brick in my chest. I can't breathe." He gripped his throat.

Dwight stepped forward. "Hey, Randall. How 'bout we go for a ride, get some perspective?"

"I can't breathe," Randall yelled.

"Sure. I understand. Just try to take one breath. Just need one at a time." He waited. "Good. Just one. Now try another one. Deep. Just in and out. Concentrate. Air in and air out." Dwight picked up the documents Randall had scattered to the floor. "How 'bout we make a date to shoot baskets tomorrow?" Dwight placed his hand on

Randall's shoulder and guided him to the table. "Tomorrow's a good idea."

"I'm worth more dead," Randall said.

"Hoops," Dwight said. "Think about that. Tomorrow."

"Don't you understand? I lost everything!"

"Not everything," Martha said. "You have your family."

"What do I have to offer?" he said. Then added, "I'm tired."

Dwight gave Martha a reassuring look and then said to Randall, "Remember those Saturday mornings when you'd bring Michael to watch us shoot baskets at the Rec Center? Give him tips. Or how about when you went to the school for Dad's Visit Day? You sat in Ruthie's small desk and made her laugh? Photo got in the newspaper and you got all kinds of ribbing about it but you said it didn't matter because Ruthie loved that picture. How about those Indian Mounds you discovered at Pugmeyer's place? Donated the adjacent land you owned to better preserve them. Didn't have to, but you did. Good works, Man. So what do you say? Let's make a plan to shoot baskets."

"The guy had all the right credentials. Offices in Fargo, Duluth, and Minneapolis. I checked him out. I asked other people who invested with him. I was getting quarterly statements and then … he disappeared. Not one trace of the money. I hired an investigator. All he could tell me was I got scammed."

"Why wait?" Dwight said. "How about we shoot some baskets now?"

"Not interested in going to the Rec Center."

"I mean right outside. The hoop you put up for Michael."

"He's a good boy," Randall said and then wailed the most mournful cry. "Oh God. I just thought of that time I made him fish cottonwood seeds from the shoreline to punish him for wetting the bed."

"Randall, don't think about those things," Martha said.

"But I did that to him."

"I turned it into a game," she said. "Michael and I had a race to see who could scoop up the most seeds." I thought of how Martha always did that, found a way to take what was rotten and make it okay. I said it was avoidance but Iris called it Martha's coping skills. Iris was right. I was wrong.

"You did?"

"He won." The way she looked at him with such concern just about broke my heart.

At that moment, Randall had to have found strength from her because he said to Dwight, "We have to shovel first."

"I don't follow," Dwight said.

"Shovel under the hoop if you want to shoot baskets."

I breathed a huge sigh of relief and hightailed it out of there as fast as I could to my car before Randall even got wind of me. I was driving off when I saw Tom Mandle walking onto the long drive leading to his place, shining a flashlight into the underbrush of his woods. "Where are you!" he shouted into the night. "Come back!"

31

Tom waved me down. I lowered my window. "Are you okay?"

"She's run off!"

"Julianna?"

"We're watching the Short children. Their mother called Julianna and brought them to our place. Now little Ruthie's run off," he said. He was wheezing like all get out.

The yard lights and my headlights only covered so much area. We used flashlights to search for tracks in the snow. My knee was aching bad. I pressed snow against it. Then I heard Tom yell, "Here!" I hobbled to him. He kept the flashlight pointed down and we followed footprints leading to one of his sheds. Inside we found Ruthie huddled under a quilted tarp on top of Lyle's dining room table.

"What a sight for sore eyes," I said. The shed was a quarter full of farm implements and some of Lyle's things.

"We're a good team," he said.

We walked slowly not wanting to startle her. "Ruthie?" I said. "Ruthie. It's me, Trudy." I rubbed her hands. "And Tom, too. It's too cold to hide out here."

She opened the front of her coat. "I found this." She revealed a scrawny black and white cat. Ruthie looked so soft and sweet, innocent and I saw so much of her mother in her as she tended to that cat.

"We were worried about you," Tom said.

"Sorry." She nuzzled the cat's face. "I think I broke something."

"Nothing in here worth getting upset about breaking," Tom said.

"Over there. When I pulled the blanket down. It fell."

He lifted a car battery. "This old piece of junk?" he said. "Well, it's just a good thing it didn't fall on you." I imagined assuring and doting Tom talking to young Julianna in a soothing voice, free from the hoarseness that now plagued it. I wondered if he had perpetually tried somehow to make amends to his little girl because of her mother's unhappiness in having to marry him. I thought about Julianna in a new and kindly light, how she was maybe just trying to do her best while hiding under her veneer.

"I saw the kitty from the window and wanted it."

"We'll show it to Julianna," Tom said.

"Daddy doesn't act nice and Mommy's always crying. This kitty is happy."

"Let's get you to the house," Tom said.

"I'm bad." Ruthie looked liked she'd cry.

"Hey. Hey. It's okay," Tom said. He patted the cat's head. "Look what you did. You found a cat. What a good girl."

Ruthie perked up. "It's a really nice kitty," she said.

"Let's take you both to Julianna." He wrapped his scarf around her neck and lifted her. "You can show the cat to your brother and sister." He stumbled backward, had to put Ruthie down. He regained his balance and struggled for breath. A bad coughing jag hit him. He bent over and braced himself against a wall until the coughing stopped.

"Mommy can give you some cough drops," Ruthie said. When Tom stopped coughing, I saw a lot of blood on his handkerchief. Ruthie held the cat up to Tom's ear. "Listen. It's purring."

He did his best to smile, to lean down and listen to the purring cat. "Julianna was always after me to bring in the barn cats," Tom said. I saw him as a young father spoiling Julianna and felt a huge pang of sadness for myself as a little girl who never felt like I was worth more than a piece of junk to my father.

32

The antiques dealer sent a courier to my house. After examining Mickey Mouse, he said yes indeed, I had found a treasure. I drove his cashier's check for $20,000 straight to the Effington Bank and opened a checking account. I needed to break this cash flow news to Don so I made a plan to show him my generous side. In my resourcefulness in selling that toy, I'd entice him back home with a van. A visible sign that I had changed and could put his needs first. But while at The Effington Gently Used lot, I got a call from Julianna.

"I warned you not to sell anything."

"Don't worry, Pluth Hardware customers aren't buying."

"Don't be flip with me." Boy was she steaming. She said she was in Ebeling's when a man came in, sat across from their booth, pulled an antique Mickey Mouse toy from a sturdy cardboard box, and talked excitedly on his phone. Wouldn't you know it; Dwight was with her and recognized the toy as the one I found at Lyle's. Suspicious, Dwight asked the man where he got it. The man said he was the courier for an antiques dealer in Michigan and had purchased it for the dealer. He showed Dwight the receipt, complete with my signature. The man would not relinquish the toy to Julianna, said she had no proof of ownership, said she could contact the antiques dealer's attorney if she felt inclined to do so and buy it.

"Wow, it's a small world," I said. Thinking, but not adding, *especially in Luce.*

"Do I need this?" she yelled. "No I do not." I decided my best defense was to keep my mouth shut. "Under no circumstances are you allowed to return to that house," she said. "And you had better hope no one appears out of the blue in search of a valuable Mickey Mouse toy and files a claim for it while the estate remains in probate."

"Okay," I said, thinking what are the chances of that happening?

"Okay what?"

"I'll hope no one does."

"One more thing of concern among many, Trudy," she said in her stern courtroom voice. "Why would you pull a gun on Mark Riepe?"

"Oh for crap's sake! That happened a long time ago. I already got my butt chewed out by Joan over it. He came to the house demanding to see the valuables he claimed were his. And for the record, Iris pulled the gun on him. Besides, it's not like your father gave us any bullets."

"My father?" Julianna said. "Did I just hear you right? My father gave you a gun?"

"But no bullets."

"All my life, he's been the most predictable man I know. I'm beside myself trying to keep up with what's gotten into him."

"Cancer," I said.

She sighed. Then I heard someone talking to her. "Just a moment," she said, covering the phone. After a few muffled words, she returned. "Dwight wants to talk to you."

"Wait! How do I know this isn't some kind of set up? Maybe you're recording me."

"Seriously, Trudy?" she said.

"Trudy?" Dwight said. "You say Tom gave you the gun you pulled on Mark?"

"Yes. No! Iris pulled the... look; it was not my idea to scare him with the gun! For the love of Martha's... oh for Pete's sake, doesn't anyone believe me anymore?"

"But he didn't give them any bullets," Julianna's voice

broke in defensively. She must have been sharing the phone with Dwight, cheek to cheek. The last time Don picked up Courtney for the weekend, he made small talk while he waited, said he heard Dwight and Julianna were dating. I told him I thought Dwight was messing around with Wanda Laconda; she'd been shadowing him. Don gave me a puzzled look and said, *Seriously, Trudy, are those pain meds screwing with your mind?* I told him that was rude, plus I went off the meds after Schemp wouldn't give me a refill.

"Smart thinking on Tom's part," Dwight said over the phone.

"What do you mean?" Julianna said. "Bullets or no bullets, that is not smart thinking." It seemed like they had forgotten I was on the other end of the line.

"Guess not," Dwight said, sounding chastened. "But of course a gun without bullets is like a man without a woman."

"Dwight, honestly, what a thing to say." But Julianna sounded like she thought it was actually funny. It sounded like they kissed, like lip-smacking action coming to me across the sound waves.

"Mmmmm. You taste like blueberry pie," Dwight said.

"Hello!" I yelled into the phone. I imagined them straightening up and looking at the phone like they didn't know whose voice they were hearing.

"Yes," Dwight finally said, "Well, it's over for now. House is locked up. I'll try to send patrols by more often to check on it."

"Trudy stay out of that house," Julianna yelled into the phone. "Nothing to do while the investigation continues until probate ends."

"Okay," I said.

"I mean it!" she said.

"I heard you."

I planned to just sit in my car, just look at Lyle's house, and then go home. But when I pulled onto the frontage road,

Martha's car was parked out front. I called her cell, but she didn't answer. Inside I called out, "Martha! You here?" She didn't answer. "We're not supposed to be here." Walking from room to room, I called her name. A book was lying open on the kitchen table, a journal apparently belonging to Martha, her handwriting, the entry dated that day. I read: *Even though grateful that Dwight saved Randall from himself, I feel really blue. I feel scared. I feel really lonesome right now. I have no one but myself to blame for not knowing how terrible things got for Randall. All those bad things I said about him and now look. All those months he was falling apart and all I did was wonder if he was cheating on me. And there he was being swindled out of all his money, our money I guess. His psychiatrist wants to talk with me. I don't know what I'll say, but I …* The writing stopped. I stood there feeling bad for Martha.

Footsteps overhead got my attention. I stood at the bottom of the stairs. "Martha, What are you doing up there?" I heard shuffling.

Martha appeared backlit at the top step. "I'll come down," she said.

"Why are you here? We're not supposed to be here."

"I'm sorry. I thought it'd be okay." I saw someone behind her.

"Who's with you?" I inched toward a table, grabbed Mace out of my tool belt, and slipped it into my jacket pocket.

Martha came down the stairs. Two figures with ski masks and bulky down coats appeared behind her. "They have a gun," she said.

The short but solid one gripped her arm. The other one slouched over. "No one was supposed to be here," he said.

"Shut up," the short one said. "We find it, we go."

"Find what?" I asked.

"Just want to look around," the tall one said. He sounded almost sorry and he sounded young, the voice vaguely familiar. "Sit down." He pointed to two folding chairs.

"We don't have any money," I said.

"Nothing here belongs to you," the short one said. I noticed he was limping. I'd seen enough movies to not ask a masked man about any identifying characteristics.

"You're trespassing," Martha said.

"Maybe she's right," the tall one said. "Maybe we shouldn't be—"

"You just stay here," the nasty one commanded. "While we look around."

I wasn't sure if they actually had a gun but didn't want to chance it. They could've fooled Martha into believing they did. Then I thought if they had one, they would've tried to scare me with it, too, showed it off. I decided to feel them out. They suddenly didn't seem so dangerous. Even the one trying to be the tough guy sounded like his voice was just a few years out of puberty.

The short boy said, "Know what a deed looks like?"

"Who are you?" I had my hand on the hidden Mace.

A crazy sounding song broke into the room. It was tinny and loud and stopped as the short boy put a cell phone to his ear. "What?" he said. "Girl. I can't make out what you're saying. You're breaking up." He walked toward the door. "It's cool. Keep cool." He hung up and said, "What kind of stuff's good to pawn?"

The tall boy shook his head. "No way, man."

"Grab them silver pieces," he said. "Them's got to be worth a shit load of money." As he reached for a serving tray, I felt like telling him silver plate wasn't worth a plug nickel unless he was a DIY kind of guy with a project in mind.

Then Martha screamed and startled me. "I'm so sick of this," she yelled. "Bastards." She lunged for the short boy and caught him off guard. "Get out!" The boy grabbed her arm, jerked her forward, and twisted her around.

I was going to punch him in the stomach and spray him with Mace, but the tall one pulled a knife, just a puny paring knife, probably duller than the boy holding it, but still, a knife. After my knee injury, I thought I'd play it safe with the knife, avoid further injury.

"Get off me." Martha stomped on the short boy's foot. Man did that send him into a rage. He shoved her hard against the wall, her hand slamming into the plaster. The old birdcage that used to adorn the entry crashed down on her head. I ran to her.

The assailants opened the kitchen door, stood there like they were unsure of where it led. "No trouble, you said." The tall boy kicked the doorframe. "See. Now what?" I lunged for him, tried to pull off his ski mask, spray Mace in his face. Skinny twerp was quick, hit my hand away then kicked my bum knee. I went down to the floor, writhing in pain.

They ran out the back door. Someone whistled. Car doors slammed.

Martha sat on the floor holding her wrist. "I can't move my hand," she said. "I think it's broken." Her head was bleeding bad.

33

Dr. Schemp studied the x-rays. "You have an impacted fracture of your radius. That's the wrist," he said. "We'll let the swelling go down before I immobilize it." He probed Martha's head and she flinched. "Sorry, Martha." He then dabbed her scalp. "You need stitches."

"I can be so clumsy."

"Clumsy?" I said. She looked at me like I was supposed to know what she was talking about.

"Knocked right into that birdcage and tripped." Her words were slurred from whatever painkiller the good doctor gave her.

"You were there, Trudy?" Dr. Schemp asked.

I nodded and didn't know what to say because I had no idea why Martha was lying.

"Fracture like this seems unlikely from someone tripping over a ... what was it?"

"A birdcage," she said.

He looked at me like I should add something to that. I shrugged.

"Can you just fix me up?" Martha said.

"That's the plan." Dr. Schemp pulled the overhead lamp close to Martha and parted her hair. "I'm gong to swab the scalp laceration with antiseptic. A slight sting." She flinched. "Now I'm injecting something to numb your scalp." She closed her eyes and took deep breaths. Dr. Schemp kept one hand on her forearm as he rearranged instruments on the suturing tray. "You okay?" he asked.

She nodded.

Dr. Schemp placed his hand on her shoulder. "Now for the stitching."

I looked away and studied the colors of a cosmetic suture chart tacked to the wall. Purple, gray, tan, yellow, green, blue, aqua, orange. *Absorbable* or *nonabsorbable.* The yellow line indicated: *GUT, plain, fast-absorbing.* I wondered what type of suture material Dr. Schemp used on Martha's wound: Ethilon, Prolene, Nurolon? I wondered what it felt like to pull a needle through flesh? I wondered why Martha was avoiding the truth about her injury.

"Done." Dr. Schemp clipped the suture thread, sat back, and touched Martha's hand. He set the needle on the tray. "Now we tend to the wrist." He lifted it gently from a frozen pack and looked at her face instead of at her wrist. "So tell me again how you managed to hurt yourself."

"I tripped into a wall, knocked the birdcage down on my head."

Dr. Schemp resumed fiddling with the instruments on the suturing tray. Seemed to be considering something, stalling. "And Trudy was with you?"

"Lucky for me." She laughed nervously.

"And Randall?"

"Randall had nothing to do with this. Don't try to pin this on Randall, he's had enough trouble."

"Had to ask, given the report filed..." He stopped talking and looked at me like maybe I didn't know about Randall's violent behavior and breakdown.

"Do you have a safety pin? I ripped my blouse," Martha said.

Dr. Schemp removed a suture needle from the glass cabinet. "This is the best I can do." He threaded the needle, whip-stitched the tear in Martha's blouse, and then said in the most scheming voice I'd ever heard, "Things have been tense between you and Trudy lately. Must make you sad."

"Friends fight all the time. Doesn't mean we don't care for each other."

I was fuming. Only way he'd know anything about fighting between me and Martha was if his mistress Greta told him. What was he getting at?

"And you were at home?"

I was about to say no when Martha said, "Yes, that's right."

"I see," he said. "And how is the bird?"

"Bird?" Martha said

"The bird in the cage that fell on your head."

Ah ha, I thought, now she's busted for that lie.

"No bird?"

"He got away?"

"The cage is funky junk," she said, laughing. He looked confused. "You know. Repurposed for decoration. No bird."

"Where are the children?"

"At home."

"Did they see you get hurt?"

"No."

"Did anyone else see you trip?"

She hesitated before she lied again. "No."

"Who's with your children now?"

Martha was not a good liar. It took her too long to respond and when she did, she didn't look him in the eyes. Then she was off on one of her nonsense tangents. "I am not a charity case no matter what you know about Randall and me."

"Of course you aren't."

"It's like the spinach thing," she said.

"Spinach?"

"They tell women to eat spinach, eat spinach. There's iron in spinach. It's good for you. Get the kids to eat it, too. Strong blood. Women need strong blood. So we eat spinach, and then what do I read? There's something in spinach that keeps the body from absorbing the iron. All that spinach and no iron. All those fights with the kids over spinach and no iron.

None." She drew a flat line through the air. "Zero. Might as well give them cookies."

"I don't understand your point?" Dr. Schemp said.

"Spinach is just another lie," Martha said.

"What are the other lies?" Dr. Schemp rested his foot on the edge of a stool as he wrapped a device around her wrist, tightened it by adding air, and kept tending to her wounds as he tried to draw the truth out of her. "I know there are often good reasons why people lie."

A nurse walked into the room. "Suzie says it's as much of an emergency at home as it is here and she insists you come to the phone." The nurse paused. "Sounds like she's got a nasty cold."

"Oh yeah?" He seemed unsure of that.

"Hope she feels better soon." The nurse fingered the holly corsage pinned to her pale yellow shirt and eyed the doctor like she had something on her mind other than work.

Dr. Schemp folded his hands and looked down like he was trying to decide what to do. "Excuse me, please, Martha. Won't take but a minute."

As soon as they were gone, Martha said, "That nurse used to work at an abortion clinic. Greta told me. And her son doesn't talk to her since she left her husband."

"Don't you have some troubles of your own to sort out? Why focus on her?"

"Because that could be me. My children will hate me if something happens to Randall. People will cross the street to avoid me just like they avoid you."

"Thanks, Martha."

"Then what will I do?"

"A more important question is why are you lying about how you got hurt?"

"I don't want anyone to know I was at the house."

"Why not?"

"Because I want to go back there to get away from my own

house and if they find out I was there, they'll take my key away and I'll get into trouble with Julianna. Greta told me she can be a real witch."

"That's ridiculous," I said. "We have to say what happened to you and report those two punks."

"Guess someone already did," Martha said. "Hi Dwight."

"Heard you got roughed up."

"I tripped."

"Dr. Schemp indicated they're pretty bad injuries." Dwight took off his leather jacket, laid it on the bed, and then set his hat on top like he planned to stay for a while. "And you say you were at home and Trudy was there?"

"I'm right here, Dwight. You don't have to talk like I'm not in the room. And yeah, I was with her, but we weren't at her—"

"Trudy!" Martha interrupted.

"Something you're afraid to tell me?" Dwight asked Martha. "Something Trudy doesn't want you to say?"

"For crap's sake, Dwight! You suspect me of hurting Martha? You actually believe I could do something like this to Martha? So does the doctor!"

"Didn't say it, but there's been a lot of tension between you two."

"Martha!" I said. "Please for the love of your … of our friendship, tell Dwight why you're lying about where you were."

"Trudy didn't do this to me," she said. "I tripped."

"The injuries don't indicate merely tripping according to Dr. Schemp."

I got right in there and said, "She was at Lyle's house and two punks came in and were ransacking the place looking for …" I went blank, couldn't remember what they said they were looking for. I couldn't think straight. "I happened to stop by."

"Why didn't you report a break in and assault?" Dwight asked. "Seems you would have called that in, Trudy."

I felt like I was right back to the day Lyle died and Hunter-meister was asking me why I hadn't called him ASAP after realizing Lyle was dead. "I had Martha's needs on my mind and just wanted to get her here. There was so much blood from her head and she kept moaning about her wrist. I focused on her. I planned to call you and file a report."

"Julianna gave you explicit instructions not to go back there and you agreed."

"That's right," Martha said.

"So where were you and how did this happen?"

"I tripped," Martha said.

"Forget this," I said, and headed for the door.

"Trudy," Martha called after me.

34

I wandered the halls trying to ignore the pain in my knee. It was kind of quiet at early evening and not that busy. I figured I might as well sneak into an empty room and maybe lift an ace bandage from a cabinet and wrap my knee that was throbbing. I also needed to pee, so I snuck into an unoccupied hospital room and shut the bathroom door. I then realized I could prove Martha was out at Lyle's. Her car was still there. I wanted to hurry to tell Dwight that. As I was drying my hands, voices came into the room. I flipped off the bathroom light, waited a few minutes, then cracked the door open just enough to hear Greta say, "Why the cool distance?"

A male voice replied, "This is not the most appropriate time or place but I do need to talk to you." It was Dr. Schemp. He shut the door. I heard something getting dragged along the floor, a chair or a cart, and then it banged against the door. "There," he said. "That will ensure some privacy."

Through the crack in the bathroom door, I could see Greta and Dr. Schemp reflected in the framed artwork beside the bed where they stood. Greta ran her fingers along his tie. "Playing hard to get?" She snuggled up to him. "You want me to warm you up?"

"We need to talk," he said.

"So your message said. Brilliant move on my part to pretend I was Suzie with a bad cold calling you at work with an emergency. How else could I have returned your call? So now talk. I'm all ears." Greta kissed his neck. "All hands, too." She stroked his thigh. He stood and stepped away from the bed out of the glass reflection.

"Whoa. You look serious," Greta said.

"Just let me say what I have to say."

"But of course."

"This is for you."

"What's this? It's not Christmas yet." She held a box and ripped the ribbon and paper off. Then it was quiet for what seemed like way too long for someone who just opened a gift. "It's lovely. You know how I love copper and turquoise, but why is my key in here?"

"I made a mistake," he said.

"So my key shouldn't be in here?"

"And so I made a decision." His voice broke. "It's bad for us."

She pointed to him and then to herself. "Us? As in you and me, us?" Her voice sounded edgy at the point of breaking.

"My yellow lights of caution are on. I got far more involved with you than I had planned." He was back in the glass reflection, leaning toward her.

"Planned? How far *you* planned?"

"I can't risk losing my children. I can't have them and you, too."

"Have me? I'm not sure I understand."

"None of the alternatives appeals to me right now."

"I'm an alternative?"

"It's my problem," he said. "I don't see a way out of my marriage without devastating Suzie, and she'd use the children against me."

"It's just a ploy."

"No it's not. She'd leave town and take them with her."

I wanted Greta to ask him how he knew that. Had he actually approached divorce with Suzie? Maybe he was just making that up.

"So I guess this party is officially over. You are turning out the lights."

"You're not on stage. Please don't pretend with me. Tell me how you feel," he said.

"You made your decision. You declared me your problem."

"I want to know how you feel."

"So you can throw it at me?"

"I want to know."

"You promised we had a future together."

"It would break Suzie's heart. It's so complicated." He sounded weary.

"What about my heart?" The room got silent and he didn't answer. "I wish I'd never taken you back," she said. "Why didn't I trust my own instincts and stick to my guns after I dropped your ass the first time?"

"I'm sorry you feel that way."

"I thought you really loved me."

"I do love you. It's just not enough."

"Enough what?"

"To compensate."

"Used."

"I don't understand."

"I feel used. How's that? Good enough for you? Used. I'm the one who took the punishment for you and your pot scheme. Me."

"I think you were less used by me than you think. I think you pursued this and you did what I asked because it thrilled you, too."

"I pursued? Me?" Now she sounded really angry. "Who approached whom on this?"

"Why make it difficult by calling me at home?" he said. "Suzie's been suspicious ever since that night you called. Why did you do that?"

"Is your memory going?" she said. "You left a message telling me it was important. I was concerned, thought maybe you'd been found out. Maybe your runner supplied your name to some patient, revealed your prescription. I called you when you were supposed to be between rounds at the hospital and the clinic, because who can get through to you at the clinic or at that hospital? Your nosey nurse in heat for you is always screening your calls, checking your e-mail, protecting your sweet butt, leaving you a box of candy to brighten your day. I told you to get a phone just for us, but oh no."

"Lower your voice."

"How's this?" She leaned close to him. "So how am I supposed to find out what you wanted after that night but to call your cell which was—surprise, surprise—at your home sweet home at seven in the morning with your Suzie?"

"Greta. I don't know what else to say. I'm torn up inside."

"Sick of phone tag, I came up with the brilliant idea to pretend to be Suzie and call you here. And this is the thanks I get." She rattled the box. I thought of the Healthy Balls that headed straight for the back of Don's head. I felt suddenly dizzy and had to calm my breathing down.

"You've been very patient."

"That's me." She raised her voice. "So you tell me what I should have done with my worry for you? Some patient spilling the beans about your non-traditional medicine."

"That won't happen."

"And don't flatter yourself with the idea that I pursued you."

"We pursued each other," he said. "We just cannot continue. I feel guilty when I'm with you and sad when I'm not."

"Well I guess you got a whole load of sad coming your way."

"Our love is important. It's just not important enough."

"Don't talk trash. That doesn't mean a thing. I knew I shouldn't have taken you back. I knew it."

"So you said."

"I knew it." Her voice was mad and I could tell she was holding some fierce anger in check. I was really rooting for her to give it to him with both barrels.

"I'll always appreciate that you didn't incriminate me."

"And now, you don't even need me. It's all going to be legal. On the up and up."

"Still. I'll always appreciate what you did."

"Yeah. Aren't I the saint? Spread the word. Hey, you know the difference between God and a doctor?"

"Greta, please."

"God doesn't think he's a doctor." Her voice was on the edge of hysterical.

"I want you to know that underneath all this, I love you very much. I will forever."

"I wish I did not love you," she sounded so sad. I wanted her to get mad again, give it to him. But she walked to the door, shoved aside whatever was blocking it, flung the door open, and banged it against the wall. Then it got real quiet. I waited for Dr. Schemp to leave but I didn't hear his footsteps. Instead my phone rang, scared the bejesus out of me. I fumbled for it and hit *ignore* to shut the thing up even though it was from Chief Huntermeister and I needed to tell him about Martha's car. The bathroom door slowly opened and the harsh overhead light came on. I blinked in the glare.

There I stood with no reason to be and all the knowledge I could have ever wanted about the good doctor and his mistress. "Oh hey," I said. "I needed to relieve myself."

"Well, then," he said. "Don't let me interrupt you." He began to shut the door, stopped. "Ever consider how being such a person who would hide so she can eavesdrop on a personal conversation solidifies reasons why people are suspicious of you?"

"When you gotta go, you gotta go," I said. And then I couldn't help but smile remembering how Greta used my joke on him. "Also, it doesn't sound like you have much room to judge me."

He shut the door and left the room before I could tell him he was lucky he had Greta to take the fall for him. I knew how it felt to be the fall guy. I wondered how the good doctor would feel driving home to his high-maintenance wife waiting for him in their mini mansion on the edge of Sucker Creek Preserve.

When I got home, I had a burning need to tell someone about all that had come down that night. I dialed Don's cell, but he didn't answer. I called Iris because it was also about time I apologized for being so rude when she had stopped by. She was bound to accept my call by now. Wait till Iris heard what I had found out. Wow! The call went right to voice mail. "Call me, please. I'm sorry. Plus I have something very interesting to share." I dialed their landline because I really wanted to talk to her and maybe she just didn't have her cell phone nearby or charged or whatever.

Nathan answered and said, "She packed and left." His voice broke. "Took the boys and said she'd send for Cobber."

"Left?"

"For Cobbers Creek. Driving cross-country on these winter roads. I've been worried sick."

"When is she coming back?"

"She's not."

"Why didn't she tell me?"

"She stopped by to tell you but apparently you were rude, so she left."

"I didn't know."

"No. You wouldn't."

I didn't blame him for hating me. Iris. Gone.

35

That night, I opened the door to find Dwight and some official-looking man in an overcoat standing on my front porch. "Trudy," Dwight said. "I hate to say this but you're under arrest for—"

"Are you for real?"

"Suspicion of encouraging or assisting in the suicide of Lyle Staybler."

"Dwight?"

"Get your coat, Trudy," he said.

I grabbed my coat, grateful that Courtney was with Don for the night. My hands were shaking. This was not supposed to happen.

"Ma'am," the other man said. "Please hold out your hands."

"That's not necessary," Dwight said.

"Ma'am." He put those cuffs on me like he enjoyed it. He was the same man who had called me back for questioning at Lyle's house on that long ago summer day. He read me my rights. "You have the right to remain silent..."

I stopped listening and when he stopped talking, I said, "I want to call Joan."

"In due time," the man said.

"Dwight?"

"You'll be able to call her, Trudy."

"Does Julianna know you're arresting me?"

Dwight looked at the man and seemed to consider something of grave importance. He seemed worried. "No, she does not know," he said, sounding so flat, it gave me chills.

By the time we got to the station, my wrists were raw. I remember thinking maybe those cuffs wouldn't have caused me such misery if I still had all my cushion of fat protecting my bones.

I was finally allowed to make a call. I dialed Don's cell, wanted to give him a warning, tell him to try to keep the news from Courtney, maybe keep her out of school tomorrow. He didn't pick up, and I wasn't about to leave a message saying I was in jail.

The man wouldn't let me make another call until Dwight convinced him otherwise. I called Joan who came right to the station. Dwight led her to the room where I was being held.

"You want coffee?" he asked her.

"No. I want my client out of here. This is ridiculous. You have no new cause or reason to arrest her. The most ridiculous thing you've ever done."

"BCI doesn't think so."

"Handcuffs, Dwight? Really?"

Joan looked at my wrists. "Bring some ice to get this swelling down or I'll charge you both with brutality." Dwight went out.

I was grateful that she had enough anger for me and her both. Couldn't remember a time when anyone stuck up like that for me. I'd pay her ASAP with the Mickey Mouse fund. I asked her what happened that they'd come after me but she said we had to just wait until BCI came in and told us. She was making me nervous though when she'd lift her pen and write notes, her handwriting so sloppy I wondered how she could decipher any of it.

Dwight returned looking all growly, ice pack in hand. The guy who had cuffed me followed him. Dwight handed me the ice and sat down. Then the other guy got right to brass tacks. "Your client has been arrested on suspicion of encouraging or assisting in the suicide of Luce resident Mr. Lyle Staybler at his home on July 28th."

"Encouraging is not against the law." She clicked her pen and looked at Dwight. "Has bail been set?"

"Twenty thousand," the man answered.

"That's a bit high. Who's the judge?"

The man scanned the sheet.

"Parla," Dwight said.

Joan smiled. "My client does not warrant such an exorbitant bail; she would not be a threat to flee town and she does not have that kind of money."

"But…" I shut my mouth when she glared at me. I was so nervous I didn't care about anything except not having to spend a night in jail. What was this going to do to Courtney? And Don? I just wanted to get out of that place and help Joan build my case. I had $20,000 in a secret bank account thanks to Mickey Mouse. I was willing to withdraw it all if it would keep me from jail. After that, I swore on Lyle's scattered ashes, I'd focus and forget about everything that did not matter to my freedom, didn't even want that house and Lyle's fortune. I just wanted my good name back, a chance to prove I didn't do it. A chance to make things right with all the people I cared about. I thought of Iris fleeing Luce, driving winter roads with her boys in the car, stopping for the night at some motel to sleep before getting on the road again. How long did it take to drive to Virginia? I wanted an atlas. I wanted to talk to Iris. I wanted to know that she was safe. I wanted another chance to be kind when she stopped by that day. I almost started crying but I didn't want that guy in the suit to think he got to me.

"We want a lower bail set." Joan stood up and read from her notepad. "I also want to go on record, sir, as saying, it is deeply saddening that people face the threat of arrest and prosecution… should they assist people they love and cherish toward death. We need a law on assisted dying that's sensible, ethical, and forward thinking."

"Yes, ma'am," the guy in the suit said. "You can take that

up with the judge in a court of law. Right after we give him your reduced bail request."

She tugged at the hem of her suit jacket. "Indeed I will. It'd be much better for the state to have an assisted dying law with upfront safeguards."

"Sounds like you've had this lecture waiting to give and I'm the lucky guy," he said.

Joan scanned her pad and then looked back up and straight at the man. "If there were safeguards, then you could better spend your time investigating real criminals."

"Need to protect the vulnerable from people on the take," the man said. "It's criminal to help someone take their life."

"Ahhh but you see, a law that allows for assisted suicide would better protect potentially vulnerable people, end suffering, prevent those who respond compassionately to someone's request to end their pain from having to endure such lengthy and distressing investigations that you are putting my client through. Lyle Staybler was her friend."

"You grieving?" the man said to me.

"Now more than ever," I said.

Joan scowled at me. She did her job though, got the judge to reduce my bail to $10,000. I'd use my Mickey Mouse funds. I eagerly listened to the conditions of my bail, mostly I wasn't supposed to leave town. Big whoop de-do. I had to obey all common laws and stay away from Lyle Staybler's house. "And this time," Joan said as she drove my sorry butt home, "You had better stay away from that house and anyone associated with a lawsuit or a claim or whoever wants to see you in jail."

The Luce newspaper hit the stands two days later with the headline: *Luce Resident Trudy Pluth Arrested on Suspicion of Lyle Staybler's Death.* The article noted *Trudy Pluth was arrested on suspicion of encouraging or assisting the suicide of 86-year-old millionaire recluse Lyle Staybler recently diagnosed with terminal cancer and under hospice care. Luce Attorney Joan Wakefield claimed the innocence of her client and said she has been in touch with the group Death with Dignity, a pressure group that has been successful in overturning prosecution for those accused of assisted suicide and strengthening its argument for a change in the law.*

The accused claims to have found Mr. Staybler dead in his bed on 28 July when she stopped by to deliver his Meals-on-Wheels. Shortly after the incident, she was released from her volunteer duties pending investigation of the strange circumstances surrounding Mr. Staybler's death.

"Don't know why she was so anxious to deliver early that day," Bertha Hewitt, manager and cook for the charitable organization said. "Not supposed to say more about it."

Mr. Staybler had changed his will shortly before his death, leaving his entire estate valued upwards of ten million dollars to Trudy Pluth and his house to her Homes for Dwelling, a charitable organization that acquires and renovates homes for low-income residents.

Luce Police Chief Huntermeister had no comments, referring all questions to Thomas Gabrielson, Bureau of Criminal Investigation lead officer on the case. He could not be reached for comment at press time.

Lyle Staybler, a long-time resident of Luce, had no immediate family members at the time of his death. Mark Riepe, a distant relative said that his claim against the will should turn things around and once Mrs. Pluth is found guilty, he will be willing to help with the distribution of Mr. Staybler's wealth. "Family's got to help family," he said.

Julianna Mandle who represents Mr. Staybler's estate could not be reached for comment.

Bail was set at $10,000 and Mrs. Pluth remains free from jail awaiting trial.

Don stopped reading, looked at Courtney, and then me. "Nathan called to tell me there's also an article in the Fargo paper."

"Geeze. Don't they have any news of their own?"

"What a mess," he said.

"Joan will clean it up," I said.

"What a mess," he said again.

"Stop saying that!" I said.

"Where'd you get bail money?"

"I sold that Mickey Mouse toy. It was worth a small fortune."

He shut his eyes and shook his head. I realized Courtney was crying really hard, snot coming out of her nose that she wiped on her sleeve.

"You're going to jail!" she said.

"Honey—"

"This sucks!"

"You'll see. Joan will prove I didn't do it."

Courtney hiccupped and tried to catch her breath. She wiped her nose and then looked straight at me. "I hate you! I want to live with Dad."

"Courtney—" I moved toward her but she stepped away.

"It's all your fault. I hate you."

"Courtney, don't talk that way," Don said as she fell against his chest crying.

At that moment, I hated me, too.

36

What time is your father picking you up?" I asked Courtney. She ignored me. "I asked you a question." She
continued to stare at the computer. "Courtney!"

"What?" She turned and glared at me.

"Don't look at me like that. I asked when your father is
picking you up."

"Not soon enough."

Christmas was less than two weeks away and I had
hoped, before my arrest, to have gotten Don to move back
home by then. Instead, I was also losing Courtney who
had her bags packed and was ready to go. The only reason
she tolerated being in the kitchen with me was because she
needed cookies for the swim team party and I knew how
to make them.

"Whatever," I said.

"Six thirty," she said, finally leaving the computer and taking an interest in the cookies. She pressed cinnamon candies
in for eyes and buttons.

"You know you don't have to take all your things. I can
bring you anything you forget."

"Why should we have to sleep in that old apartment? It's
creepy."

"How creepy can it be?"

"It smells like mothballs and stuff. Makes me want to
hurl." She brushed her bangs out of her eyes. "Dad's gonna
turn it into a photography studio. Said it'd be real easy to do,
too, and I can help him, like be his assistant."

"Oh yeah?" Hearing about Don's enthusiasm for his hobby made me sad and I had to keep from blubbering. "Thought it was creepy."

"Won't be when Dad's done with it."

"We'll see."

"Allison and Justine said they're not talking to me because of you and they're not going to talk to anyone who does."

"Their loss," I said, thinking of their mothers doing the same thing to me. "Is Ericka still talking to you?"

"Yes."

"Then that's all you need, one true friend."

"I don't want you to go to jail," she said.

"I'm innocent, so I won't go to jail."

"Ericka's mother said innocent people go to jail."

"Why would she say that?"

Courtney shrugged. "Something her and Ericka's father were talking about."

"Were they talking about me?"

She shrugged again. "If you go to jail, me and Dad will have to live here without you."

"It won't happen," I put the greatest possible conviction I could into my voice. I pressed the cutter into the dough. "Let's talk about something else."

"Ericka's mom's giving her an iPod for Christmas."

"Oh yeah?"

"I put an iPod on my Christmas list."

"I thought you wanted a digital camera?" I slid a pan of cookies in the oven, set the timer.

"I do."

"Pretty expensive gifts you're asking for." My knee ached so I sat down, looked up at her, and wondered if I'd ever win my daughter back.

"If Dad was here, he'd say I'm worth way more than ten iPods put together."

"You cannot just have—"

"If you weren't so bossy, maybe he'd still live here. Why'd smelly Lyle Staybler have to die? It's his fault." Courtney slammed the spatula on the counter. "Ericka told me Justine's father never came back after he left." Courtney glared at me. I thought of Justine's mother, Darcy, flirting with Don at swim meets, calling the house for photos, snubbing me at the Mini-Mart. She must have been lonely, I reckoned. "Justine hardly ever sees him now. That's what's going to happen to me unless I live with Dad like forever."

"No, Courtney. It's not." I tucked a strand of hair behind her ear.

"I like staying at Ericka's house. Her mother and father do stuff like play Wii with us. They laugh a lot and her father says mushy stuff to her mother. They're not all uptight. Her mom told me I was the best houseguest ever."

"Me and your father have been talking," I said, feeling like I was losing my daughter to another mother, someone who laughed and sang. "We're going to try and—" The doorbell rang. Before I even finished washing my hands to answer it, Greta walked into the kitchen.

She dropped her jacket on the floor. Her too-large black sweatshirt declared *Wenches Want Me* across the front. "I let myself in," she said. "You should keep your doors locked." I didn't have a chance to remind Courtney to remember to lock the doors because Greta headed right for the cookies and bit the head off one.

"Hey!" Courtney protested.

"Where on earth did you get that shirt?" I asked.

She looked down at her chest. "Oh ha ha. It's a gag gift I bought for a friend who I'm not friends with anymore. So I thought, what the hey, might as well wear it myself." She bit the head off a cookie. I imagined Dr. Edward Schemp wearing that shirt in the privacy of Greta's bedroom. "I came to turn in my key to Lyle's house."

"You already turned it in," I said.

"Did I?" She broke off an arm. "Really? I thought I still had it."

"No."

"Oh maybe I've got that key mixed up with someone else's key."

"Maybe," I said. "None of us have keys anymore since Martha's accident."

"I'm really sorry about you being arrested. I know exactly how it feels."

"Greta..." I frowned and nodded toward Courtney. "Not now."

"Sorry kid," Greta said to Courtney. "Guess I'm cutting in on your time with Mom. I know how that feels, getting shoved aside." Greta poured milk into a glass. "My mom and I always made sugar cookies together when she was sober enough. Good for you two for upholding tradition." She snapped a gingerbread man in half.

"Hey!" Courtney said.

"That, my dear girl, is what I'd like to do to Edward Schemp." She lifted another one. "And this is Mrs. Edward Schemp."

"Hey. I have to take those for the swim team."

"Sorry."

"You're acting kind of weird," Courtney said. "Besides, I like Dr. Schemp."

"Do you have a boyfriend?" Greta asked. "Pretty girl like you must have." Greta stuffed her mouth full and smacked her lips. She reached across the counter, grabbed another cookie, and broke the head off. "Poor us, too. I miss ... well, I miss a lot of things." She was drunk. "And now Edward." She brushed crumbs from her mouth. "Do you think I'm high-maintenance?"

"Just like an old house," I said.

"That's so funny," Greta said. "Your mom's so funny." She gouged candy red eyes from a cookie.

"Stop busting the cookies," Courtney said.

"Sure, okay."

"You're not a good listener," Courtney said.

"What else am I?"

I leaned over and whispered, "You are drunk or stoned." I moved the cooling rack full of cookies to the other side of the kitchen.

Greta laughed. "Yeah so I—"

"Courtney, hand me the sprinkles," I interrupted.

Greta struck a match.

"Not supposed to play with fire," Courtney said.

"This kid's busting me all over the place. You're right, though, Courtney. I should not do that." She sat down. "Man I am parched." She reached for a glass but something caught on the back of Courtney's sweater.

"What the ...?" Courtney said.

"Don't move," I said to them. "Greta's bracelet's caught." I freed the clasp from Courtney's sweater.

Greta unfastened the bracelet. "Let me see your wrist." I held out my arm. "You really lost some serious weight, huh?" She kept fumbling with the clasp. "Man those cuffs Martha said they put on you really left a mark." I pulled my hand away but Greta grabbed it back. "Let's see if this fits you." She couldn't get the clasp closed. "Oh for the love of ... Courtney, see if you can do this."

After easily clasping it, Courtney said, "There. It's really pretty. You should wear jewelry, Mom." She sounded kind and forgiving. "Ask for some for Christmas."

Greta covered her eyes and started crying. Me and Courtney looked at each other. Then Greta started laughing.

"You're acting totally weird," Courtney said.

Don came in the kitchen. "Hey there."

"Finally," Courtney said.

"You ready to go?"

"Get me out of here," she said.

"Don!" Greta yelled. "You should forgive Trudy. She can't help it. Come home. She didn't do it. I'd bet my own life on her innocence."

What the bejesus was going on? Greta of all people coming to my defense.

I guided Don into the dining room. "She's stoned and drunk," I said. "Edward Schemp ended their affair."

"What affair?"

"Can you drive her home?"

"What's this? The very woman you cussed me for dancing with, you want me to drive home?" Don shook his head.

"Okay. Let it go. How many times do you want me to say 'I'm sorry'? Just take her home."

"Let her sleep it off here."

"Here?" I said, the idea sounding ridiculous.

"I told Courtney I'd take her to the movie and it's starting in ten minutes. That's what I'm going to do."

They left and I was stuck with Greta.

I built a fire. We sat on the couch watching it. Greta smoked a joint. She handed it to me but I just held it. "Really, Trudy." Greta released smoke. "Never smoked before?"

I thought what the heck. What could happen? Arrested for smoking pot in my own home. Not likely. I took a drag and held the harsh smoke in for as long as I could before coughing. "It's not legal yet, you know?" I felt myself relaxing.

"Close enough to being so." Greta said. "Even Lois." She smirked then gestured to button her lip.

"What?" I nudged her with my elbow. "Tell me."

"Lois thinks it should be legal, too."

"For Lyle?"

"For anyone in need. A real angel of mercy."

"Get out," I said, wondering if it was her high or the truth that had her tongue wagging. "Maybe deep down Lois even believes assisted suicide should be legal. That's how Joan feels."

"No kidding?" Greta said. "You know you can tell me. I won't tell anyone. Did you help him die?"

"I'm not supposed to talk about it."

"Oh yeah. That's cool. So let's talk about me. I've got this new way of thinking. I'm going to try to focus on logic over emotion. Now that she's sober, my mother tells me to try that." She took a drag, handed it to me. I took a deep drag, held the smoke in and then let it out. "And I'm practicing celibacy." Greta's words were spreading in my ears; the syllables were long and kind of rubbery, and the room was huge. The flames in the fireplace seemed really long and slow. Then I noticed the Christmas music from the radio should've been faster. Fa La La La La wasn't moving along. I was on the last La and it still sounded like Fa. So I sang "Fa Fa Fa Fa …"

"Girl, what are you doing?"

I laughed and so did Greta. We leaned into each other and laughed until I snorted, which made us laugh harder. "Look at the fire," I said. "It's still burning." We found that incredibly funny and laughed until our sides hurt.

She grimaced and held her cheek. "Damn."

"What's wrong?"

"Went to the dentist yesterday. My tooth feels kind of weird."

"Maybe you should get it checked out."

"Never going back to Percola. Pervert. I know a slick move when I feel it. Dragging his fingertips along that paper bib covering my chest. Cheap feel. Jack hole."

"Slimeball." We cracked up. The mantle clock chimed. It seemed to take hours to get to eight.

"You used to call me Felon," she said.

I looked at her, wondering how to make amends. "Sorry."

"Sometimes it matters what other people say."

"Speaking of other people. I think Dwight is secretly seeing Wanda Laconda."

"Ewwww," Greta laughed. "No way!" She pretended to shiver. "That woman reminds me of a jittery squirrel."

"I see her hanging around after him."

"Let's get something to eat," Greta said. "And I'll tell you about my secret: Edward."

"Let's," I said. "I'd like some of Iris's fish chowder right this very minute and some of that ginger beer punch." I felt weepy. "It's all my fault she left."

"It's Virginia's fault," Greta said. "Never trust a state with a female name." I looked at her and thought what the heck does that mean? But then she laughed and snorted so hard, I laughed too. Then she grabbed my hand and got real serious. "I miss Iris, too."

"She didn't even take Cobber," I said. "She loves that dog."

We were quiet.

"I think Nathan is really sexy," Greta said.

"Hands off," I said and then we laughed really hard.

Greta made herself stop laughing by putting her hand over her mouth. "You know there are two things to be careful of with this stuff." She held up two fingers. "The first. You get really, really hungry."

"Like now," I said.

"The second is. You get horny." Greta looked at me and waited.

"Not with me you don't," I said. "Hey. I just remembered something. Me and Don got in a fight over you."

"Me?" She touched her breastbone. "Me?"

"You danced with him." I sat up straight.

"Ah, you saw that photo. That's why you two separated?"

"Don't flatter yourself."

"He just happened to be in the right place at the right time."

"You mean wrong place?" I said.

"What did I say?"

"About what?" I said. We looked at each other and laughed.

"Oh. No. Wait. I know." Greta took the joint. "He danced with me because he felt sorry for me. But wait. Wait. Let me back up. Give you the story in the right order. I was a fool on a barstool at the Cactus Corral. The hospital party was going on and I was hoping lover boy Edward would come out and sit with me."

"Officially: Your Lover Boy?"

"Well, yes," she said. "Fool that I am. I actually thought he'd brave it, leave his little Suzie to sit alone for a moment and at least come to the bar and say hi. He didn't, but Don walked in. He seemed really edgy, not his usual affable self. He sat next to me, maybe to make me look less pathetic. *How is it, Don, that you never left Luce?* I asked. I mean I remember when his parents died, how sad he always was when I'd see him around town, but still he could've ditched the grief for a different place to live. He just said obligations over dreams. When he said he used to think he could be a photographer with his own studio, I told him he was still young and he should go for it."

"Great advice, Greta. Absolutely great."

My sarcasm didn't stop her from talking more about him. "So then I asked Don to dance with me. He's so thoughtful and Edward was missing in action."

"Hey." I put my arm around Greta. "Don't cry. "

"Honestly," she said. "That's all." She pulled her cell phone from her pocket. "Call Don and tell him he must come home this minute. It was all a mistake."

"It's about more than that. I took him for granted."

"It happens. Hey!" Greta said. "Look, a text message. She hit a button on her phone. "Oh no. Look what he's done." She showed me the message: :{ :.(

"Doesn't look happy, that's for sure."

"He misses me." Greta punched a button and another.

"Are you deleting it?" I asked.

"I should reply. Let Edward know I'm okay. Maybe he's worried about me."

I put the phone on the table. "Don't do it."

"But he misses me," she said.

"He's not worth a penny nail," I said. "For your own sake. Do not call him. I wasn't going to tell you this, but I heard him break up with you."

"You're too funny."

"I was in the bathroom of that hospital room when you two walked in and barricaded the door."

"Get out!"

"Got trapped in there. Heard it all. I know where this came from." I lifted my hand and she rubbed the bracelet. "Seriously, Greta. He misses how you make him feel good and grow his pot."

"You heard that, too, about his medicinal crop. Please don't tell anyone! I don't want him to go to jail." And did that ever open up a floodgate. I never thought a person could cry so much. In between all the crying she told me how she grew marijuana in her greenhouse for the good doctor to prescribe through some dealer directly to his terminally ill patients. Now that the state had approved medicinal marijuana, what did he need her for?

"He said that?"

"No, but what the hey. It's probably true."

"Who was the dealer?" I asked.

She shrugged. "I don't want to get anyone into trouble."

"Lois?" I asked.

"Just for her patients. Not for everyone. Edward wouldn't tell me who the main dealer was."

"No kidding," I said. I had a new respect for Lois, hiding Lyle's stash in that fancy porcelain gravy boat, sitting there trying to keep her composure when Dwight lifted it and asked me about the weed.

"It's top quality. I babied those plants."

"So what is it about Eddie that mesmerizes you?"

"Oh no. Do not ever call him Eddie or Ed, always Edward.

Course my pet name for him was Mr. Tambourine Man because his hands could play me like music."

I plugged my ears. "Stop. Too much information."

"The sex was stupendous," she said. "We're talking fall-off-the-bed sex. I miss it ... I mean him. I love him."

"Sure you do."

"The last night I was with him, I thought we'd make it." She sat straight up and took my hand. "Trudy. I forgot to tell you. Julianna was in Lyle's house with an antiques dealer."

"Why would she tell you?"

"She wouldn't. She disdains me."

"Why?"

"Because she believes the rumor that I'm having an affair with Judge Parla. She said so to my face, sticking up for his wife who's in her circle of friends. Haven't you heard that one about me?"

I shook my head. "Are you?"

She gave me the funniest look. "Hello. I'm not Wonder Woman. One affair at a time is all I can handle. Besides the judge isn't my type, though he was once engaged to Julianna. The first one she jilted. Along the same lines, have you heard this rumor about me? I posed naked for Jon Drahmann in his studio over Cleone's Gift Shop."

"Get out!"

"Indeed, but not true. Though I would if he ever asked to paint me."

My life seemed to suddenly pale in comparison to Greta's pursuits.

"Hey," I said, "We're off track. How do you know Julianna was at Lyle's with an antiques dealer?"

"Edward and I had some of our stash hidden in Lyle's cellar. Edward helped me get it out of there. That's why he was with me the night you fell. We went to get it but found you on the floor with your busted knee. We had to go back later that night." She looked pensive for a moment, frowned. "I wondered why he was so hot to trot to get it out of there and now I know. He wanted it before he broke up with me. Or wait, did he break up with me because it's going to be legal?"

She got real quiet until I nudged her with my elbow. "He said it was because he was afraid he'd lose his kids."

"Oh right. Right. His children."

"So how do you know about Julianna at Lyle's?"

"We went to the cellar, but the stash wasn't in the coal bin. Someone stole it. So we got out of there fast. Edward was seething because that was the last of it. He said he needed a drink but was on call so he couldn't imbibe. He settled for a cup of coffee at the Mini-Mart. I waited for him in my car parked in the dark near Lyle's woods. I was sitting there when Julianna pulled up to the house; a man and a woman got out with her. They all went inside. The woman came back out and I recognized her. She operates an estate auction business. She's got her name and face plastered all over the place. I waited for Edward who slinked over in the dark. I dropped him off at his car parked on the other side of the Highway 10 overpass. He tried to convince me to go back and search for the stash and put it in a storage unit. I said no way I was going to do that after I was the one who got busted for him once before. Not going to happen a second time. No sir."

"That's right Buster," I said. She laughed so hard this time she snorted and so I laughed too. "So, who was the guy?"

"The guy?"

"You said it was Julianna, a man, and the antiques dealer."

"Oh, yeah, Trudy." She grabbed my arm. "I almost forgot to say. It was Dwight."

37

I wanted to know exactly why Julianna had gone into my house with an antiques dealer and Dwight. A note on the front of her office door said: *Closed.*

I drove out to Tom's and banged on his front door, which he eventually opened and told me to stop with the racket. He looked like death warmed over with an oxygen tank beside him, the tubes at the base of his nostrils. "Tom." I didn't know what else to say.

"Sorry you got arrested," he said. "Shouldn't have happened."

"I got out so I'm—"

"Tom," a female voice said. "I told you to..." Lois Urho stared at me.

"Oh no," I said. "Not you." Lois in the house meant he was closer to the end.

"Not me? What a thing to say."

"I didn't mean ... it's just ... Didn't come out right," I said. "Just surprised to see you here." I sniffed the air for marijuana.

"Oh." She raised an eyebrow like I was up to something fishy. "Hiding something?"

I wanted to check Tom's shed but had enough sense to understand I shouldn't burden him with it. "Can I talk to Julianna?"

"She's out of town," Tom said. "Run off with the Chief."

"Now, Tom," Lois said, "You don't know that for certain."

He was coughing and trying to yank the oxygen tube away. "Sure I do. I can read my girl like a book and she has it bad for the Chief."

"I'll just catch up with Julianna when she gets home." I left quick and got in my car.

My phone rang and the man identified himself as Jerry Wanderi. "Not supposed to talk to you," I said.

"Then it's in your best interest to listen. Not able to reach anyone else connected to Staybler's house. "

"Call Joan Wakefield with your nonsense."

"Not nonsense," he said. "I got some of your things, thought you'd be interested in getting them back."

"You stole from the house?" I said.

"Not me," he said. "You got some thieves coming and going."

"Did you call Huntermeister?"

"He's out of town." Well, well, I thought, Tom was probably right about Julianna and him. But what did *run off with* mean?

"Then how about some other cop?"

"They're on their way but I thought you'd want to know someone's inside the place."

I didn't trust him but I had a burning need to see for myself. Besides, I didn't have anything to charge Jerry with other than being a pain in the butt and stealing wood.

I pulled up to the Mini-Mart to see two police cars parked in Lyle's front yard. One car had its back doors open. I was trying to be more logical and less emotional and figured I shouldn't go into the house. Jerry stood by the wood stacked outside his store. "What's going on?" I said.

"They filled a garbage bag with silver and coins," he said. "I found it in my shed." He knocked snow from his tennis shoes. "Nunda was supposed to shovel this walk," he said. "That girl's getting fired. Plenty others could use a job. Customers complain. They come into the store and no one's here. Then she comes rushing in from somewhere. If it's not that, she talks on her cell when she's ringing up customers. She's over there. The police are inside."

Another cop car drove into Lyle's front yard. A county sheriff had some skinny kid with him. He pulled him along by his collar. It was the pizza delivery boy. His hair tinted yellow and orange. Then I had a shiver-down-the-spine sense that he was one of the punks who hurt Martha.

Lyle's front door opened. The cops led two people out and down to the cop car. I recognized Mark Riepe's son, short and stocky. He got close to the pizza delivery boy and said, "Krueger, I'm gonna flatten you."

"Freakin' snitch," the girl yelled. It was Nunda.

"Screw you both," Tony said. "Your old man too, Arnold."

The boy tried to break free but the cop held onto him. "Pussy," he yelled at Tony.

Two days later, me and Leon Hopper sat in Joan Wakefield's office. "I understand your client wants us to believe he didn't put his son up to this," Joan said. "Evidence and the kids' statements indicate otherwise."

"You can't prove Mark was involved," Leon said.

"He'd leave his boy hung out to dry for him?" Joan said.

"The boy just thought he was helping his father get what he deserved."

Joan smiled. "I guess he did at that. Doesn't explain the garbage bag full of marijuana though, does it?"

"Mark Riepe may be a lot of things, but he's not a criminal and he doesn't know nothing about the dope," Leon said.

"Maybe you should look at your client's case a bit more realistically and talk some sense into him. The way I see it, the will still holds up in the court of law. Probate ends. He can drag this on and continue to cause trouble, though why he'd want his legal debt to continue accumulating while he fights a losing battle is beyond me." She paused and looked at him intensely. "You know he has no case. You should be ashamed of yourself for leading him on to believe he did in the first place."

"It's my job to help guys like Mark."

"Taking advantage is more like it. Just cut the case free. If he wants to continue his pursuit, he most certainly can. In the meantime, his kid's in Juvy for vandalism, terrorizing, and theft of property. Charges are being considered in other incidents as well. You think Mark wants you to represent his losing case for the Staybler estate or to save his kid's hide from all that's coming?"

"Our rightful ownership case relies on who murdered Lyle Staybler. Trudy had the most reason." He nodded toward me.

"Leon," Joan said. "If you had any decency, you'd apply whatever Mark paid you to defend his kid."

Three days later Joan called me back to her office for a meeting with Leon and Mark. It was supposed to be simple enough with Mark agreeing to remove his contesting of the will.

"Maybe I ain't so sure about changing my mind," Mark said.

Joan leaned forward and stared at him. "You're in trouble. Nunda and the Krueger boy are willing to tell even more than they already have."

"Who's going to believe those delinquents over me? Don't worry me squat over them."

"No? Well let me tell you something. You ought to be thinking more about your boy than whether or not those kids you got to do your dirty work worry you."

Mark hit her desk. "This is crazy stuff, man."

"No, what is crazy stuff is that you still believe you have a case. Let's drop this idea that you contesting the will is going to make you wealthy. Deal with what's important."

"That land belongs to the family."

"Face it, Mark, you are not family to Lyle."

"My grandmother... "

"And her illegitimate daughter from another man shacked up with Rufus Staybler for a couple of years. I know all about the connection. I like to do research. That makes her familiar but not family. And speaking about things that grow … the kids are claiming you told them to hold onto your garbage sack of weed until you had a chance to sell it."

"I don't know nothing about where they got that dope and you can't no way pin it on me."

"How about your boy?"

"How about him?"

"Think he needs possession on top of all these charges? Maybe the judge might be interested in giving him a break."

"Why'd he do that?"

"Favors."

I left that meeting not knowing what to think, and I felt kind of bad knowing that was Greta's stash those kids got busted with but I kept my mouth shut because, like Martha's god, the law works in mysterious ways. Sure enough the next time Joan called was to say she got Mark to drop his claim against the estate. Seems community service for the juveniles might also do them some good. When I told Greta about where her bag of marijuana ended up, she said. "They only had one bag? Where's the other one?"

I wasn't about to go into Lyle's looking for it.

38

Christmas arrived with all the doom and gloom of a funeral around me. I was still sweating out charges and awaiting a preliminary hearing to determine a trial. I focused on trying to lift people's spirits for a Christmas Eve get together at my house. It took most of my former pushy self to get them all to come. Martha wanted to stay home and cry because—as she said during a low point—"life sucked." Greta wanted to stay home and cry because she had a hole in her heart. Nathan wanted to wallow in his loneliness misery. Courtney was mad at Don who wouldn't let her stay out past nine on school nights. And Poor Randall, recently released from the psych ward, was a shell of himself. I didn't think we all needed to give up the ghost on Christmas Eve, so I put myself in charge and figured I'd let the cards fall where they may once they all arrived. The only people who seemed to have Christmas cheer were Julianna and Dwight, having returned after eloping to California. Course, Tom's declining health put a mark of sadness on their lives, too.

So there we were all under one roof. Like the patient person she still was, Martha sat with Randall staring at the Christmas tree. They were facing foreclosure and who knew what all else was beneath the bomb he dropped on their lives. Martha said his psychiatrist reported giant improvements. From my view, it looked more like baby steps, but I just lied and said it sure seemed that way to me, too.

Courtney and Greta opened cans of Play-Doh and made sculptures with Martha's kids. "No, don't put it in your mouth." Greta made a strange face and Grace laughed.

"I miss Marcus and Curtis," Ruthie said.

"We all do, Honey," I said, feeling the vibes of Nathan's deep sadness. He got up, stoked the fire, added another log, and settled back in his seat. Cobber stayed close beside him. Not one day went by that I did not miss Iris and feel ashamed for not being more attentive to her fears.

In the dining room, Julianna spread the green tablecloth out. While she smoothed it with her hand, Dwight set two bottles of champagne on the table. "To toast to love," she said.

"And the hot pursuit of happiness." Dwight stood behind her, put his arms around her waist, and rested his chin on her shoulder.

I never thought I'd see two people more in heat for each other than Nathan and Iris had been. But there they stood all warm and fuzzy, practically glowing and tripping the lights fantastic. Just goes to prove I should never assume anything; it wasn't my case that brought them together. It had been his need for a restraining order against Wanda Laconda who'd been stalking him. Julianna and Judge Parla got Wanda to understand that if she didn't want to face court again—she had a pattern of misbehavior—she had to agree to stop sending him love letters, stop calling him, and stop sitting in front of his house. She had to relinquish her police scanner and promise not to follow Dwight on calls.

"So why all the secrecy about you and Julianna," I asked.

"If Wanda had seen us together, she would've menaced Julianna."

"Why elope?"

"Didn't want to risk being number three left at the altar," he said and then laughed.

"Dwight, honestly," Julianna said.

"Plus, it's enlivening to have a love secret. Living in this town all our lives, we wanted to see if we could stay below the radar."

"Wish I would've stayed below radar," I said too quickly.

"Oh?" He gave me a suspicious look.

"I mean … you know what I mean. Just the two of you in on a secret."

Julianna then called me back to the present moment of Christmas Eve. "Where do you keep your champagne flutes?" she asked.

I laughed. "Will a nice set of jelly jars do?"

"Sounds good." I thought she was messing with me that she'd actually drink expensive champagne out of a jelly jar. But darn if she didn't put them on the table. You have to be ready for the way people surprise you in a good way. Like finding out the reason Julianna and Dwight were in Lyle's house with an estate dealer. Tom wanted the player piano appraised after Lois expressed interest in it. She was afraid to come directly to me because she figured I held a grudge against her. As personal representative, Tom had a say in things. So what the hey? If that old piano floated her boat, let her have at it.

Dwight finished setting the table and then helped Tom to an overstuffed chair next to Randall. Julianna wrapped a woolen throw around Tom's shoulders.

"Don't make a fuss," he said. "I'm not dead yet."

Randall actually smiled at that. "Here. Here," he said.

"You're looking better," Julianna said.

"Sure," Randall said. "Sure why not?"

Over in the corner of the living room, Nathan sat like a lost puppy even though Cobber stayed close by his side. The group's goal was to get Nathan on a plane bound for Iris. Cross the Mississippi and fight for the woman he loved. Love. What a roller coaster.

We soon sat down for the feast of turkey, mashed potatoes with gravy, green beans, lefse, wild rice hotdish, cranberry relish, and a whole lot more. "Randall, mind carving the bird?" I handed him the knife and fork. He looked confused, then grinned, and stood over the bird. He hacked more than he actually carved. It took every ounce of my will not to step in and take over. But he managed. Sometimes that's the best anyone can do. Manage.

After dinner, Dwight popped the champagne. "For all the reasons to celebrate," Julianna said. Dwight kissed her. Don poured non-alcoholic champagne into Randall's and the children's glasses.

"Come on, Dad," Courtney protested. "It's Christmas. Let me have the real stuff." He honored her request by pouring a few ounces in her glass. "Better than nothing," she said.

We held our jelly glasses up for a toast. "To what?" Julianna asked.

I'd gotten better at realizing people's emotions and I noticed that Nathan was looking sadder as the evening progressed. "Well, how about Happy Holidays and Merry Christmas to those near and far," I said.

"To there's no man like a snowman," Greta said.

"Okay, enough," Don said. "Let's drink."

Then we gave Nathan his gift: a voucher for a plane ticket to Virginia. He looked stunned like the thought of actually getting off his duff and doing something about his loss had never crossed his mind. "But she ..."

"Go win her back!" Martha said.

"I'll take care of Cobber while you're gone," Greta offered.

"My father also has a present to give," Julianna said. "Go ahead, Dad. You're on."

Tom removed the oxygen from his nostrils and slid the tube to his chin. He sniffed and cleared phlegm from his throat. He pinched the bridge of his nose beneath his glasses. "You know I got a neighborly way about me. Most folks don't think so, but I do." Tom blew his nose. "Old Lyle never thought his plan would..." he stopped and looked around the table. "Heck we all used to be under Lake Agassiz. I got the land it left behind. A glacial lakebed's a darn good place to be. My wife's buried in it. I'll be joining her soon." Never hurry a dying man, but Tom seemed to weaken as he talked.

"After all those years of hard feelings, Lyle got to be a friend before I…" He stopped and waved like he couldn't talk anymore.

Julianna said, "My father is leaving his house to Homes for Dwelling."

"But you should have your parents' house," I said in all honesty.

"Dwight and I plan to retire to California."

"Get out!" I said.

"We can get lost in a crowd there," Dwight said.

"The land will go to the Natural Conservancy to remain protected as Dad requested. The house is to go to Homes for Dwelling. This is all in the initial planning stage, but my father wanted to be the one to tell you."

"Thank you." I felt like I'd start blubbering if I tried to say more.

"More news is coming," Tom said. We all waited for him to reveal something else. He pointed at me. "That bump on your head all gone?"

"What?"

"On your head when you fell?"

"No it was her knee that got busted up," Don said.

"Yeah, it was my knee," I said, "My knee, Tom."

"Don't look so worried, Trudy," Julianna said. "The transfer of ownership will go smoothly." Maybe she emphasized that because she knew I had jitters over my upcoming preliminary hearing and maybe a felon couldn't own anything.

Nathan's phone rang. We all stared at it ringing on the table. He smiled and connected the call. "Merry Christmas, Iris."

Greta yelled out. "Iris, girlfriend. We love you!"

"Iris. Merry Christmas!" I yelled. "We miss you, sister."

"Randall, it's Iris," Martha said.

"Why isn't she here?" he asked.

"She's in Virginia," Martha said. He nodded. I got a sense Martha had to repeat herself a lot those days, even more than usual. He was a shell of the man he used to be but maybe his core was filling up with stronger stuff than it formerly held.

Though I wanted Nathan to stay at the table and talk so we could all hear, I understood why he left and disappeared into another room. It all rested on his shoulders to woo her back.

I suggested we clear away the dishes, but Greta said, "That can wait. This is a perfect night for winter bubbles. Got the idea from Pinterest."

We bundled up and then traipsed out the door, along the sidewalk Don had shoveled out for me that morning. It was mild, in the high 20s with just a breeze. The back yard patio light illuminated us. Martha blew bubbles. They froze, landed on the snow, and rolled until they popped. Courtney blew bubbles. One landed in Don's beard.

Martha held the wand for Grace and said, "Blow." Bubbles floated above Michael and Ruthie's heads until they froze, fell to the snow, and bounced.

"You do it, Dad," Michael said. "Dad. Try it." I had not ever before heard Michael sound so happy. Randall dipped the wand into the bottle. He blew bubbles.

Ruthie said, "Close your eyes and make a wish before the last one pops. That's what I do."

Nathan came outside, scooped Grace from Martha's arms, and twirled her around. "I've booked a flight to Iris."

39

Three days later, Joan called to tell me the preliminary hearing date was set for the next week. "It's to determine if the prosecutor has enough substantial evidence that you committed the crime," she said.

"Did they find something to stick on me?" I asked.

"As far as I know they only have circumstantial evidence, a lot of hear-say and speculation," Joan said. "First you'll be arraigned. You'll plead not guilty."

"But I'm not guilty," I said.

"And that's what I'm going to argue if it goes to trial," she said.

"You just said it was going to trial."

"I said ... really Trudy you need to learn to listen ... I said 'preliminary hearing.' They'll have to show just enough evidence and testimony for probability."

"What will we present?"

"Not a thing. There's no chance of getting the charges against you dropped, so our plan is to see if the judge finds sufficient evidence to try you. If there is no convincing evidence, the judge can dismiss it."

"Will I have to testify? Take an oath to tell the truth, the whole truth?"

"Does the idea of that worry you?"

"Could I go to jail after this hearing?"

"No. It's a hearing, not a trial. You're out on bail. Remember?"

"Every morning I wake up, I tell myself that." I hung up and could hardly breathe, seeing myself standing in front of a judge, maybe someone who had already determined my guilt because of all the rumors. It wasn't supposed to come to this. I paced my kitchen and felt like if I didn't talk to someone, I'd go insane. All these months of worry, trying to keep the story straight in my head, not doubt myself.

I called Don, needed to tell him I might be in bigger trouble than I'd ever believed possible. I wanted to say I was sorry for dragging him and Courtney down. His phone rang and rang. I was just about to hang up, didn't feel like leaving a message, was tired and sorry. No one could be more sorry and worried than I was. "Hello," he said. I couldn't talk, just couldn't say even one word for how much fear stuck in my throat. "Hello?"

"Don."

"Trudy? What's wrong?"

"I didn't think it would come to this," I said. I did not want to give in to the tears trying to come. But I did want Don's compassion, maybe even wanted him to pity me if that would move him to care. I used to hate anyone to pity me. At that point, I wanted it from Don. If he could pity me, maybe he could love me again.

"Talk to me, Trudy."

"You know how you once told me I had the bad habit of looking at people like they were projects in need of repair?"

"Must have been during one of our heated fights."

"Yeah." I wished he were in the room so I could look at his handsome face that I never fully appreciated because it drew other women to him. "You were right," I said, then took a deep breath to keep my voice from breaking. "It occurred to me one day that maybe Lyle saw me as a project in need of his help. Maybe I was his charity case. All that time I was bringing him my charity and he was actually seeing that I needed something." I wasn't sure I was making sense. I just wanted Don to understand that I changed. "I guess what I'm saying is that I was the biggest mess in the room. Other people—even a dying man—saw it, but I didn't realize it until the night you moved out."

"I appreciate you telling me all this," Don said. "We'll get through the preliminary hearing and take it from there."

"I have a meeting with Joan tomorrow." I wanted him to say he'd go with me. I wanted him to say he'd come over. I wanted his physical comfort. He didn't offer any of those things and I wasn't about to ask, for fear he'd say no. I couldn't take any more rejection.

The next day there was good news, sad news, and salvation news. Made me feel like I was on a path to some other land. I hadn't slept well, had the jitters, and could hardly drink my coffee that morning; but I needed to drink it to help me be alert for my meeting with Joan. My phone rang and when I saw it was Iris, I thought maybe I was still asleep and dreaming. How many times had I wanted her to call me back? Wasn't that typical? Stop wishing and the thing you wanted appeared out of nowhere. My heart skipped ten beats ahead and then settled down when I heard her beautiful voice. "Nathan's visiting," she said.

"I know," I said.

"Just have one question for you?"

"Shoot."

"Those windows still waiting for us at Pugmeyer's?"

"Need two people for the removal work."

"I'll keep your offer to help in mind," she said. "Gotta go. Auntie, Nathan, the boys and I are heading to Sugar Nymph's for breakfast."

I had no sooner hung up and was flying high when my phone rang again to bring me back to reality and Joan. I figured I was in more trouble when I heard her say, "Julianna and her father want us to come out there right now."

"Did she say why?" I was really anxious.

"Could have something to do with his role as personal

representative of Lyle's estate or his own. He's not doing well, so perhaps he wants to square something about his estate."

I was locking up the house when Don pulled into the driveway. "Thought I'd go with you to your meeting."

"Need to go to Tom's first. Something urgent. Will you come with me?" I waited. Then joked, "You'd get to see Julianna."

When we arrived, Dwight answered the door. Took me by complete surprise when he said, "Tom's in bad shape."

His words sent me right back to Lyle's house, sitting there with him, knowing his days were numbered, wishing he didn't have to suffer. I walked into the room where Tom lay in bed struggling to breathe with the help of oxygen. Julianna held his hand and he nodded at me.

I nodded my understanding.

"Good. Now it's time, Trudy," he said.

Joan and Dwight stood near Don in the doorway.

Tom tried to speak again, "You need…"

"It's okay, Dad. You don't have to say anything."

"Yes, Julianna, I do." He pointed to a wooden trunk near the bed. "Open that." He watched her lift the lid. "Take out that green box." She removed something the size of a shoebox. "Inside there's a box with a ring. Lyle wanted you to have it."

She held up a small gold band with a diamond chip. "It's beautiful. But why would Lyle want me to have this?"

"The ring," Tom said. "I got it before Lyle died. I finally found it before Lyle died."

There was the salvation of my soul.

"I don't understand," Julianna said.

"It was your mother's."

She examined the ring. "It's engraved *LS & IF*."

"Took some time, but I finally found it for you. In his room right before I helped him die."

Julianna looked stricken. Everyone looked surprised. I kept my focus on Tom, stayed level, and took deep breaths. My head was spinning.

"I did a favor," he said. "He didn't die alone. I was there. Ida will know. I was there."

Dwight stood next to Julianna who was clearly shaken by her father's confession.

"Trudy. I'm sorry you got hurt," he said.

"Tom," Dwight said. "Are you saying you were the one in the room who pushed Trudy?"

"I was." He pointed to his bedside table. "Open that drawer."

Dwight slid the drawer out. "What am I looking for?"

"There's the other part of the note. Right on top. See it?"

Dwight read, "*to the grocery store. What kind of ice cream do you want next?*

"It's the rest of my note," I said.

"I didn't hurt him," Tom said. "Lyle told me where his medicines were. I crushed them all up, put them in the ice cream. He ate it. And then he was gone."

"Dad—" Julianna was crying really hard. "Dad, you helped him kill himself!"

"I'm tired now," he said.

We all left the room so she could be alone with her father. Downstairs, Don took my arm and turned me around. He hugged me. "You're going to be okay now," he said. "I am so relieved." He hugged me harder.

"Now do you believe I didn't do it?"

"What kind of a question is that?" he said.

"A good one. Now you know," I said.

"Never thought otherwise."

That night I lay in bed thinking about things, how different it was all going to be now that my head was off the chopping block. I thought about the bump on my head and how hard it is to inflict pain and how killing oneself or helping someone die is not the easy way out; it's just not easy either way.

All charges were dropped against me. I wasn't about to

spread the word about Tom Mandle, but it didn't take long and people were trying to dig up the dirt on a love triangle grudge carried on for decades. Those of us who knew Tom knew there was no grudge about it. Whatever ill will Lyle and Tom had at one time was mended when one friend made sure the other friend did not die alone.

40

I pulled into my driveway one evening happy to see Don's new van parked in back. I had used my returned bail money to buy it and was relieved when he accepted my peace offering. He'd been stopping by unannounced more often since Tom died. After my name got cleared, Courtney moved back home. When I walked into the kitchen, I found her and Don hunched over the table, a stool on top of the counter. Courtney was drawing. "Hey," Don said. "Come see Courtney's new talent."

His photographs were spread out on the table. Courtney looked up at the stool, then down to her paper, up at the stool, then down to her paper. "I'm looking at negative spaces," she said.

Don pulled a chair out for me. "Want to try?" he asked.

I shrugged. "Sure." This maneuvering back to a kindness between us scared me. Change is slow as molasses and thick, too. But it's also possible.

I'd just been to the Pugmeyer place to get the stained glass windows with Iris, who not only made her home in Luce again with Nathan and the boys, but owned land in Cobbers Creek where the four of them—five counting Cobber—would spend as much time as they could every year.

"Ready?" Don asked.

"Okay," I said. "What do you have to teach me?"

"Photography is all about seeing and requires active perception in the moment. Drawing also puts you in the moment. You have to see." Don touched my back. "You try it."

"Never been good at drawing," I said.

"We'll see." He placed a pencil and paper in front of me. He smelled good, like ink and musk. "In order to make pictures, you have to shut off your language. Don't sit and think 'I'm going to draw this stool.' Instead, see the spaces around the stool and draw them. See how lines come together and what the space is," he said.

"Like when I look at a house and see *it* rather than all the stuff in or around it?"

"Sounds right. When you put that pencil there," Don touched my paper and then my hand, "make a mark and you have to look at it. You have to see it. You cut off the internal chatter and respond to what's in front of you." He placed his hands on my shoulders.

Courtney's phone rang. She soon hung up and said, "They're outside so I'm outta here." She grabbed her overnight bag and headed for the door. "Allison's mom will bring me home tomorrow."

"I thought Allison wasn't your friend," Don said.

"That's when her and her mom didn't like Mom. Now everyone knows Mom didn't do it."

I looked at our daughter, finally freed from the cloud of doubt I had put her under. I hoped I'd be as quick to forgive and forget as she had been.

Me and Don fixed dinner, a new recipe from my *Heart Healthy Cookbook*: Butternut Squash and Spicy Black Bean Enchiladas. We sat close at the kitchen counter and Don talked about the weight of allegiance he'd carried to his family's name and business. "It's killing me, Trudy," he said. "All these years, sorrow over losing them kept me committed to the store. Maybe I was secretly glad when Tool Mart moved in and freed my mind from wishing our store would somehow catch fire and burn to the ground." He stabbed at his enchilada, put down his fork.

I stopped eating as I took in all that heavy info. "I had no idea. I'm sorry." And then I thought maybe I did suspect that the store wasn't for him, but to face what we'd do without even that measly income maybe worried me.

"Living on my own gave me time to think."

I got suddenly scared that he was going to ask for a divorce. "And?"

"I'd walk through that store at night and hear voices from the past. It was like some door opened up to reveal my brother and I working with our parents on weekends and summers. All those hours in a place they both really loved. Then Scott left for college. Four years later, it was my turn to take off. Going to college freed me, but their deaths brought me back. Scott had completed his Peace Corps stint by then, but said he'd never return to Luce. So there I was, the one meant to carry on the family business. Anyway, after I moved out of this house, I'd go to the store and up the stairs to the apartment, resenting the growing debt on my back."

"Emotionally and financially," I said in understanding.

He took my hand and I thought my knees would turn to rubber for how good that felt. "I'm just saying maybe now we can put the store to rest. I contacted Scott to let him know that I—"

"You don't owe him any explanation; he never lifted a finger to help you."

"Not a battle to fight, Trudy. I called to tell him and he said it was about time I unburdened myself and let the place go. I want to auction off the store's inventory and sell the building. We'd get a good price for it. And then I want to set up a photography studio in town."

"We could find a place where we could also sell the antiques from Lyle's and Tom's houses. We could be business partners!" I said.

"Maybe we could," he agreed.

Caught in his new dream, I said, "That rocks."

"I cancelled having the hardware store name printed on

the van. Want to leave it blank until I know what to call my photography business."

Don stayed the night, and it was just like I knew it would be. I don't like to brag but having sex again after a long spell, well like I said, I don't like to brag. I had to pinch myself in the morning to believe he was still there. He soon moved back home, turned his old apartment into a temporary photography studio, and reduced the store hours. I stopped seeing his photography as a hobby and saw it for what it was: his true calling.

As the days moved along, the truths continued to spool forward. Mark Riepe was charged with contributing to the delinquency of minors and awaited his comeuppance. Nunda Ward told the judge that Mark gave them money and alcohol whenever they could prove they'd done damage to the house or scared *the women*. I had thought the menacing racist phone calls to Iris stopped after she got a new phone, but they kept coming. I had no idea until Nunda and Tony confessed. They took advantage of Iris's kindness when she pulled over to help Nunda on the side of the road, her car hood up. She let Nunda use her phone after Nunda said she didn't have hers and needed to call for a tow. That's when Nunda stole the number off Iris's new phone and kept menacing her. Nunda and Tony were sentenced to a year of community service working at the homeless shelter.

Arnold Riepe admitted to setting the trap on Cobber's tail. He originally planned to set it by the back porch steps, hoping one of us would spring it, teach us a lesson. Then when he saw the stray dog, he said using it on him seemed like more fun. It was also his idea to steal from Lyle's house. His community service sentence was to work for the county animal shelter for a year, maybe learn compassion for animals and take responsibility for his actions.

Tony had such a crush on Greta that he took a chance and

told her he was sorry for going with Arnold the night they menaced me and Iris out on Mandle Road. Said after Iris ran over Arnold's toes, he was madder than ever and that's when he decided to break into the house and start stealing stuff. Tony never wanted anyone to get hurt like Martha did that night. To make it up to us, he told Greta she could find the other bag of weed at an abandoned farmhouse in Effington. She dragged it back to Lyle's and hid it in the attic, set aside some for her own personal use. Maybe it helped her focus, or maybe it helped her stop crying in her beer over Dr. Schemp.

The same judge that stuck me with Greta—I now say that with all due respect—granted us permission to begin work on the house. We had tons of cleaning to do. Julianna knew all along that her father planned to give Homes for Dwelling his house and had figured if I was going to be too bullheaded to get Lyle's stuff out of the house and into a safe place, it was best kept in her father's sheds. "See, now you don't have to hurry to sell it," she said. "You can sort through it carefully."

After she told me, I just thought, well why didn't you say so in the first place? But to each their own in their own time, I had grown to say.

Jerry Wanderi decided to pay out of pocket for a surveyor who determined he was right: Lyle had set his fence five yards onto Jerry's land. I tore down the chicken wire and made it right between us, wanting to start over and be a good neighbor. I suggested we plant trees there. Jerry said he'd think about that. Would I also hire someone to rake up the leaves? We agreed I'd plant a line of evergreens.

Anyway, who had time to complain about who did and said what and when? We had work to do to get Lyle's house ready for the low-income residents who would occupy it. We hired a mover to haul the player piano out to Lois Urho's. Man did that open up a lot of space in the living room. I refused to take her money. She said she'd bring us homemade bars as often as possible.

We got right down to the repair work. Before we knew it, we were in the cleared-out living room cutting cracks that ran through the plaster to the lath. Greta wasn't obligated to help us any more. She'd done her time; but she was hooked on us as friends, so she stayed to learn the work.

Martha showed her how to angle the chisel's beveled cutting edge to the crumbling plaster wall. Greta tapped the hammer on the chisel head and knocked a plaster chunk to the floor. "See, you're getting the hang of it." Martha wanted to encourage her as much as possible. I just kept quiet knowing Greta had a whole lot to learn about using tools and Martha had the patience to teach her.

I helped Iris carry in the SawzAll so she could cut the tiles she made for the kitchen backsplash: yellow buttercups on a bright blue background. "Beautiful," I said.

I walked through the house that was out from under the weight of all the things Lyle had collected. The rooms smelled of Zip Strip, varnish, and paint. A musty scent mingled with a disinfectant's lemon fragrance. Tucked within corners of the house, the sage's cleansing aroma lingered and I heard Lyle's voice: *Come in. Come in.*

41

Probate officially ended and we women planned a bonfire to do one last important cleansing. "I still don't like wasting this." Greta wasn't pleased that she had to haul her last bag of marijuana down from the attic and out to the woods.

"The house inspector is coming," I reminded her.

"Can't we just hide it somewhere in the woods until he leaves?" Greta said. "Think of the fun we could have." She looked really bummed. "Or get it to pass for official medical use."

"That's pretty closely regulated by the state," Iris said. "You'd have to start from scratch and go through all the hoops."

"No more trouble with the law," I said. I also had a sense that Greta might always be tempted to get the stuff back to Schemp, resume that relationship in one form or another. Burning it was the best way to burn that bridge to him.

We stood at the pit that me and Iris had stumbled on all those months ago when we went in search of Cobber. Nunda told Dwight that her and her friends dug the pit. They went into the woods to drink and search for sacrificed dog graves. Said if someone unearthed the bones, they'd get reward money from Mark Riepe once he owned the house.

I pointed at the pit. "Okay, Greta."

"Best crop of weed ever." She dumped marijuana into the hole.

"Let's at least stand upwind and inhale," Martha said, which made me laugh. We were all shifting in surprising ways.

But as the crop burned, the smoke mostly went straight up

to the trees and no one felt like climbing after it. We were all boots on the ground and focused.

A couple months after the one-year anniversary of Lyle's death, Randall and Martha were awarded Lyle's house and four acres; so in a roundabout way, Randall got what he wanted. He was getting back on his feet, so to speak, by completing the rest of the repair work there. I set aside six acres of Lyle's land for a special project that Lois suggested I consider. She said a lot of patients under hospice care feel lost and without purpose once they receive a terminal prognosis. What if Homes for Dwelling had a project just for terminal patients to work on? Sounded good to me, so we planned to have them help build a cabin at the opposite point of the lake. Once completed, the cabin would be available for patients to enjoy during their last months, weeks, and days on earth. The rest of Lyle's land belongs to Nature Conservancy and can never be developed. On that point, him, Tom, and Ida would always be on similar ground.

Martha and Randall had installed new kitchen cabinets and I was anxious to see them. I went around back and found Martha on the porch shaking out throw rugs. Ruthie and Michael were playing in a nearby sandbox with Curtis and Marcus. Greta lazed in the hammock swinging Grace.

Iris called out to me. "Come see what I did." She had installed Pugmeyer's stained glass windows where the blackened dining room windows and plywood had been.

"But those were supposed to be for your studio," I said.

"Two in my studio and two for Lyle," she said. "Enough color to go around."

"Very nice," I said, but nice didn't quite seem the best word. It was bigger than nice. The sun streamed through the windows to warm us where we stood side by side. I thought about how I almost lost Iris forever and that I'd never be so selfish to not see when a friend was in deep need.

"See how the sunlight plays through the colors?" Iris said. "That's how people are, casting various hues, letting the light shine on."

"It's pretty," I said.

"I'm taking the largest one back to Cobbers Creek. We're drawing up plans for a cabin there. Nathan's knee deep into studying the Tidewater region, so when we stay on our land in Cobbers Creek, he'll feel the familiar of it. He'll feel at home."

"That's great, Iris." I didn't know what else to say. Happiness often left me speechless.

"Got to thank Auntie for helping me see straight again. She asked me to think about how running from heartache was one thing but running from love was another. *Where's your mind? Find it, Child. You have got to find it and make it right.* She saw how low I was missing Nathan. And then, he came to visit and I fell in love all over again."

"I'm really sorry, Iris. I didn't understand just how bad it was for you."

She nodded. "Well, we're all back to measuring twice and cutting once, now aren't we?"

Later us four women sat on the back porch steps. I thought of Lyle, didn't think he was looking down on us, as Martha believed, but that he did live on around the place. His wood-carvings were on display at the library along with a write up about him as folk artist. Luce residents would see just how talented he was, and he'd be known as more than just the recluse out on Highway 10 who died under a cloud of suspicion.

Robins flew into the arbor where vines were heavy with grapes for their taking. We'd make jelly soon, use Lyle's old Mason jars. Life's a circle. Sometimes it takes time to get back on track within it. Cobber came running up from the lake and shook himself near the children who had returned to the sandbox. They all squealed.

"Oh, I almost forgot," Martha said, "Listen to this." She

pulled a yellowed clipping from her shirt pocket. "Found this stuck in a kitchen drawer. It's dated 1892: *A recent instance of man's inhumanity to women. After she milked the cows, strained the milk into the stone crocks, carried the crocks down from the cellar, skimmed the cream, washed the crocks, hung them on the fence to dry, fed the calves, churned the cream, put her husband's supper on the table, and then hurried to the crying baby, she said to the farmer she was tired and wanted a portable creamery in order to lighten her labor. The farmer replied that he couldn't afford it, and the next day he went to town and bought a riding plow, paying for it with the butter money.*"

"Hmmmm," Greta said.

Martha looked at us. No one said anything, waited for her to connect it to something. "Well, I felt really sad for that lady," she said.

"Bet he died and she ended up buying a portable creamery with the life insurance money," Greta said.

"Well, that's even more sad." Martha had cleaned up a bunch of old pop bottles and lined them along the railing. Iris lifted a bottle, blew against the rim, and made it whistle.

My knee was aching, so I stood up to stretch it out. "If we start now, we could help Randall paint the north side before dinner," I said.

Greta sighed. "Hmmmmmm. I suppose so. But wouldn't you rather dance?"

Iris hummed. "Or sing."

Martha blew into a soda pop bottle. The whistling surrounded us.

No one moved.

"Just let me know when you're ready." I sat back down.

There we were, the four of us. Perched on the steps like birds of a feather, Lyle might say.

I looked towards the woods, thought of Lyle's ashes scattered there, some of Tom, too, since he had requested it, the two of them at peace on the land.

What a plan those two had come up with. Lyle told me what he had asked Tom to do and I sure as heck didn't try to talk him out of it. Those *Do Not Resuscitate* orders Lyle had posted on his door were his voice of authority. If it was what he wanted, it was what he wanted. Not saying it didn't make me sad, but his wanting to die and get away from pain wasn't about my sadness.

I didn't want to have any part of the actual suicide. We agreed I'd deliver Lyle's lunch and walk in to find Lyle dead. Didn't want him lying there dead any longer than that. He was dead when I arrived. That's the truth. It's my story and I'll take it to my grave with me. It's true. I didn't do it. Tom helped Lyle die but I agreed to say I found him dead. We came up with the sure plan; no one would believe I'd be stupid enough to do it and stay with the body. Tom was dying of lung cancer and had nothing to lose for paying what he saw as a debt to Lyle who did not want to die alone in pain.

It was sad to see Lyle lying there dead in his bed, but I had to keep telling myself he just did what was inevitable. Tom didn't want to push me like we planned to give me a visible wound to back my story. So I opened up the dresser drawers and said, *just shove me a little, surprise me, and I'll make sure I hit it hard.* You'd think I had asked him to kill me the way he said he didn't like hurting me. Finally I forced myself to hit that drawer. Hurt like all get out.

Then, when Dwight and Lois started interrogating me, I knew it wasn't a foolproof plan; but no matter what, I had promised Lyle I wouldn't give up Tom. I also knew that if it came to me going to trial, Tom said he'd confess sooner rather than later and go to jail if he had to. But it all worked out when Tom told his story on his deathbed and presented proof with the other part of my note and that ring. Plus, he had written his story down and stuck it in his will just in case he never had the opportunity to confess.

The one huge surprise to me was that Lyle left me his fortune. I swear on this entire story and the lives of everyone in it. I did not know that was coming.

I've learned a lot of lessons. From now on when I think someone is causing my friends trouble, level straight I'll be a better ally. Kick some butt for others. That's my new motto. Not for just one Luce woman, but a whole lot more.

Acknowledgements

I offer thanks and gratitude to Nick Dimassis and Forty Press for believing in this novel and for providing thoughtful professional guidance and editorial expertise.

I acknowledge with thanks the many friends (Angelique Kube with an eye for detail) and colleagues—notably Lin Enger and Al Davis—who read various drafts and offered feedback and encouragement through the years. Tom Meinhover and Debra Gluesing generously shared their land and sense of place and believed in this work from the beginning. Kathy Freise graciously read and offered valuable discussion, buoyant energy, and steady light from the very first draft to the very last.

The writing life is more enjoyable and full shared with John D. Early whose patience, insights, and suggestions mattered immensely along the way.

Numerous years have passed since I began work on this novel. I am grateful for the many voices from the past lingering within the pages and for the stories of my parents, Adam and Erna Kisacky, and my grandmother, Emma Matz Johnson, that color the setting. I'm also grateful for those whose voices are present, close, and familiar: Aaron, Katie, Leo and Mae Severn; Alyssa Severn and Craig Harding. I value the voices I am still getting to know: Richard, Nick, Alex Early.